What Reviewers Said of J.

"Steinfeld has a gift of humour, wit, and ironic social comment … His stories show … that he sees the absurdities of life, and understands the jokes that fate plays on almost everyone. [*The Apostate's Tattoo*]"
— Canadian Literature

"He's a competent craftsman with a rich imagination, obsessively recording every experience touching him … Are we nurturing a Canadian Kafka on Prince Edward Island? One can't help thinking that, especially upon reading the stories in *The Apostate's Tattoo*."
— The Globe and Mail

"[*Anton Chekhov Was Never in Charlottetown*]… In Steinfeld's fiction, appearance and reality are often subject to strange twists of fate. His characters are believable, as are their ideals and motives, and what they prove to be in the harsh light of reality."
— The Toronto Star

"Grand leaps of the imagination … appear in Steinfeld's writing."
— The Calgary Herald

"His stories [in *Forms of Captivity and Escape*] emerge with a sharp, satiric edge, defying evil and celebrating the good in humanity."
— The Whig-Standard Magazine

"*Would You Hide Me?* … feels more like a love letter to the written word … That's the best quality of *Would You Hide Me?* – the way these people swim in their language, dive into it, soak in it."
— The Hamilton Spectator

"… This book of stories [*Forms of Captivity and Escape*] should do much to consolidate his reputation. His imagination is rich, his touch is assured and his eye comfortable detailing life in more parts of the country than most writers attempt."
— Atlantic Provinces Book Review

Acting on the Island
and other
Prince Edward Island Stories:
New & Selected

J. J. Steinfeld

Pottersfield Press, Lawrencetown Beach, Nova Scotia, Canada

Library and Archives Canada Cataloguing in Publication

Title: Acting on the Island : and other Prince Edward Island stories, new and selected / J.J. Steinfeld.
Other titles: Short stories. Selections
Names: Steinfeld, J. J., author.
Description: Includes new and previously published stories.
Identifiers: Canadiana (print) 20210354542 | Canadiana (ebook) 20210360836 | ISBN 9781989725733 (softcover) | ISBN 9781989725740 (EPUB)
Subjects: LCGFT: Short stories.
Classification: LCC PS8587.T355 A6 2022 | DDC C813/.54—dc23

Cover painting: Brenda Whiteway, *Acting on the Island* (oil on canvas)

Cover design: Gail LeBlanc

Pottersfield Press gratefully acknowledges the financial support of the Government of Canada for our publishing activities through the Canada Book Fund. We also acknowledge the support of the Canada Council for the Arts and the Province of Nova Scotia which has assisted us to develop and promote our creative industries for the benefit of all Nova Scotians.

Pottersfield Press
248 Leslie Road
East Lawrencetown, Nova Scotia, Canada, B2Z 1T4
Website: www.pottersfieldpress.com
To order, phone 1-800-NIMBUS9 (1-800-646-2879) www.nimbus.ns.ca

Printed in Canada

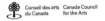

*Dedicated to the memory of Island artists
Hilda Woolnough, Erica Rutherford, Lionel Stevenson,
Brian Burke, Carl Phillis, and Catherine Miller.*

And for Island artist Brenda Whiteway, as always.

Acting on the Island is a work of fiction and all the events and characters described in its stories are imaginary, not based on anyone living or dead.

Contents

Godot's Leafless Tree

*I*ve lived my entire life on the Island, and to tell the truth,
haven't wandered much outside Kings County, which to me
is God's county, or God's country, depending on the figure of
speech of your choice. I have my job on the road crew, work
my butt off for a chunk of the year, then collect pogey or find
me little jobs to do the other months. Once a year, I do take
a one-week trip off the Island. My mother, pregnant with
me, along with my father, his head full of dreams of a simple,
uncluttered life, and their three-year-old daughter, came to the
Island in the late 1960s as two of those free-thinking, idealistic
back-to-the-landers, and stayed. My parents were both already
nearly forty, but needed a new life, or so they used to tell me.
That makes me an Islander, and my mother, even though
she lived three decades here and died on her cherished red
soil, as did my sister who died not far from here in her early
twenties, and my father, who still calls the Island home, were
not official Islanders. You know, born here, you're an Islander,
no matter where in the world you live the rest of your life or for
how long; arrive one-day old, live into old age, and you're still
unalterably a "come from away."

My parents came all the way from San Francisco, in a beat-up old Karmann Ghia via Vancouver and several points in between, to the woods of eastern Prince Edward Island. Where I was born. At home, in a secluded little cabin. The 1963 Karmann Ghia is behind the cabin, and I have been intending for the longest time to get that sweet little car in running condition but my skills and the parts are lacking and it sits there in antiquated disrepair, a museum piece. The cabin, with a few additions and some modernizing over the years, is still there, cringing at progress and development, and it's my home. I moved back in after my mother died peacefully on her adopted Island home, to be with my dad. I live alone now, have since I had to put my father in a nursing home a couple of years ago, his mind back at Haight-Ashbury, mumbling paeans to drugs and Janis Joplin, who still seems to be singing to him. I guess he escaped the Island without really leaving. I never want to leave.

Don't get me wrong. I'm not a narrow-minded, narrow-thinking bumpkin. I read and contemplate all sorts of worldly things and listen to every kind of music around, but I do have a fondness for music from different times and places – Irving Berlin, Jacques Brel, Bessie Smith, Edith Piaf. That's how I travel hither and yon, near and far, through reading and listening to music. And that's why I was so amazed I found this place, on a dirt road off an out-of-the-way side road in the woods that I never paid much attention to, thinking that I knew every inch of Kings County, Prince Edward Island. You see, this here spot, this rarely traversed dirt road, is how I imagine the setting in Samuel Beckett's *Waiting for Godot*, one of the books I've read during my lifetime Island residence. I mean, the play could have been set right here.

Coincidentally, it is evening now, near a leafless tree on a country road, as is the setting and time in Act I of *Waiting for Godot*. Small world, wouldn't you say? The Island is full of smallness and coincidences – that's part of its islandness. Just knowing this out-of-the-way piece of paradise exists makes me dance, not that I'm much of a hoofer. Perhaps it might be illuminating to point out that I've been greatly influenced by the works of Beckett, especially *Waiting for Godot*, which I have read over a hundred times, and seen many times, off the Island during my once-a-year sojourn elsewhere. My personal everyday look, which I must concede is somewhat affected, what with my wire-rimmed glasses and wearing patched jeans and a ragged jacket with large pockets, is how I imagine a Beckettian character might appear on such an evening. Isn't that a lovely adjective, Beckettian?

That's enough dancing for now. Some days are so filled with possibilities, you're just happy to be alive. How can I suppress my joyous dancing? To be dancing and flinging your arms in all directions and breathing in the air, and so close to the soil in which a tree would grow. Oh, the beautiful Island red soil. I love to behold it, to hold it in my hands, to inhale its aroma. Possibilities. Yes, a magnificent, possibilities-filled day. Today Godot finally arrives. I have this on good authority. The best authority. This tree, scrawny and forlorn as it may appear, is magnificent. I can't help but stare at it, want to nestle up close to its naturalness, shake hands. Oh, but I don't want anyone thinking I might not have a full complement of branches myself. I'm no tree hugger, no way. I'm a respecter of trees. Good luck to shake hands with a tree. Not that I need good luck. I don't believe in luck. I don't believe in all that much. But I do believe in possibilities. And that Godot will at long last arrive. Here. This very spot. The anticipation makes me burst with joyousness. I'm just overcome with the urge to throw the soil high into the air. Silly, irrational, foolish, but it's what I want to do. It's raining dirt. The sky is falling. The sky is not falling. What does it matter?

As a matter of fact, it does matter. Godot would not arrive on a day in which the sky fell. I was going to sing a medley of Irving Berlin songs in honour of Godot's long-awaited arrival. But I think Godot might not like Irving Berlin songs. Why take chances? I could go for a medley of Jacques Brel songs. Godot might like that. Or Bessie Smith songs. You think Godot would like Bessie Smith? How about Edith Piaf? My sister wrote some catchy lyrics but I get too sad when I sing them. Looking at this tree, at any tree for that matter, reminds me of that great sadness. But that was a long time ago. I was young. Didn't understand the significance of such things. Not that I understand now. I'm counting on Godot to explain things like that to me.

Sometimes I can't bear to look at a tree, when I remember what my sister did. There's only so much you can learn from books and TV and radio and press releases and heat-of-passion disclosures and overheard phone conversations and the internet and words in foreign languages. But one person's foreign language is another's personal tongue. My uncle spoke in tongues. He also drank and pissed his life away. My uncle was my father's identical twin brother, and he visited us every summer, stayed and drank and raised hell and departed. You could not believe how much they looked alike. Yet my father never drank and my dear old dad pissed moderately.

Beckett makes absolute sense to me, even if he never set

foot on Prince Edward Island, let alone Kings County. Can you imagine Beckett taking a little vacation on the Island and bumping into Lucy Maud Montgomery at a kitchen party, fiddlers playing, stepdancers entertaining the celestial beings? I'm just assuming they had kitchen parties in those days. Can you picture Beckett and Montgomery, in a kitchen together, talking about literature and the world, and Beckett, man of the world that he was, maybe getting smitten by the illustrious Lucy Maud? But I'm delving into the world of the absurd, and on this day I have some real possibilities to consider.

Yes, just the tree and myself, in anticipation of the momentous arrival. If I needed to take a piss, which I do not, a leafless tree would be as good as any other place. But what if I was pissing, a natural act, harmless in and of itself, and Godot arrived at that exact time? No, that would not be right. Not of the magnitude of blasphemy or moral transgression, but a disruption to the natural order of things nonetheless. A natural act not being right, that doesn't sound all that right. Right and wrong. I'll leave those concerns until Godot arrives. Soon. Very soon.

I'm not ashamed to admit, I'm nervous and somewhat impatient. I've gone to ten different productions of *Waiting for Godot*, dozens of performances, and whenever I could swing it, I would sit in the front row, as close to the centre as possible. And along with the characters in the play, I would wait for Godot. But those were theatrical productions, and this is real life, my real life, and Godot will be arriving today. This tree, it looks exactly like the tree in the first production of *Waiting for Godot* I saw. Not a leaf on it anywhere, as it is supposed to be in the first act. In the second act, if you follow Beckett's stage directions, the tree should have four or five leaves.

In my pocket I have a well-worn script of *Waiting for Godot*, here, presto, just like magic, the aforementioned script. I found this old script on a sidewalk when I was a kid. I was going to the store in the nearby village by the river, on an errand for my parents, and didn't know what in the world to make of the find. I didn't show it to my parents, thinking they might want to take it away from me. I saved it all these years. My theory, developed when I became older, is that a retired professor from Massachusetts, a summer resident in the village, lost the old script or threw it away. But no, he would never throw a Samuel Beckett autographed script away. That would be an absurd if not an insane act. Unfortunately and sadly, I never did show it to my mother. But I cannot allow sadness to ruin this evening.

I grew into this script. My most valuable possession. It has the author's autograph on the title page, which makes it priceless to me. I've never tried to find out if the signature is authentic. I love looking at this script, reading it. It states unequivocally at the beginning of the second act that the number of leaves should be four or five. Beckett was still alive when I found this script – he died in late December 1989, the same year Irving Berlin died. But what does that irrelevant coincidence mean? Nothing. I doubt if Beckett ever sang "Alexander's Ragtime Band" in the shower, but you never know. It feels so good to hold this script against my face.

I also have many book copies of the play, but my favourite is my old Grove Press Evergreen Book edition, thirty-fourth printing, $1.75 cover price, which I picked up in a secondhand bookstore on one of my off-Island trips for *more* than the original cover price. I have it at my place of residence. There on the classic black-and-white atmospheric cover,

Estragon and Vladimir in shadow, wearing their bowlers, and the tree, the leafless tree from Act I. I've always been partial to leafless trees, don't ask me why. Among my strongest memories from my youth are images of leafless trees. Late fall, a powerful windstorm, the last leaves being blown off the trees. This tree is as identical to the one in the first production of *Waiting for Godot* I saw as my uncle was to my father, and you couldn't tell the two of them apart, except when my uncle was speaking in tongues or pissing his life away.

I should put the script away before Godot arrives. I could be completely absorbed in the play and miss Godot. What would that do to my psyche, after all my waiting? My mother, my dear, departed mother, on her deathbed told me she had had an affair with a man who had seen *Waiting for Godot* in 1957 while he was a prisoner in San Quentin penitentiary. An affair during her early years of marriage, before I was born. She had me late in life, yet she had married young, too young, she told me. An affair, she whispered with her little remaining strength, that lasted nearly ten years, and he broke it off, not her. I was an infant when she heard that her ex-convict had died. Died of natural causes. In his sleep. But alone. Alone in a stark, barren, airless room. That was my mother's description, for which there is no verifying evidence, no corroboration whatsoever. But why contradict a deathbed divulgence? Before that revelation, I did not know my mother even knew of *Waiting for Godot*.

Once I had gotten over my astonishment over that revelation, my mother having had a decade-long affair with an ex-convict, I told her about the old, autographed script I had found as a young boy, and she said it might have been the script of one of the actors who had performed at San Quentin in 1957. I wanted to show her the script but I feared that if I went home to get it she might be dead by the time I returned. Instead, I started to ask her questions about the play, what type of tree she thought that the 1957 San Quentin production had used, artificial or real – real like this tree I'm standing near. But she died. Died before she could tell me. My father was not in the room when my mother took her last breath, her last words being of Beckett and his immortal play, a play I have seen ten different productions of so far in my life, dozens of performances, and I hope to see many more, assuming I live a long life. My father, who is very ill these days, unless he is hiding nearby, listening to my words, *my* revelation, does not know of my mother's affair, and I'm sure not going to tell him. I mean, what would be the point? But I could show him the script, not that it would interest him at all.

My nervousness and impatience aren't dissipating. Not a great deal happening, but it will, once Godot arrives. I have, after all, been waiting a long time. And I have had what one might call an uneventful life, and that would be a generous assessment of my worldly comings and goings. Apart from attending ten different productions of *Waiting for Godot*, dozens of performances, what have I actually done in my life? Yes, uneventful would be a most generous assessment.

If I mine my memory, mine it deeply, I do recall an eventful occurrence. The only eventful occurrence in the last long while of waiting. I got into a scuffle with a theologian. A scuffle that almost turned into a prizefight. Would have, but I caught a punch to the jaw and hit the ground, not all that far from this road. He was gone when I came to. I got up, ready to do real battle, but the theologian had hightailed it to wherever theologians go after sucker-punching a stranger. A stranger whose only crime is that he has been waiting for years and years for Godot's arrival. I still kind of feel the pain, in memory at least. Pain remembered and pain experienced, of course, are two different things. What had prompted my pain, in actuality and now in memory, was nothing more than an argument between two strangers.

We argued over who was the greatest athlete of all time, right back to the ancient Greeks. It was an endless argument, really, no resolution possible. When you consider all the sports and near-sports, all the athletes, male and female, all the countries, all the civilizations. You think Godot is an athlete? the theologian asked. Godot a jock, I said, erupting into laughter, and I a person who is not quick to laugh, who sometimes goes days or weeks without cracking so much as a smile. The theologian assumed a boxing position, the kind the old-time bare-knuckled boxers used to assume, if you've seen those old photos or paintings. I thought it was a joke, a vast silliness, until he sucker-punched me. Well, I'll ask Godot myself about being an athlete, and who the greatest athlete of all time is. We'll have lots to discuss, and that might as well be one of the items on the agenda.

One day I'm going to write a play about my life, such as it has been, with all my stumbles and failures, and I'm going to set it in a spot just like this, which might be the perfect spot to reflect on one's existence, near a leafless tree on a country road, if existence isn't too fancy a word for my days on this earth. And surely Godot will be a character in the play of my life, a major character.

I know Godot is on his way and it won't be long before our orbits in life intersect. Wouldn't it be great good fortune if Godot had expert mechanical abilities and could help me fix up my parents' Karmann Ghia? Then Godot and I could both take a spin in the old car, taking in the beautiful Island countryside, talking about anything and everything. If I had the eyes of a hawk, or some other bird of prey equipped with acute eyesight, I would be able to see Godot at a distance, a distance much farther than my miserable eyes can detect. I have been waiting an inordinate length of time. I could say years, but who would believe me? Edith Piaf? Bessie Smith? Jacques Brel? Irving Berlin? Years. Years and years. Most of the time without many possibilities. But today, this glorious evening. A day of possibilities. Godot will be here soon. My patience will be rewarded. My earthly stay will be redeemed the instant Godot arrives. The very instant. If only I had the eyes of a bird of prey ... Godot is about to arrive. Oh, I'll have to go to the bathroom soon, but I can't risk going away from this spot. You know, I would never piss on a tree. This tree is so lovely. Touching it gives me such comfort. Thank merciful merciless God, Godot is about to arrive ...

19

A Television-Watching Artist
(With apologies to Franz Kafka)

During the late fall of 1982, on the hundred and ninth day of sitting in the window of a Charlottetown department store, Patrick Warlin was nearing a state of total peacefulness. A Hindu mystic sanctified by deprivation could hardly have appeared more placid and otherworldly. Sitting under fluorescent lighting, as he watched for the ninth consecutive time a three-minute video replay of himself being interviewed by a local CBC television reporter, Patrick was unaware that it would take an Act of God to shatter his serenity. After all, by the hundred and ninth day, Patrick believed that he could go on watching television in the department store window indefinitely.

Patrick was oblivious of the small afternoon crowd that had gathered to watch him watching television. He was concentrating on himself, mesmerized by his own image, his beard then only one week long. He had told the interviewer as she held a microphone near his face that the more he watched television, the less real he became. The expression of the interviewer's face indicated that she wasn't taking Patrick seriously. Those were the days when he still didn't mind speaking, and enjoyed the attention he was receiving. He was once one of the city's most unusual tourist attractions but now he was just part of the scenery. People still stopped and looked at Patrick but it was almost as if he were another mannequin in the window. At first, he used to turn periodically from his TV set and gaze through the glass to see who was observing him, picking out friends and relatives, waving at tourists, smiling for the photograph takers. But he had lost interest in the viewers even before he had surpassed his original goal of thirty days. Soon he did not have any desire to stop watching television – *ever*.

Patrick had gotten the idea for his TV-watching marathon two weeks after he had lost his job. During a late-night party, three of his friends drunkenly attempted to come up with ways to get into *The Guinness Book of World Records*. Patrick was too depressed and preoccupied to offer any suggestions that night. He had worked at one job or another for all of the nine years since the day he turned sixteen, when he had quit high school. To his friends' disbelief, Patrick was upset by the prospect of receiving unemployment insurance. The day after the party, he once again found nothing for himself on the Employment Centre's job board, and struggled to think of something that would keep him occupied and earn some money also. Nothing frightened Patrick more than not having a job.

Then he noticed the department store window with the display of television sets. He had been saving money in order to replace his seven-year-old black-and-white set with a colour one, but losing his job forced him to abandon that plan. Now a window full of TV-watching mannequins seemed to mock his unemployment.

TV SPECTACULAR EXTRAVAGANZA ... DISCOUNTS GALORE ... MANUFACTURER'S REBATES ... NOW IS THE TIME TO BUY ... FROM 5 INCHES TO 48 INCHES, WE HAVE THE PERFECT MODEL FOR YOU ... WE DEFY ANYONE TO BEAT OUR PRICES ...

The idea struck Patrick like a revelation. He rushed home to his basement apartment, and as his old TV blared, he began to compose a letter to the manager of the department store. He offered to attempt entry into *The Guinness Book of World Records* by sitting in a store window and watching TV. Publicity, he emphasized with thick underlining, could have a positive effect on sales during these difficult economic times. Three days later, Patrick received a phone call from the department store manager and was asked to stop into the store to discuss his interesting suggestion.

The manager was impressed with Patrick's initiative and imagination. Even the owner, whom the manager had talked with earlier, thought that Patrick's proposal had possibilities.

"The retail business always needs fresh ideas," the manager said, and they settled on a modest thirty dollars a day remuneration and a bonus of any television set other than the model with the 48-inch screen, along with picking up his apartment rent for the month, if Patrick made it into the record book. At the time, neither man knew what the record was or if anyone had ever attempted such a feat, but as the manager said with a damp smile, "If Christopher Columbus had never set out, where would we be now?"

The guidelines were quickly worked out: Patrick would have a "home" set up in the ground-floor centre window of the store on Grafton Street, be provided with the finest 26-inch colour television set, good food, and a comfortable reclining chair from the furniture department. Reasonable length bathroom breaks were allowed. Patrick, awake or asleep, would be expected to sit in front of the operating television set and watch for a minimum of sixteen continuous hours each day. Cable TV and a video cassette recorder would be provided so that he could record his favourite programs and watch them again. Once he had completed a sixteen-hour viewing day, he could sleep or rest behind a screen that could be drawn around the reclining chair for privacy. An exercise bicycle would be stationed next to the chair so Patrick could maintain his health. Patrick wryly requested that the four mannequins remain in the window display with him, for company. The store would take care of publicity and advertising; all Patrick had to do was watch television.

"If this doesn't increase sales, nothing will," the manager claimed. They agreed to begin in two days. Patrick predicted he could last for a month but the manager said the owner would be satisfied with two weeks. "No need to go overboard," the manager said as he gave Patrick a robust handshake. There were only two weeks left in the TV promotional month, a month that so far was not going well at all.

The first day in the window, Patrick felt awkward and uneasy. Although he was friendly and outgoing, he wasn't an exhibitionist by nature. He changed channels frequently with his remote-control channel changer and ate nervously. On the second day, a TV crew from the CBC gave him his first media coverage. The next day, the local newspapers ran photographs of him. A local radio station picked up the story of the TV Watcher on the fifth day and began to issue periodic progress reports. Before the first week was over, Patrick felt comfortable, as if he belonged in the department store window watching television.

By the start of the second week, a marked upturn in TV set sales was noticed. Other stores in the mall that housed the department store were eager to capitalize on the publicity. Merchants donated a variety of items – from monogrammed pillows to a specially designed pendant – to the determined TV Watcher. The department store set up a rack with a lavish assortment of the latest men's fashions for Patrick to model during his stay in the window, but he insisted on wearing his favourite outfit – patched jeans and an oversized Boston Bruins jersey – day after day. Patrick told the manager to let the mannequins wear the fancy stuff: they were the clothes-conscious ones.

Signs, of course, were placed in the window, giving full credit to the generous donors. Employees of the fast food outlets on the second floor of the mall took turns bringing food down to Patrick, no limit on what and how much he could eat. One civic-minded businessman offered to donate one dollar to charity for each hour that Patrick stayed in the window and challenged the other store owners in the mall to match his pledge. Within a day, nearly every story in the mall plus several nearby downtown stores had promised to donate one dollar to charity for each hour of Patrick's unusual endeavour. Before he knew it, Patrick was raising thirty-eight dollars an hour for worthy causes. His publicity increased. Local church leaders commended his effort to help the less fortunate. City politicians and business leaders wandered by the window and had their photographs taken with the twenty-five-year-old who wasn't allowing the bleak unemployment situation to get the best of him. No one really believed that Patrick would stay in the store window longer than two or three weeks.

Yet Patrick watched and watched TV. He watched with the obsession of a man determined to sail solitarily across an ocean, damn the threatening weather and the dreamless critics. On the twenty-fourth day, he even made the national CBC news broadcast. The reporter, doing her story from inside the store window, asked the TV Watcher at the end of the segment, "What if the great thinkers of history had been forced to watch TV all the time?"

To the multitude of Canadians watching the national news, Patrick answered, "I guess other people would have had to become the great thinkers."

The story on Patrick the TV Watcher and fundraiser provided relief from the gloomy economic stories and the usual barrage of worldwide crises. It was near the end of the tourist season and a visit to the Island wasn't complete without seeing *Anne of Green Gables* at the Confederation Centre *and* Patrick Warlin watching TV in the department store window across the street. No one knew how many photographs were taken of him, but the tourists certainly found the TV Watcher as worthy as the scenic Island landscapes.

For the first two weeks, Patrick posed obligingly; later, he paid little attention and kept his back to the window. Being a local Island celebrity ceased to have an effect on him. As far as Patrick was concerned, he had a job to do and was determined to do it better than anyone could, no matter what.

On the day marking the completion of one month in the store window for Patrick, the manager paid his regular daily visit and related the sales figures for the last thirty days. They had outstripped the manager's most optimistic expectations. Two weeks earlier, the manufacturer of the brand featured in the promotional sale had sent a representative to the department store to announce that the sale would be extended for as long as Patrick could hold out.

But Patrick's sales-stimulating magic proved to be finite. On the forty-fifth day, the manager, realizing that sales figures had levelled off and were beginning to decrease, suggested to Patrick that he could end his TV-watching. Surely he was now eligible for enshrinement in *The Guinness Book of World Records*, not to mention the hearts of Islanders and tourism department officials. "We could try it again next year," the manager said, standing behind a mannequin and patting it affectionately on the back.

"I'd like to go a little longer," Patrick said as he stared at the TV screen, not the manager. The manager offered Patrick a real job as a salesman in the home-entertainment department if he was ready to finish his TV-watching.

By the end of the second month, TV sales were lower than before the publicity stunt had started and the manager was more insistent that Patrick give up his obsession. The manager wanted to use the strategically located centre window for another display. "Merchandising should be fluid, never allowed to become static or stale," he lectured Patrick. When Patrick refused to respond, the manager argued with an unexpected burst of vehemence that the novelty of the promotional gimmick had completely worn off. "Let's not beat a dead horse," he added in a more reasonable tone. Patrick brought to the manager's attention the flip chart in the window exhibiting the running charity pledge total, then at $57,720. Did the manager want to be responsible for ending that?

A handful of the less prosperous merchants in the mall were getting nervous. One store owner visited Patrick and joked about the financial consequences to his business if the TV-watching went on forever. Patrick merely smiled and claimed that three years would be a more realistic goal – *nothing lasts forever.*

The worried store owner removed a small calculator from his pocket and punched the buttons. "There are exactly 8,760 hours in a year," the man said uneasily.

"That's good to know," Patrick responded, as if just informed of a bland weather forecast. Then Patrick instructed the store owner to multiply 8,760 hours times thirty-eight dollars times three years ...

On the seventieth day, the owner of the department store, through the manager, *ordered* Patrick to stop watching television in the window. Patrick refused. "You going to remove me bodily?" Patrick challenged as he watched an entertaining children's program. "Wouldn't that provide excellent publicity for the store," Patrick said with the precise timing of an accomplished television comedian. "We're over $63,000 already – and that's just the beginning." Without a trace of enthusiasm in his voice, Patrick stated he had calculated that at thirty-eight dollars an hour he could raise a million dollars in a little over three years.

By the seventy-sixth day, Patrick had earned $2,280 for himself. The manager, acting on the owner's instruction, offered the stubborn TV watcher another $500 to stop. On the seventy-ninth day, the owner raised this to a $750 bonus plus a video cassette recorder of his own, but Patrick said no. It would take force – and perhaps violence – to remove him from the store window, he explained.

"I could get a court order removing you," the manager threatened, unable to contain his frustration. Patrick responded without irritation that if the manager got a court order, the department store's name would replace Scrooge's as a synonym for cold-heartedness and miserliness.

On the eighty-first day, a journalist from Nova Scotia arrived on the Island especially to interview Patrick for an in-depth magazine story. The journalist had already decided to call the story "What Makes Patrick Watch?" Patrick had no desire to talk to him. He only wanted to watch TV. The required sixteen hours a day had on Patrick's initiative become seventeen then eighteen then nineteen hours by the end of the first month. By the end of the second month, it wasn't unusual for Patrick to watch TV for twenty hours or more a day, viewing video replays of his favourite programs and sports events when there was nothing interesting to watch. There were a few days when he watched TV for twenty-four hours straight and his record for continuous TV-watching, except for bathroom breaks, stood at forty-three hours.

When the journalist from Nova Scotia commented that Patrick's TV-watching was a form of captivity, a voluntary imprisonment at best, Patrick reacted calmly and said softly, "I feel unbounded, unlimited. I really feel free in front of this TV. I can tape a war scene or a love scene or myself on the local news. With the video recorder, I can keep The Beatles together or Elvis Presley alive for as long as I want. TV allows me to be in command." Then he refused to answer any more questions.

On the eighty-seventh day, while Patrick was on one of his bathroom breaks, which seemed to be less and less frequent as the days passed, two men entered the store window and began to dismantle his TV-viewing room. The manager was eager to do a feature display on winter wear before the Island's first snowfall. Patrick arrived back as the two men started to lift the sturdy 26-inch set out of the window. Patrick grabbed one of the men, and the other let go of the television set in order to help his startled accomplice. The TV banged to the floor with a thud. An infuriated Patrick, weak from sitting and watching TV for nearly three months, managed to push the intruders of his store-window home. One of the men attempted to re-enter the window display, but Patrick punched him in the stomach with a strength he was astonished to discover he still had. Patrick warned the two men that if they came back, he would kill them. He hurriedly hooked up the set and resumed watching television.

As the third month ended, weekly TV sales were down to their lowest level in twelve years. Patrick was more content than he could ever remember being. The manager threatened to stop Patrick's food supply, and Patrick muttered that an emaciated corpse in the store window would be a marvellous testimonial to free enterprise. The truth was that Patrick ate very little anymore. He could live on fries, blueberry muffins, and coffee. If only he had bathroom facilities in the store window, then he wouldn't have to leave his TV at all.

When the manager told Patrick that he was going to send documentary material he had been accumulating to the Guinness organization for verification, the TV Watcher was indifferent and uncooperative. Without documentation and verification, the manager complained, the Guinness people would never enter Patrick's accomplishment into the record book. Patrick said that he couldn't care less about *The Guinness Book of World Records*.

Each day the manager continued to beg, plead, bribe, and

threaten, but Patrick refused to leave the store window or even discuss the subject with him.

"Don't you know that fluorescent lighting is bad for you?" the manager said, pointing to the rows of overhead lights. "And watching too much TV from as close as you sit will do who knows what to your insides," he added, with conviction.

Patrick merely grunted in reply. Now he rarely spoke and slept no more than three or four hours a night. He no longer used his exercise bicycle and started to feel lightheaded if he stood too long. Even the fries and blueberry muffins seemed excessive. He ate only so he would have the strength to watch TV. Untroubled, relaxed, and with a firm sense of purpose, Patrick Warlin was genuinely happy.

On the ninety-sixth day, as he was watching a midnight movie, a rock was hurled through the store window, but Patrick was unhurt. He endured a chill draft that night – the first fresh air he had breathed in ninety-six days – and the next morning the broken window was replaced. Two days later, a beer bottle was thrown through the new store window, again around midnight, and Patrick cut himself when he picked up a piece of glass that had fallen near his reclining chair. He bled heavily before he bothered to take a tie from the clothes rack near the TV and wrap it around his deep cut. When the manager arrived in the morning, the floor was covered with dried blood, yet Patrick was watching TV unperturbed. The manager insisted that Patrick go to the hospital.

"Bring a doctor here," Patrick replied.

"You're insane, you're insane," the manager screamed at the TV Watcher.

"Perhaps," Patrick whispered. A store staff member with first-aid knowledge was brought to the display window and attended to Patrick's wound as he continued to watch a morning exercise program.

On the hundred and ninth day, during the first major snowstorm of the season, there was an Island-wide power blackout. In the downtown area, where the department store was located, the power wasn't restored for an hour and forty-five minutes. Flashlights in hand, the manager and the store's lawyer rushed in and informed Patrick that the terms of the agreement with the department store had been violated: he had failed to watch television continuously during store hours. Patrick was too weak to fight as two men carted off the television set and three more store employees stood guard to make sure the TV Watcher didn't go berserk. Patrick gripped his remote-control channel changer and pressed futilely as the manager said, "Thank God it's over ... thank God ..."

Patrick stood up, feeling faint and dizzy, took a parka off a nearby mannequin, and slowly walked out of the department store. As he stumbled toward his apartment building a few blocks from the store, the lights came back on, as if to salute the conquering hero. Once in his basement apartment, Patrick's first action was to turn on his old back-and-white television set. Later, when the night's local news came on, the newscaster announced, "It took an Act of God to stop Patrick Warlin, but earlier today the twenty-five-year-old Charlottetown man ended his one-hundred-and-nine-day TV-watching marathon after raising nearly $100,000 for Island charities ..." Patrick sat still in front of his television set, fighting not to lose consciousness, intent on continuing his television-watching.

The World of Our Hero
in the Cradle of Confederation

Nowhere on the planet could Our Hero exist other than in Charlottetown, Prince Edward Island. Not in Toronto, Ontario, or in New York City, New York, or even in Paris, France. Well, perhaps he could exist in Toronto or New York City or Paris, but he wouldn't be the same man with the same dreams or demons. There's something enchanting and transformative about Charlottetown and Prince Edward Island. Let us defy time and go back to Sunday, October 21, 1984, the day, if one day can be picked out, that is the turning point of Our Hero's entire existence. Let us go back and be there as witnesses in the present, even though it is the past already. Let us see what happened, is happening, in the world of Our Hero in the Cradle of Confederation.

As we join Our Hero he is on his bed, paralyzed by depression, a gun pointed at the peeling ceiling, surrounded by the stale and unromantic odours of his room. The décor is pure urban indifference, only a perfectly working, seven-foot antique grandfather clock, a sturdy electric typewriter, and a lovely old radio hinting that more than a transient lives here.

Our Hero keeps the radio set to the same local CBC station all the time, even when he rarely pays attention to what is on the radio. It keeps the room from being too silent, Our Hero from being too alone. The old radio is one of the few possessions left by his father to Our Hero. It usually works well, but when it does sputter or fade, a slap to the side casing always brings it back to clarity. Our Hero has lived in this room of a downtown Dorchester Street rooming house for nine years, actually having had to bribe the previous tenant to move out so he could have this specific room, no other would do.

Without thought, Our Hero fingers the trigger of the gun, a gun he bought for twenty-five dollars in 1975, a week after he moved into the rooming house. The gun is loaded, was loaded nine years ago and still has the same bullets, but Our Hero has no intention of firing it. Through his work and wanderings, for Our ambulatory Hero is ever the wanderer, he always carries the concealed weapon with him. It is not a big gun, very small and light in the hand, perhaps the size and weight of a large stapler. He likes the thought of having the gun, just in case; he knows how cruel and humiliating life can be, has been, will be. But he does not boast of or flaunt the gun, and no one on the Island knows he has it. The man he bought the gun from moved away to Ontario years ago and died there from a self-inflicted shotgun wound in 1980. His dear father should have had a gun, Our Hero thinks whenever he looks at the object of potential extinguishment or considers throwing it into Charlottetown Harbour.

Our Hero wades through countless fantasies, but his most frequent ones deal with the gun: A beautiful ballerina, after a performance of *Sleeping Beauty*, steps out of the Confederation Centre of the Arts; she is quickly surrounded by six burly villains from out of town; Our Hero is wandering by the Confederation Centre of the Arts, just wandering and bemoaning the unfairness of his life, when he sees the villains from away about to harm the beautiful ballerina. In Wild West fashion, Our Hero pulls out his small gun and fires six shots. Six villains from away strike the pavement in front of the Confederation Centre of the Arts in the glorious clunk-bang of retribution. Our Hero knows the fantasy is silly – he is forty-five years old and has seen the realities of life – but still he enjoys this fantasy and its many variations.

Our Hero, the morning miasma in his mouth, lowers his gun, not out of plan, but because his arm tires. His depression strengthens, and he hears the Screamer the floor above his – Second Floor, South Quadrant – up to his usual vocal outpourings. The Screamer, bless his screaming soul, cannot let a day pass without an outburst, usually several outbursts, ranging from whimpers to the screams of a man on the rack. But Our Hero does not mind the screams. He finds them fascinating, a high-pitched commentary on life, on injustice, on the dolorous compartmentalization of the rooming house. It is impossible to put an exact age on the Screamer. When sober, he can look ten or fifteen years younger than when he is drunk. He refuses to disclose his age, but is an otherwise warm and open person. Our Hero thinks he is about sixty years old.

During the screaming, Our Hero counts one-one thousand, two-one thousand, three one-thousand, up to sixteen. A record! Our Hero carefully gets out of bed – there are eleven mousetraps set in the compact room – and goes past the large oval table in the centre of the room which holds his electric typewriter, to his little desk against the wall near the room's only window. It is a desk for a child of ten, but it is Our Hero's writing desk, where he creates. A thick notebook and an old journal are all that occupy the desktop. In the notebook, Our Hero records the time and length of the Screamer's latest pronouncement. In the same notebook, he also records the bits and pieces of his life: a to-the-penny account of his income, savings, and expenditures, the number of beers he drinks, the days he has lived in the rooming house and on earth – currently at 3,296 and 16,622, respectively – his dreams, the rejections, humiliations, things to do, the books he reads, and, of course, the Screamer's screams. It is volume ten in his collection of notebooks. The others are on a shelf over his writing desk.

The old journal on the desk had belonged to Our Hero's father. It contains eight years of neatly printed entries, from March 1947 to his death in February 1955. They are short entries for the most part and written erratically, sometimes every day, other times weeks or months between entries.

Our Hero reads from his father's journal often. It is the link with his father, a sixth-generation Islander, born 1914 in Charlottetown, died 1955 in that same Charlottetown. He started the journal the day he moved from the country back to the city after nine unhappy years living thirty-five miles outside of his beloved Charlottetown. His wife had insisted that they live on her family's farm and raise their only child in a wholesome rural environment. Our Hero's mother was the first one in her family born on the Island, her parents – Our Hero's maternal grandparents – having bought their farm in 1911, after moving to PEI from Boston, four years after their daughter was born.

While turning the pages of his notebook/volume ten, Our Hero notes with a ripple of nostalgic sadness how the price of beer has been increasing since 1975, when he began keeping his notebooks, after moving into this room and trying to cope with his divorce and his wife's remarriage, 11,497 beers ago – think of all the pissing, he thinks. His former wife is now married to a Member of the PEI Legislative Assembly, and Our Hero still curses the day he voted for that incompetent, not knowing at the time that his wife was in love with the man. Our Hero prints very small in the narrow-lined and thick notebook, and hopes that the notebook will accommodate all of the year.

After thinking about how futile politics is, the nest of patronage and subterfuge about which he often writes letters of condemnation to the editor of the Charlottetown *Guardian*, Our Hero turns back to the Screamer's log. The Screamer really isn't a nuisance, he thinks. The Screamer is a true character and a lot more exciting than most of the people Our Hero sees in the bars and churches he frequents in his search for material to write about. In fact, Our Hero likes all the residents of the rooming house: the eccentrics, the abused and the abusive, the borderline living, the passed over and the passed by, those caught in strange dreams and those dreamless. Our Hero genuinely appreciates them all, the three floors of them. He is a great lover of the misfit, the malformed, the out of tune, and the out of step. They are part of his immediate $175 a month for the room/no cooking/no pets/quiet after eleven/no smoking in bed reality.

But many of the men in the Dorchester Street rooming House smoke in bed, in the bathrooms, everywhere, and Alfred Dofferhone of the Third Floor, East Quadrant, has two dogs and is a gourmet cook with a microwave oven. Alfred is a culinary genius, making do on his old-age pension cheque, eating like a king, and treating Our Hero or others in the rooming house on Saturday evenings to gourmet dinners.

In his mind, Our Hero hears his ex-wife calling him a failure, a nothing mouse; her voice is difficult to erase. "I am a success and will be a greater success," Our Hero says softly, adroitly avoiding the mousetraps and returning to bed. He hates mice, waging a relentless battle against the little creatures that leave their droppings all around his room, even on his typewriter, and creep into his nightmares.

Our Hero's father, according to his journal, also despised mice. He once caught a mouse in his bare hands and squeezed it to death. Our Hero could never do that, but he has the scene in the novel he is working on – his second novel. His father was drunk at the time. In the novel Our Hero is writing, Our Hero's father, when he does appear, is sober and much older than the forty-one years he died at in 1955. There are many mice in the novel, individual mice and nightmarish armies of mice, along with bars and churches and many of the streets in Charlottetown. Also in the second novel are all of the residents of the rooming house.

Forcing his thoughts away from the mice, Our Hero places the gun under his pillow and rolls over to his side, still depressed, wrapped in more gloom than a man should rightly possess. He decides against having another morning beer. Vacant Sunday, he thinks with overworn frustration and bitterness. Sunday is a toilet day. The Public Library on Queen Street – located in the Confederation Centre of the Arts, which also contains the Art Gallery and two theatres – does not open until one o'clock on Sundays. Our Hero enjoys going to the library and reading newspapers from all over the country, studying the human condition as it unfolds in the cities of

Canada, reassuring himself that he does not miss anything by living on an island and in such a small city.

Later he will dress and go to church, with his gun, and relax until the library opens, safe in a familiar pew. The church is a pleasant and restful place to visit, and Reverend Willow's Sunday sermon is wonderful entertainment. Although Our Hero cares little for organized religion, he does care a great deal for God and the Houses of God. Sometimes Our Hero thinks God wants him to live in the rooming house, but he knows that God is not that interested in his life.

Our Hero could move from the rooming house, move wherever he wanted, even to the expensive apartments overlooking Charlottetown Harbour. He is not impoverished or immobilized by alcohol or crippled by failure like most of the residents in the rooming house. Goddamn it, he admits to himself, he likes the area, likes the rooming house. It shelters him, hides him like a wooden womb, provides him with inspiration, keeps him close to the memory if not the very spirit of his father.

And the rooming house is alive with history. It was built soon after the Great Fire of 1866 destroyed the previous house on the site. From his window, if he situates himself at a certain angle, Our Hero can see Owen Connolly's sandstone head on top of a three-storey building on Queen Street. Our Hero's great-grandfather on his father's side, a fourth-generation Islander, helped to construct that building in 1889 and 1890. That old and somewhat shabby building is directly across the street from the liquor store and also faces the three main spires of St. Dunstan's Basilica, which can be seen rising up from behind the liquor store. Those three church spires reaching toward Heaven can be seen from nearly every part of the city, even miles away. They are God's punctuation marks, Our Hero wrote of the three spires in his unpublished first novel.

Coming from outside his door, Our Hero can hear the unmistakable voice of the Actor using the first-floor hallway as his rehearsal hall, the man pacing back and forth as he assumes *all* the roles of *The Two Gentlemen of Verona*. The Actor claims to have been a great Broadway actor, Lionel Barrymore – or was it John Barrymore, the story changes – once spitting in his face for forgetting his lines on stage. The dirty brownish-grey gloves the Actor always wears, white as snow decades ago, were supposedly a present from Lionel Barrymore, before the spitting episode. Now at eighty-four, having been born in 1900, he is planning a comeback, auditioning for every play – professional or amateur – staged on the Island. The Actor and Our Hero have the only two rooms on the first floor of the rooming house.

As Valentine, one of the gentlemen of Verona, utters his last line, "One feast, one house, one mutual happiness," Our Hero's depression starts to float away, like exhausted smoke after a minor and unspectacular fire. He gets up once again and notes the Screamer's next paean to incarceration, a lacklustre four seconds, drinks down his third beer of the morning, then takes another look at the best-seller list from this week's *Maclean's* magazine and shakes his head, shakes it as if shaking a rectal thermometer back to its former temperature after registering a high fever. One day, he vows with much conviction, he'll be on the best-seller list.

Our Hero moves past his small refrigerator and two mousetraps, and bends down next to his writing desk. He removes the last letter from a shoebox – there are many shoeboxes piled in a neat pyramid of boxes to the left of his writing desk, between the desk and the illegal hotplate – and rereads it. It is a long, passionate love letter from a lovesick youth to an older woman, and Our Hero is pleased by its contents. This letter is a prize. On the envelope are printed in Our Hero's neatest printing – he only prints, even his signature on cheques – the date and subject matter and a few other notes about the wondrous letter. Like the other letters he has, this one is numbered and the number circled in red: 4017. Everything neat, in order, in its place.

Our Hero, his bare feet and hands cold, is standing dressed only in undershorts despite the inescapable fact that it is a chilly late October morning and the room's heating is vindictive. Always too hot or too cold, never right. He shivers but does not dress. His shivering is a dance, a graceful exercise, a harmless bit of choreographed suffering.

After three readings of the letter, Our Hero returns it to the top shoebox of the pyramid of boxes. The shoeboxes are full of photocopies of letters, each letter numbered, indexed, and annotated. Our Hero works in the Post Office on Queen Street, a job he likes in the same way he likes the rooming house, and each and every working day he cautiously removes two letters and photocopies them, placing the photocopied letters into new envelopes. He could steal dozens at a time, he is smarter and craftier than the Post Office's security system, but he thinks that two letters a day are all he can digest. If he takes a letter that contains cash, he returns it like any other; he is not that sort of thief. In hardship cases, he even adds a little money and some gentle words. Our Hero despises greed and insensitivity.

Our Hero has developed an incredible knack for pilfering good letters, ones that provide glimpses into real life.

In the beginning, back in 1975, after a period of brooding and idleness over his ex-wife's marriage to the MLA and his departure from teaching high school English, Our Hero began working in the Post Office and took letters at random; then there was no art to his vocation. But soon he became more selective and then, in time, developed his uncanny ability to snatch interesting letters. Although he looks sceptically at ESP and any such parapsychological phenomena, he knows in his heart that he possesses an extraordinary gift. Sure, once in a while he lifts a dud – a maiden aunt writing about her bursitis or a humdrum account of the month's weather in rural PEI – but he manages to fish out so many winners.

Our Hero's first novel, five years and 709 typed pages in the writing, makes good use of these appropriated letters. He shakes with anger and rage thinking of his unpublished novel and the best-seller lists and the eight rejections he has received so far, most incensed about the Island publisher who told him he wasn't ready to have a book published, that he wasn't really capturing the true spirit and essence of the Island. He went to the publisher's office and shouted at her that he was a seventh-generation Islander, a writer with vision.

Yet he believes that in time he will become accustomed to the rejections. Humans are marvellously adaptable, aren't they, even to squalor and exitless madhouses? Our Hero wrote those exact words in the novel he is working on now. He believes with unswerving faith that his time will come and when his ship arrives, it will be a luxury liner on an around-the-world, full-speed-ahead cruise.

And when the recognition and success come, he will not flee his beloved Charlottetown, not for Toronto or New York City or the Left Bank of Paris; he will savour his fame right here in the Cradle of Confederation, in the rooming house that has been more than a home for nine years, the rooming house sure to become a shrine just like Lucy Maud Montgomery's house. No one can convince Our Hero that *The Incurable Stubbornness of God* is not destined to eclipse *Anne of Green Gables,* and his mail-sorting hero, Garth McGrath, is not destined to evict little freckle-faced, red-haired Anne Shirley from the hearts of Islanders.

After he becomes famous and rich, what with paperback and movie rights, along with translation into numerous languages, Our Hero plans to purchase as many rooming houses in the downtown area of Charlottetown as possible and realize his dream of a utopia for winos and derelicts and down-and-outers. He wants to renovate the rooming houses, lower or eliminate the rents, and make them comfortable residences for the misfits and downtrodden. It is another one of his innumerable dreams. Our Hero does have enough money saved to buy one or two run-down rooming houses, but that money is security against the possibility of a miserable future. His father died penniless and the thought of an impecunious expiration haunts Our Hero.

Yes, he will become famous, a success dwarfing the petty triumphs of an MLA, no matter what obstacles stand in the way. He writes beautifully about life and suffering, why shouldn't he achieve fame and fortune and have major motion pictures made from his work? His thinking pushes Our Hero back onto the bed.

Our Hero's fantasies dissolve with an irrepressible obscenity and a morose thump of his aching heart. It is a thump declaring the injustice and unfairness he feels. He curses the unseen editors, he curses the local publisher who dared to tell him that he did not understand the Island, he curses the entire publishing industry; he curses the PEI Council of the Arts which thinks that his current project – a second Garth McGrath novel still untitled but more than three-quarters finished after four years of writing – is a joke and refuses to give him an arts grant like other creative people on the Island receive; he curses and shakes with even more anger and rage. Like a dung beetle set spinning on its back, Our Hero spins with anger and rage.

Creativity is the only tranquillizer for this revolving state. Our Hero spins off his bed and rushes to his writing desk, no longer the insect trapped, but a man of letters prepared to write, his surging spirit ready to become ink. He grabs his startled Muse and whirls her into orbit. He is about to do more to his Muse, but it is a time for creating, for writing beautiful prose, not for having any diverting sexual fantasies.

Our Hero releases a scream that makes the Screamer seem like a listless whisperer; a scream that rumbles all the liquor bottles in the rooming house; a scream that makes Owen Connolly's sandstone head wonder what in the world is going on in the rooming house on Dorchester Street.

After his screaming subsides, Our Hero prays like a lifetime devotee for his big left toe not to hurt so much, wishes that God would become a benevolent physician. He has never experienced physical pain to this penetrating extent, not even when the boys at the Post Office threw him headfirst into a cart of letters five years ago – to help celebrate his fortieth birthday –and he almost suffocated until he was dug out by three laughing mail sorters.

That's what temper and recklessness get you, Our Hero scolds himself. At least he didn't have rat traps set, he could be thankful for that. A rat trap would have chomped off his whole foot. Our Hero, through his agony, almost has sympathy for mice. There had been bleeding after the mousetrap had sensed his toe was a rodent and snapped shut for the kill, but Our Hero had stopped that after a frantic five minutes of direct pressure, cold compresses, and, finally, an entire box of adhesive bandages mummifying his tormented toe; but the toe was smashed, lifeless, a fleshy relic.

Our Hero hobbled over to his writing desk, determined not to allow his latest misfortune to further hinder his dreams. He began to write about his accident, in great detail, and after nearly two hours of painstaking printing, he had completed a new chapter in his novel, deciding the pain was more than adequate compensation for what he considered his best writing in the last four years. Pain or no pain, he sensed his novel was nearing completion, and now he had a title that would ensure success: *The Freedom of Pain.* Yes, he exclaimed to the walls and to his new Muse, pain, *The Freedom of Pain* will one day see the literary light of day.

Reach Out to Anita

After receiving 150,000 letters from 1927 to 1989, and personally answering over 28,000 of them in my advice column, here I am writing to all my friends and loyal readers an open letter without a bit of advice before the publication of my second book, *Bursting the Double*. I don't know whether it's decency or guilt or some strange twist of mind that compels me to have this letter printed in the newspaper that for sixty-two years has carried my column. But after meeting old Clifton McDollip in town I knew I couldn't just bury my head and hope for the best.

Even though *Bursting the Double* is being published by a big Toronto publisher, has a chance to reach a wide Canadian audience, and fulfils a lifelong dream of mine, I'm having second thoughts about the book. Why, when I should be reposing in the serenity of eighty-five years well lived, am I worrying like a lost and frightened little girl? I would have been fine, I suppose, if I'd outlived all my old loves and friends, but a few of them are still kicking around – not to mention their children and grandchildren and great-grandchildren. It's one thing to cave the roof of scandal down on oneself – that

I would relish – but I'm going to short-circuit a whole slew of minds around here. I might even sink the cherished Island I was born on in 1904 and where one day I will breathe my last breath, although I have every intention of seeing the bright side of the year 2000.

Damn it, had I not bumped into old Clifton McDollip in town everything would be a breeze – I'd be waiting for the adulation, the reviews in Toronto papers, my royalty cheques. But poor old adorable Clifton, away with the fairies more often than he's with us, put his arms around me right in front of the Confederation Centre as a double-decker bus full of tourists was emptying. He shouted as loud as his eighty-nine-year-old voice let him, "I love you, Anita girl, always have, always will." His wife, my dear friend Lillian, died only a year ago. I wrote the obituary for the precious woman, as I will no doubt write the obituary for Clifton when he joins his wife. I tried to hush the excited old devil, but he was a lovestruck, irrepressible lad again, and kept shouting away: "I would have been proud to have been your husband ... The beautiful children we could have had ... It's not too late to tie the knot, Anita girl ..."

I tell you, the crowd that gathered, you would have thought someone was having a heart attack and not merely proclaiming his undying love. We sure were the main attraction in downtown Charlottetown that hot afternoon. Some of the tourists began taking photos of us. It's instinct for them, their cameras being like vital organs that work away on their own. "I love you, Anita girl, I love you," old Clifton went on in a confused state of melancholy and overexcitement, tears starting to form in his old eyes that are not without their occasional glimmer of mischief. Then he wept openly like a baby. The words I might have been able to face up to, but seeing old

Clifton weeping in front of half the town and more tourists than you could count in an hour started me having my doubts about the book right there on the Confederation Centre's concrete plaza, under the fluttering flags from all the provinces and territories of Canada. Fluttering flags, a weeping old man of eighty-nine, declarations of love – maybe I should backtrack a little. After all, to you, eighty-five-year-old Anita Adams is just a sweet old thing, not someone capable of scandalizing our whole Island.

My first plunge into literary fame coincided with winter ten and a half years ago. Before the spring thaw I was a toasted "literary figure," at least on Prince Edward Island. I should have been all aglow after my first published book but I was downright sad. Sad about my sham fame. A compilation of letters selected from the first fifty years of my three-times-a-week, three-letters-a-column output, and I was a celebrity in a place so small you can't get lost even if you're blindfolded and three-quarters stunned. I had dreamed for the longest time about having an honest-to-goodness hardback book after all those years in perishable newsprint, but that dream hardly seems a snore now. My literary début should have been more creative and more mine.

Truth is, my first book was nothing more than the letters of others, neatly divided into categories, and my responses, reasonable and witty and wise as they may be, but old stuff, veined through with attic smells and airless inspiration. Advice dealing with everything from knitting to hysterical pregnancies, philandering husbands to head lice, stain removal to proper funeral etiquette, proved to be a bigger hit with my Island fans than what any of the big shots of CanLit were publishing. Yet

I could have done a collection of my best obituaries for all the thrill I got out of that book.

My real dream was to produce a work of art, within my limitations, of course. Deep down I wanted to be the toast of Toronto, even after all the nasty things I've said and written about those deluded souls who desert our Island for the lure and perfumed stench of the big city. I'd rather live in the woods with a ramshackle outhouse, inhaling the effluvia, than anywhere near Toronto, I used to say when someone tried to bring up the disadvantages of Island living. I've already had two "Anita Adams Appreciation Days," twenty years apart, and five years ago got to sit on my very own float in the Gold Cup and Saucer Parade; now I want Toronto to stand up and take notice of me. I want to be taken seriously as a writer.

At eighty-five, believe me, I'm a long way from being burned out, as anyone who knows me can verify. A kiss from old Anita, even on the cheek, is no mere show of affection – it's a battery charger! At an age when too many people are content to rest in the shadows, to accept the dim flickering of their lives, I was about to blaze brighter. Then I had to bump into my old friend Clifton.

This forthcoming book will create more cracks and crevices on the Island than any earthquake. It will shroud completely that feeble excuse of a first book I put together, and one friendly local reviewer described as "the perfect tonic for world-weary minds ... an unbeatable, uplifting read." The last thing in the world I desired to be was someone's tonic. I wanted to roar; I needed to soar to the literary heavens. My second book I wrote exactly as my heart dictated, no compromising, no holding back, no bowdlerizing whatsoever. The reception on the Island to this second book of mine may well break my heart – or my neck, I can't be sure. But the actual writing of it, I tell you, sure as heck rejuvenated me.

I keep asking myself, what in the world can they do to an eighty-five-year-old woman? I won't lose any sleep if the critics pillory me. Let the wardens of propriety impale me on their morality. Am I afraid of impalement? Like I say, what can possibly be done to an old woman? *Especially when she's an old man.* Oh well, fair Island, home of my heart and brittle bones, the secret is out at last. The double bursts ... My fans, forgive me. My friends, try to understand. My God, laugh with me.

Wait till my next round of talk shows and interviews and personal appearances. I'll give the public ear-to-ear revelations. The deception that chap Grey Owl once carried out will seem like a minor sleight of hand when my story is told. Of course I'll never be allowed on any local radio or TV stations, not by those people who treated me so kindly after my first book, who considered me the ultimate granny. All those sedate teas and tranquil church socials I smiled through. I look back, and wonder how in the world I did it.

Universe and Toronto, prepare yourselves, here comes Anita Adams of Charlottetown, Prince Edward Island. Here comes Delwin Fuller of the very same locality. Yes, the both of us, hand in hand, id in id, ego in ego, private parts once well concealed now all over the place. And for those who are offended, whose senses of curiosity and adventure and humour are overridden by a vision of a universal chastity belt, spare yourselves even a single word of my second book, turn away right now. For you others, here comes the heroine of the advice column and the hero of the sports page. Heroine/hero. A love affair with life unfolded twice.

To be honest, for as long as I can remember I yearned

to be literary, never considering my obits and advice column as any more than well-crafted scribblings. Say a poetess, that would have been more rewarding. Unfortunately, all I can do with any flair are limericks that make my friends blush. I also chased dreams of being a novelist. But you can't wish a great novel into existence. Or even a novella. I certainly wrote my share of novels, no less than one every three years for the last sixty-two years, but rottenly. They still stink up my attic like mouse-nibbled, yellowed newspapers bundled away. Putrid little exercises of romantic gibberish. But how I love romance, as you'll find out if you read *Bursting the Double*.

I even wrote a play once, a romantic musical in three acts called *Ambiguity for Two* that played twice a week for one entire February in 1938. Some of you old-timers might have seen it, but I hardly expect you'd remember a line or lyric. I was forever telling people that there's more to life than meets the eye, occasionally dropping hints and clues, yet no one ever picked up on them. People have always demanded that Delwin and I be exactly what we appeared to be. How sad for me: no poetess, no novelist, no playwright of any stature. Just a playwrong. To be buried at Cavendish next to Lucy Maud Montgomery herself, with sweet Anne Shirley perched atop my tombstone, what a satisfying interment that would be. Or next to George Sand or maybe George Eliot, if you get what I mean. Probably I'll wind up being burned like Joan of Arc. Anita of Arse, that's me.

But I shouldn't avoid the fact that I do have a prodigious talent for answering letters. Sensible advice ... down-to-earth guidance ... verbal embrace. How I hate that talent. It's confined me all these years as surely as any steel chains or prison bars. Sixty-two years of my life and it pains me. Oh, I was sincere in my replies, even if I didn't want to be, so don't lynch me yet. I never did my obits or columns in a slipshod way; I always fussed and fretted over each word. I built up a following – actually, three generations of followings – being conscientious and "good." But finally I wrote for myself, damning propriety and goodness. Read the book, if you dare, and you'll see a side of old Anita that you couldn't have imagined in a million years.

Don't get me wrong, I'm not renouncing my past. I can't – it's me, however shaped or constructed. Besides, I have a certain affection for those unseen letter writers, especially the ones who wrote to me from desperation and need, who opened their hearts or dared to unlock dark doors. I hope they don't feel I'm betraying them. The very thought of having received 150,000 letters in sixty-two years makes me feel like I'm part of something much bigger than myself. Perhaps I should stop the publication of *Bursting the Double* this very instant and incinerate my foolhardiness. But I might as well cease my bodily functions. I never felt like a deceiver. It became natural to be two people.

So, no moving poetry to evoke a youth's tears. So, no romantic epic of scope and grandeur tracing two centuries of tempestuous Island life. So, no fabulous Broadway play that runs until doomsday to thunderous bravos. You're probably asking, in between curses, what did I squeeze out of my old grey head and blackened heart? Well, it's an autobiography of sorts. Really, half autobiography, half biography. I wrote it. No use troubling Delwin. He had enough on his mind, the poor dear. He's the morose one, subject to gloomy spells, living and dying with his sports teams, always pulling himself out of mounds of regrets, worrying like a fool about being old, drinking immoderately as if there's no tomorrow. In his prime Delwin used to be quite the high liver; however, the old boy did stretch his prime a little too far and much too thin. Mind you, he is a living legend on the Island, particularly around the race tracks and with the bootleggers and, of course, with the ladies. Delwin retreats to the past far too frequently for his own good, and I can't help but hear the talk around town that he's crazy as the crows. Delwin *is* eighty-five in every sense; he didn't sidestep with my agility those traps and pitfalls leading to spoilage. I sure hope Delwin, who was dead set against the book from the start, survives *Bursting the Double*.

I was careful not to make my second book confessional in the least. It's more like a chronicle of duality, of the struggle to make sense out of a world that has a knack for turning into a giant loony bin too often, even on the Island. Perhaps it's fair to call *Bursting the Double* a remembering or a going-over, a description of how Delwin and I existed virtually side by side yet independently for sixty-two years. No matter what Delwin's frame of mind is, *I* feel full of hopeful beginnings. When you construct yourself, you can keep your figure a little longer, in a manner of speaking. I hear you calling me a charlatan and fraud and a thousand worse things, but just wait. The laughter was always genuine. And so were the tears.

I hope I haven't lost too many of you so far. But I'm trying to break things to you nice and slow, leaving the details and the unravelling for the book. But there's no avoiding the big, glaring question: How does a nice boy from our fabled Cradle of Confederation, unsophisticated as a person can be, who once only wanted to play professional hockey, get to be an attractive advice columnist who doubles – excuse the pun – as the newspaper's obituary writer? The story, at the root of it, is rather simple and unspectacular.

My secret, which you Island readers now share before the rest of the country finds out –against the wishes of my Toronto publisher with his planned Anita Adams/Delwin Fuller publicity blitz in the fall – has been kept for sixty-two years, quite an astounding feat, I might add in all modesty. I had friends who loved me, I had bosses and colleagues and family, yet no one knew, not a soul. I didn't even have the heart to tell my clergyman, although both Delwin and I were once regular churchgoers – different denominations, however.

Just to give you a flavour of the rich, full lives we were able to live on the Island, a few little peeks into our pasts might not be out of order. In *Bursting the Double* there's a whole chapter on the time I broke both legs and an arm, and was in casts for two months at the end of 1929, right about the time the stock market collapsed. It was after Delwin went absolutely wild over a trapeze artist from Boston who came to Charlottetown with the most incompetent, ridiculous travelling circus I'd ever seen. I told Delwin not to try that romantic stuff so high in the air, safety net or no safety net, but there was no stopping his hormones in those days.

During the late 1930s, Delwin and I dated fun-loving fraternal twins for two years and neither of them knew. In 1945, at the age of forty-one, Delwin became engaged to be married, determined to end his bachelor days, until I paid the woman a visit and informed her of Mr. Fuller's incurable and unspeakable hereditary disease. Delwin didn't heal from that wound easily.

I personally turned down eleven proposals of marriage, all of them described with sensitivity in the book. (That doesn't include old Clifton McDollip's recent emotional proposal.) Out of necessity, I developed a definite genius for putting men off. Oh, I'd tease and hug and kiss and get quite affectionate at times, but the expression of my passion, needless to say, was circumscribed by heavy-handed biology. Delwin was much more generous with his person, too generous for my tastes. I couldn't begin to list all of Delwin's flirtations and flings, but the more interesting ones certainly aren't left out of the book.

So you don't think that everything Delwin and I did concerned the flesh or a panting Cupid, let me tell you that we once decided to try to run in a provincial election, Delwin for the Conservatives and me for the Liberals. It was a time when we were both itching to get more political on an Island that is very serious about its politics. But that endeavour, believe me, wasn't easy to pull off, not along with our jobs at the newspaper and all our other civic activities. Delwin begged out because of ill health before the campaign began – I know it was only nervousness and fatigue – and I wasn't able to get my party's nomination, although I gave it a good try and had some strong male support.

But I suspect the part of the book readers will most enjoy will deal with the close calls both Delwin and I had. Some of them, I tell you, were hair-raising if not heart-stopping, like the time one of Charlottetown's most prominent lawyers got too amorous and I had to knock him cold; or when Delwin was arrested for public drunkenness and was defended by the aforementioned lawyer still with his black eye. But I'll leave the juicy anecdotes and incredible adventures for the book.

Since that lovely August day in 1927 – the day after Sacco and Venzetti were executed in the States – Anita Adams has existed, splendidly I'd like to add. I often wonder if she was always there, hiding within Delwin, waiting for the appropriate time to emerge. It was when Delwin was twenty-three, atwitter with youth and dreams. There was no other way he could get the job he wanted, and therefore Anita Adams, young fresh thing of three and twenty in all her virginal splendour, was born; from away, so I could explain her sudden appearance in a community where strangers are always noticed. I claimed to be from London, England, because it seemed such a cultured and literary place to be from. I know that when speaking of birth it is customary to speak of babies, but not with Anita. She was born full-bosomed then and there in 1927 to do her sixty-two years of the "Reach Out to Anita" column. During my jittery early days as an advice columnist no one knew if I could fill the enormous shoes Muriel O'Flaherty had left.

Muriel had been writing the advice column in the newspaper for ten besotted years – her only conspicuous failing seemed to be a taste for a fiery homemade brew – and she had a loyal readership who needed her homespun wisdom to fortify their existences. She was a firm and unwavering believer that the Island way of life was the best way of life. It was uncertain whether her readers would take to an unknown upstart from away. Poor Muriel, she was kicked in the head by a horse on New Year's Day 1927 and went blissfully into a coma for almost eight months, then awoke, spoke rapidly in perfect Russian for over two hours, and died, just like that. We didn't have any fancy facilities like the modern Queen Elizabeth Hospital back then, no life-support systems. People from one end of the Island to the other prayed a great deal for Muriel. The really peculiar thing about Muriel's accident and demise was that relatives and friends swore to a person that she didn't know a word of Russian, not even *nyet*. Within hours of her death some bizarre rumours began circulating that Muriel had been a Communist agent. Those rumours never picked up much momentum but for a few days our placid Garden of the Gulf had its very own Red Scare.

When the barrel-chested editor who ran the newspaper in those days looked around the office for someone to replace Muriel O'Flaherty, Delwin Fuller eagerly volunteered. Delwin was enthusiastic and ambitious in 1927, and wanted to develop his writing skills in whatever ways he could. Once he realized he couldn't make it in professional hockey, Delwin wanted to be the best damn newspaperman in the Maritimes. The barrel-chested editor – who preferred to be called "Newsy" – laughed at Delwin like he had never laughed before. His usual dirty, gravelly laugh became dirtier and more gravelly. Delwin was a young sports reporter and Newsy said his credibility as an advice columnist would be nil.

Over and over again Delwin told him how much he wanted to help people, how he desired to keep Muriel's spirit and work alive, but Newsy scoffed at the idea, telling Delwin to stick to his sports writing and chasing the gals. "Give me a woman with an honest, sincere, compassionate face," Newsy bellowed in his barrel-chested way through the newspaper office. He could rarely say anything without stringing together more adjectives than a sow has piglets.

Muriel's column was a strong feature, one of the most popular the newspaper had, and Newsy was reluctant to discontinue it. During the time Muriel had been in a coma, Newsy reprinted columns from earlier years. Muriel's funeral was the biggest and most tearful the Island had seen in some years, dignitaries everywhere you looked, including Premier

Saunders and every member of the Legislative Assembly. The readers wanted Muriel's tradition carried on.

So along came Anita Adams, honest, sincere, compassionate, and believable, neatly dressed in the fashion of the day. (Until I developed my own tastes and style, I copied my more stylish neighbours.) It was harrowing that first month, take my word for it. All that women used to wear. The outward appearance took work and dedication – I did have to shave very carefully and altering my athlete's deportment and movements was no easy task – but inside Anita unfolded effortlessly. Thanks to an inheritance, Delwin and I were able to share a lovely house in town, on Fitzroy Street, one floor for each, keeping our lives tidy and separate. Delwin was the landlord and I his dependable tenant, always paying my rent promptly.

Where Delwin had failed with Newsy, Anita triumphed. What a charming talker young Anita was with her delightful English accent. An enchantress. After thirty minutes she had that job despite not having an authentic past. A little creative forgery, some convincing lying, and there was "Reach Out to Anita." Muriel's popular column had been "Messages to Muriel."

Newsy wrote an adjective-laden obituary for Muriel in which he asked that all future letters for advice be sent care of the newspaper to Miss Anita Adams, formerly of London, England. The barrel-chested editor also wrote that Muriel O'Flaherty had hand-picked and trained Anita Adams, having given the young Englishwoman her deathbed blessing. Newsy, struck a little too hard by the hammer of grief, intimated in a non-journalistic manner that Muriel and Anita would be "communicating" regularly. Poor man, he had to sell newspapers and cope with the fact that he had been in love with Muriel for a decade. After a brief reviving flirtation with Muriel's replacement, requiring my sharpest skills of evasion, Newsy returned to his debilitating pining. His once exemplary work and inspirational leadership skidded downhill. It was pitiful to witness the barrel-chested editor, of the sturdiest and most redoubtable Island stock, so reduced. He lost his dirty, gravelly laugh. He took to drinking and babbling and conducting elaborate séances right in the middle of the newspaper office. He wore the same faded suit day after day until he smelled worse than a barnful of slops. Newsy was eventually replaced, but not Anita Adams, who gradually shed her cumbersome Englishness and became as true a red-clay Islander as possible for a person from away.

I chuckle to write that I'm an Island institution now. But who knows what will happen to that institution when *Bursting the Double* is published in the fall. Maybe my column will be suspended after sixty-two continuous years. But it's summer as I write this letter and I'm always bolder in summer, so onwards I press. Open your hearts, open your minds, and I hope my book doesn't make you hate me. After sixty-two years, Anita still needs your love. Remember, my friends, no matter what happens, you can still "Reach Out to Anita."

The Existence of Posters

*I*t was a Sunday, early in the morning, on the first day of summer, when an amorous young man of twenty, leaving a married, older woman's apartment, in rural Prince Edward Island, saw the beautiful poster adorning the window of a vacant store. The poster so arrested his attention that he stood in front of it for a full minute, even though he had been in a hurry to get home. I MIGHT NOT EXIST was printed in luminous tiny capital letters at the top of the poster, which depicted a Heironymus Bosch-like scene. Except he recognized it as the shopping and commercial district of his town. The town he had grown up in and almost left countless times.

A week later, a complaint was phoned in to the local police chief that vandals were at large. More complaints quickly followed. The police chief investigated, and counted thirty-six of the posters around the shopping and commercial district. On storefronts, the sides of buildings, a mailbox, telephone poles, trees, parked vehicles …

The police chief thought the posters were impressive, but he instructed one of the town workers to remove all thirty-six of them. After all, there was a bylaw against displaying posters without prior approval from town council. No one on town council had been contacted.

A few days later, amid a swirl of rumours and gossip and speculation about the appearance of even more posters, the editor of the local weekly newspaper sent her youngest, least experienced – yet most enthusiastic – reporter to take a few photographs and see if there was some sort of feel-good story behind the enigmatic posters.

The reporter came back with several photographs, and the information that he had counted ninety-three of the posters.

"The quality of the posters is high. The artwork is professional," the enthusiastic reporter said.

"Who around here would go to all that trouble?" the editor asked.

Closing his eyes, and contemplating what might be going on, the reporter said, "I wouldn't mind having one of the posters in my bedroom ..."

At the next town-council meeting, during new business, the issue of the posters was brought up. One councillor said they added to the shopping and commercial district. Another saw a potential tie-in to tourism. Junk, nothing but junk, another councillor argued. "Isn't it amazing," the mayor said, holding one of the posters and fingering the gooey substance on the back, "that whoever is doing this is using a biodegradable adhesive?" "It may be biodegradable, but it wasn't easy to get it off my car," the mayor's brother-in-law complained. The debate became strident, the most strident since the dispute last year over the cost of sewer expansion and increased taxes. The councillors agreed to put off a decision until the next meeting. Perhaps cooler heads would prevail then.

A reporter for a big-city newspaper telephoned the editor of the local weekly and asked about the posters. The reporter's sister, who had never been given to exaggeration, had told him about the phenomenal number of fantastic, incredible posters during an earlier telephone conversation. She had also told him the bad news about her medical diagnosis.

"All we know," the editor said over the telephone, "is that there are close to eight hundred posters around town, more springing up every day, and no one has ever seen anyone put them up." The big-city newspaper reporter expressed incredulity and the editor of the local weekly became annoyed, and they got into an argument over investigative journalism and the relative merits of living in a small town as opposed to a big city.

On the day the big-city newspaper reporter arrived in the town, to visit his ailing sister, but also to see if there was a story worth pursuing, why waste the trip, he thought, there were well over a thousand posters. Besides, he could combine visiting his sister and researching what might turn out to be strangely interesting story with a little summer vacation. He had joked with his sister over the phone, attempting to lift her spirits, that writing a story in such a beautiful touristy area certainly qualified as a journalistic version of "summer fun."

"It's a big mystery," one of the patrons at the town's largest coffee shop said to the big-city newspaper reporter, on his second day in the town.

"You know what? This kinda reminds me of the Alfred Hitchcock movie *The Birds*. Where the feathery creatures take over the town," another patron said.

"Birds and posters aren't the same thing, for Heaven's sake," a third patron said, shaking her head at the ludicrousness of the comparison.

"That terrifying 1963 movie, directed brilliantly by Alfred Hitchcock, was based on a story by Daphne Du Maurier," the big-city reporter said, as if he were lecturing to a class of slow learners.

"My, don't you know a lot," a sunglasses-wearing counter clerk, a slight sneer curling her upper lip, said.

"I happen to be an Alfred Hitchcock fan, that's all," the big-city reporter defended himself.

"Well, we're being taken over by posters, the way that other town was taken over by birds," said the patron who had first mentioned the film comparison.

"*The Birds* was a movie, and this is reality, in case you've forgotten," the sunglasses-wearing counter clerk, pouring a cup of coffee, said.

"Sure, but wouldn't this make a great movie?"

"Yeah, a horror movie."

"There's nothing horrible about those posters," the big-city newspaper reporter said, jotting down notes as the patrons and staff offered their opinions. "They are exquisitely artistic," he stated, doing a mediocre imitation of Alfred Hitchcock that no one in the coffee shop recognized.

One of the town councillors, on his own initiative, nearly a month after the first poster appeared, had a couple of drinks and then went around ripping down posters. He was stopped by the local weekly's young, enthusiastic reporter, and they got into a shouting and shoving match. Comments such as *freedom of artistic expression* crashed loudly against *friggin' eyesores, I'd rather look at an attractive poster than a blank wall* against *there's enough garbage around here,* disturbing the otherwise tranquil, uneventful afternoon. The councillor, holding on to a portion of a ripped poster, fell to the ground and banged his head on the sidewalk. Banged it so badly that he bled on the sidewalk and all over the portion of the poster he had ripped down, and which had wound up under his head like a flattened pillow.

An ambulance, a poster on the driver-side door, took the injured man to the hospital. As the two ambulance attendants approached the hospital, they saw on a wall near the emergency entrance several more posters, and two doctors and a patient nearby. One of the doctors was staring at a poster; the other was drawing moustaches and beards on some of the faces of a second poster.

"It's you who's plastering them ugly things up," the patient, standing outside having a smoke, accused.

"I find them quite lovely. However, I have better things to do than put posters all over town. And you shouldn't be puffing on a cigarette," the moustache-and-beard-drawing doctor said.

The posters, and the stories about the posters, had a magnetic effect. People from all over the province came to the town. From all over the country. Some even from other countries, as if they were journeying to a miraculous shrine. A national TV crew arrived to do a segment on the sleepy little town and the "mushrooming posters," and shortly after that a foreign TV crew that in the last year had also done shows on a Himalayan family of hundred-year-old mountain people and on telepathic contact with UFOs. Many of the businesses in the town prospered. A few new enterprises emerged as a direct result of the interest in the posters.

I MIGHT NOT EXIST …

A month after the first poster appeared, one caller to the local radio phone-in show stammered, "We should be getting rid of those posters, like we would do with noxious weeds …"

The host, discarding objectivity, responded, "Stupid to look a gift horse in the mouth …"

Of the seventeen calls that morning, twelve were in favour of the posters, saw them as contributing to the town, and five were against, two vehemently.

The official count – run prominently front-page in the weekly newspaper – on the sixth week was 3,132 posters. (This number did not remain accurate for long, since posters were being removed as souvenirs or by members of a self-appointed town-beautifying crew, and replaced or added to by a yet-to-be-discovered individual or individuals.) A history buff, and well-known local eccentric, sat in the town's largest coffee shop and pointed out to anyone who would listen that the current number was exactly twice the year of Nostradamus's death in 1566. Another local eccentric, both more patriotic and more skeptical, said that if you took the year of Canada's Confederation, added it to the year of Nostradamus's death, threw in his age of forty-four – it was his birthday that day, he reminded the other patrons – and subtracted 345, his lucky number, he claimed, you would also get 3,132, the number of posters. By the next week the twice-the-year-of-Nostradamus's-death number was out-of-date, and the history buff announced that the new figure of 3,389 was twice the year of the 1692 Salem Witch-Hunt, plus five.

Then there was a report from another town, less than fifty kilometres away, that I MIGHT NOT EXIST posters had appeared. What one local artist, in a conversation with a vacationing lawyer who had recently purchased two of her paintings, described as a Sistine Chapel ceiling-like scene, with the townsfolk depicted in religious splendour. And then other towns. People lost interest in the first town, which still had under 5,000 posters. There were at least five other towns within a two-hundred-kilometre radius with more than that amount, and their posters having proliferated during a shorter time.

The big-city newspaper reporter stayed in the town, to be with his sister, whom her doctor said could not cling to life much longer. And the reporter thought there was a significant story in the recent murder – the small town's first murder in nearly ten years – of a young man who had been caught, in the less than sympathetic words of the reporter to the sunglasses-wearing counter clerk at the coffee shop, *in flagrante delicto.* Then someone told him that the murder victim had been, three months ago, the first one to see an I MIGHT NOT EXIST poster. This has to be the most elaborate, largest hoax ever, the big-city newspaper reporter said at the coffee shop, which had become his regular haunt in the town, when he wasn't at his dying sister's bedside at the hospital.

"Think of what people would say if these posters start showing up all over the world. In every single country," said the sunglasses-wearing counter clerk, taking off her sunglasses for a moment, her eyes seeming to be peering at a faraway place.

"Some things just aren't explainable," philosophized a patron, staring into her coffee.

"There has to be an explanation," another patron, finishing his third doughnut of the morning, stated adamantly, and pointed to the six posters on the coffee shop's window, one more than the previous morning.

A little girl and a little boy, walking hand in hand by the town's largest coffee shop, were the first to notice that one of the posters was different from the others. As with the thousands of other posters, words were printed in luminous tiny capital letters at the top of the poster. The two children read aloud at almost the same time, "I MIGHT EXIST."

Continuity

*I*t was 1989, and no one who knew Albert believed that he would ever leave Prince Edward Island, let alone get on an airplane and fly to Vancouver. Albert, after all, was ninety-seven years old and had never left the Island, rarely even went outside Charlottetown anymore. He almost left in 1914, seventy-five years ago, when he was twenty-two, but the family farm needed attention, and Albert, the oldest son and afflicted with a bad leg, stayed. One of his younger brothers died in the First World War and for years afterwards Albert wished he could have exchanged places with him.

You could count on the fingers of your two hands how many times Albert had left his current residence, a Charlottetown nursing home, in the last eleven years. He simply did not like to travel, feared airplanes, hated the very thought of invading the domain of birds. Yet Albert suddenly had the need to fly to the other end of the country. The first person he told of his desire to visit Vancouver was his grandson, Bobby, who was fifty-four and had left the Island several times over the years, but always came back. Bobby was the one, with the help of two of his aunts, who had recently completed the first part of the family's genealogical history, tracing every descendant of Albert and his dear wife, Edna. Edna had died forty-one years ago, but not before raising nine children with her husband, and Albert never remarried. Their descendants lived all over North America. Bobby had even traced down some relatives living in Europe and one in South America. Currently he was going further back in the family's lengthy Island history, to Albert's and Edna's parents and grandparents.

Albert told everyone who visited him in the nursing home – relatives, friends, staff – that he wanted to take an airplane to Vancouver as soon as possible, but no one took him seriously except Steve, Bobby's youngest son and one of Albert's many great-grandchildren. Steve, who looked much younger than his twenty-three years and whose ambition in life was to be a poet, even encouraged the grand old man in his dream.

"A trip like that will kill him," one relative claimed.

"You think he can make a rational decision?" another relative scolded Steve.

Several family members told the twenty-three-year-old to spend his energy trying to find a decent job on the Island, not encouraging old Albert's preposterous notion. The young man had already written five poems about his great-grandfather, and intended to write many more for a book he was working on about the only person he knew who had been born in the nineteenth century.

What had sparked Albert's desire to travel to Vancouver was the birth of his latest great-great-grandchild, a boy born a month before to an unmarried great-granddaughter, nineteen years old, whom he had met only once, when her parents brought her to Prince Edward Island when she was seven, and Albert personally took her to see *Anne of Green Gables* at the Confederation Centre. A year later Albert was put in a nursing home against his will and lost most of his desire to travel, across the province or even around Charlottetown.

The infant in Vancouver was very ill, but no one would tell Albert. One relative suggested that they "borrow" a local baby and bring it to the nursing home, telling Albert this child was his great-great-grandchild from Vancouver, and several other relatives thought it was a great plan, but Steve almost punched the man who first suggested the idea. Albert is a human being who has lived a long life and deserves to do something he wants so badly, Steve argued with conviction and love. "Goddamn it," Steve yelled, losing his temper at some relatives who discouraged even talking to Albert about Vancouver, "a person doesn't stop dreaming because they're old."

As the arguments and bickering continued among family members – it was the largest, most intense family argument since the time their richest Island relative died intestate a quarter century before – Steve bought himself and his great-grandfather airplane tickets to Vancouver, getting them in advance so he could get a discount fare. As it was, the young man used nearly his entire savings to buy the tickets, and planned on using his credit card to cover their expenses on the West Coast. He told the old man they would be leaving in three weeks, and not to discuss it with other family members.

The three weeks were important ones for Albert. He filled his time thinking of the little boy in Vancouver. And of all his years on Prince Edward Island and on the farm and the fishing he loved to do. He even had some conversations with his younger brother, the one who had been killed in the First World War, but no one paid much attention to Albert's rambling utterances, except Steve, who tried to turn them into coherent poems. Albert thought a great deal of the good, long life he had lived on Prince Edward Island. But now he needed to go to Vancouver. The old man sensed something, something very important: that his life would not be complete unless he held the child in his arms. Albert fought his fear of going into the air with thoughts of the little baby. And every single day during the three weeks, Steve visited his great-grandfather, bringing him pictures of the faraway place they would be visiting soon and sharing in the old man's dream.

Telling the staff that he was going to take his great-grandfather to the harness races – how can you deny a ninety-seven-year-old man the chance to rekindle his old passion, Steve argued against the staff's cautiousness – the young man called a taxi and they were driven first to his apartment for the suitcases he had already packed, one for himself and one for Albert, and then to the airport.

Albert cursed the idea of flight and airplanes, but his fear was much less than either he or Steve had anticipated. All through the long flight, the old man talked to his great-grandson, and pretended they were on a boat, out fishing where he used to as a boy. In the most vivid detail Albert described and relived his outings. He could even hear the sound of the line being cast and the fish being pulled out of the water. Steve told Albert that he wished he had lived then, and wrote a short poem before the airplane landed about his great-grandfather's youth and love of fishing.

When they arrived in Vancouver and Steve contacted the young mother, Albert's great-granddaughter, she cried throughout the telephone conversation. The child, after a two-month, incubator-confined struggle, had died. It had happened several days ago, and the small, private funeral service would be tomorrow.

The great-grandson did not know what to say to his great-grandfather. The old man looked into his eyes and knew right away that something was horribly wrong. He said that the Good Lord must have a reason, even before Steve could tell him of the unfortunate death.

Steve, who had been certain, even adamant, that he should take his great-grandfather to visit a living child, decided that Albert was not strong enough to go through the sadness and stress of a funeral service. In the hotel room the two men were sharing, Albert talked of the past, of life on beautiful Prince Edward Island. He had seen many relatives and friends die during his ninety-seven years of life. Holding his gnarled hands against his face, Albert said that it was not the length of a life, but what a person accomplished and the peace felt within at the end. Steve told his great-grandfather that he loved him more than anyone, even his own parents, and promised to take him around Vancouver tomorrow, if he was feeling well enough. After Albert fell asleep, Steve stayed up late working on his poetry.

The next day, while Steve was sleeping, Albert sneaked out of the hotel room, found a taxi, and went alone to the cemetery long before anyone else arrived.

When the mourners started to arrive, Albert was standing close to the gravesite. All morning he had been thinking about the child he had never been able to hold.

Nothing seemed right here, so far from home, birth and death without the intervening journey to take, the road to follow, the life to live. Albert began to weep. People at the cemetery tried to help him, but he did not need their assistance. No one knew who he was, except for the young, grieving woman, even though she had been with the old man only a week, and that was twelve years ago. Albert continued to weep through the entire service for the dead infant, two months old, and his great-granddaughter held her ninety-seven-year-old great-grandfather, feeling beneath her grief that life somehow still had meaning and love. She remembered her trip to Prince Edward Island and the day the old man took her to the Confederation Centre. She remembered it as the happiest, most senseful day of her life. After the funeral, Albert and his great-granddaughter spent the day at her apartment talking, but before they said goodbye to each other, the young woman promised to visit Charlottetown and the old man during the summer. He, in return, promised to take her to see *Anne of Green Gables* again.

Late in the evening, when the old man returned to the hotel room, his great-grandson was frantic with worry. He had called the police and then roamed the streets looking for Albert. No one had thought of going to the cemetery or the young woman's apartment.

"Where did you go?" Steve asked.

"I want to go back to the Island ... to Charlottetown," Albert said, not paying attention to his great-grandson's question.

"Where were you all day?" Steve demanded to know.

"It's time for me to get back home," Albert responded, his eyes and mind elsewhere.

"The return tickets aren't until Tuesday – a week, like we planned," Steve told him, feeling that the old man was losing his hold on reality.

The old man sat down on one of the beds in the hotel room and said, "I'll wait right here."

"Don't you want to see Vancouver?" Steve asked, afraid that the old man would fall into a deep depression if he stayed in the hotel room too long.

"The Island is all I care for."

"But we came all this way."

"I have to get back to the Island, where I belong. I was born there, and I'll die there."

"Don't talk that way," Steve said, forcing himself to smile in a hopeful manner.

"My life has been most rewarding and I sure as heck can't complain that I've been shortchanged by the Good Lord. Ninety-seven years is more than fair."

"You still have many more years," Steve told the old man in as cheerful a tone as he could bring forth.

"No doubt, no doubt," Albert said, no sadness or fear in his voice. "But they'll have to be on the Island ..."

Acting on the Island

*I*had this image in my mind of a heavy coffin, heavier than wood. Then I heard the words come right through the lid: *It's most unfortunate, but you have to be released ...* It wasn't the first time I had ever been fired from a job, and I was somewhat used to the feeling of vocational expulsion, yet I still wasn't able to quell the sensation of queasiness. Every time I get fired my sense of being out of place or unable to fit in becomes deeper. I've been digging my little ditch of nonconformity for eight years now. Not that I mind fancying myself an outcast or outsider – after all, I have chosen to be an actor – but it's disconcerting being bounced around all the time, having people who aren't particularly concerned about your well-being passing judgement on your life like cold-hearted theatre critics.

This last job went on for nearly seven months, a personal record, and my father thought that I, at twenty-nine, had finally settled down and was going to do the family proud. He told me in that damn imperturbable voice of his that he couldn't keep getting me jobs forever. Only Shakespeare is forever, I argued mischievously.

Well, I was doing all right at this clerical job except that I came in medicinally drunk a few too many times and every so often did what I felt, therefore shaking terribly the equilibrium of the office. It's merely my thespian calling pushing through, telling me to get on stage, to do something with my psyche before it ossifies. For me performing is a dance to keep the gods of lunacy off my back, simple as that. But I suspect that my real sin at my patronage-secured job was not getting a haircut for seven months, although I could never fathom the connection between good grooming and worldly success: look at Samson, look at the Bard of Avon himself ... don't forget The Beatles. My supervisor considered hirsuteness a transgression next in magnitude to premeditated murder. Who would think a little afternoon Shakespeare sonorously delivered by a long-haired – actually, ponytailed that day – actor would lead to the final curtain. As they say, give someone enough hair and he'll hang himself.

I was withstanding the supervisor's rebuking surprisingly well, including his laudatory references to my father's and my grandfather's contributions to the Island, enduring even the discourse on acceptable behaviour and good grooming, when he magnanimously informed me that the consensus of the office staff was that they felt only pity for me, that my reprehensible actions were indicative of a troubled person, and it was unfortunate that I had to be released. *Released?* That's when I lost control and erupted with laughter. I managed to prove my sanity by sticking a thumb into each ear and waving my fingers as I offered a stumbling version of Jaques' "All the world's a stage speech" from *As You Like It* before I became completely submerged in my own volcanic laughter.

I wonder if I'll ever be able to make a living from acting so I won't have to wade through these jobs anymore. In a couple of weeks I'll ask my father to forgive me. He'll cough a few times in thought and manage to find some temporary job for me. Too many people owe him favours for me to dare collect pogey and disgrace five generations of pillars of Island society.

I might as well be waiting for Godot for all my luck. A week out of work and I thought this last little audition would be my salvation. Another audition down the drain. It's that vindictive director, darling of the Island theatre community. The man hates me, and he seems to be lording over every audition lately. He remembers when I had the great idea to do Anne of Green Gables in drag. How seriously everyone was taking themselves that day, trying to determine what else would appeal to the tourists, what plays would pack them in, when I suggested that an alluring, scantily clad, perhaps a touch lascivious Anne Shirley would be a stupendous theatre innovation. I told everyone that we could put it on simultaneously with the real McCoy, get some hot publicity, shake up the tourists and the local theatre community a little. Sex and Anne would be an unbeatable combination, I argued.

That harmless flight of fancy evoked cries of derision that declared me to be no better than a heretic or foul-mouthed blasphemer. Trapped on stage, surrounded by grim leftovers from the Spanish Inquisition, I bravely vowed that I would play a sensual Anne if it were the last role I ever played. A few stalwart friends and I did manage to put on one performance at a small theatre downtown, boldly adding a little frontal nudity for spice. I'll never know who tipped off the police for our second performance. If my dad would have seen my modified Anne and less than masculine Gilbert Blythe, his arteries would have hardened on the spot.

Bad enough I lost my sweet provincial government job, now I can't get an acting job to save my frayed soul. I've played fifteen different roles on the Island – I've got the glossies pinned to my walls to prove it – but work, challenging acting work, is hard to find in this land of red soil and rampaging tourists. So why don't I leave? Because my fragile mind crumbles at the sight of a skyscraper or the virulence of a big-city traffic jam. Charlottetown is small and navigable; my failures less gruelling and eviscerating in the Cradle of Confederation. I left the Island and tried New York City eight years ago, after graduating from UPEI, and believe me, the Big Apple is thoroughly rotted. I got two roles in my half-year, big-city sojourn, one of which will go down in theatre history as the ultimate in histrionic puke. In an avant-garde off-off-Broadway production, I played a giant squirrel who mates with a successful accountant. I swear to God, that was the play. It could have been a sensational role had the director and the playwright both not insisted that I play the part straight. I never understood the social comment that piece of theatre was trying to make, but the walleyed playwright told the actors that it was a metaphoric statement on the debate between heredity and environment. Incredibly, that job lasted six weeks, thirty-six lunatic performances, and I was always hot and smelly after each two-hour squirrel-suited show. Just when I was getting used to being a giant squirrel, at least on stage, the playwright in a fit of inspiration changed the lead role to that of a dwarf monkey and got a shrill-voiced kid to replace me.

Enough of this nostalgia. To keep my sanity intact on the Island, I need to keep acting, to play roles on stage or elsewhere. I cope as best I can. A little makeup and a costume change can do wonders. During a time when so many people have difficulty figuring out who they are, I can be anyone.

My actor's instincts took me to the Confederation Court Mall with its honeycomb of mind-numbing stories encased in climate control. God, I don't want to be here when the world ends. I hurried into the bookstore, a favourite haunt of mine, left immune from the mall's commercialism and sterility through glorious words. The bookstore is most enjoyable when least crowded but Saturday afternoons leave the store flooded with bit players and supernumeraries. Watching the others on stage closely, I moved through the abundance of books. I took various books off shelves or from displays, read a paragraph here and there, and replaced them.

After replacing a current self-help best-seller, I noticed an impeccably attired woman, around my age, maybe a few years older, standing in a corner, and stealthily reading *The Joy of Sex*. She was beautiful, and her large sunglasses added just the pinch of mystery on an overcast spring afternoon. She was no bit player; she would be my co-star. I had to see her eyes, I had to speak to her. Full of opening-night jitters, I travelled through the crowd to the mysterious woman in the corner, still uncertain what voice or identity I would assume to go along with my three-piece blue suit with matching silk handkerchief, finely crafted cane, and curly-haired, sandy-coloured wig I had used when I play a psychopath in *One Night Stand*. Improvisation, my man, I directed my emerging afternoon persona.

Tapping my cane once ceremoniously on the floor and trying a slight British accent, I asked, "May I be of assistance, madam?" Startled, the woman quickly closed the book and tried to hide it along with her purse behind her back, as if she had been caught fishing out of season.

"I'm just browsing, you know," she told me apologetically.

"I noticed you were examining *The Joy of Sex*," I said in a voice rich in warmth and erudition, my nervousness replaced by on-stage confidence, the British accent growing a little stronger.

"*The Joy of Sex*," she echoed, absently. "I was only curious. I only wanted to –"

"It's an excellent instructive work of scientific objectivity. First-rate," I said and tapped with my cane at another copy of the book on a shelf over the lovely head of trim brown hair.

"It is? ... Yes ... yes ... it is," the woman stammered.

"You should add it to your library," I told her.

"I should?"

"Certainly. Years ago, when the book first came out, there was so much sensationalism and controversy but people have had a chance to give it serious thought, and *The Joy of Sex* has become a classic of erotic instruction. We so mystify Eros. We make Eros an enemy instead of a friend."

With a smooth hand the woman removed her sunglasses and looked very seriously at me, an engrossed student peering at her knowledgeable professor. In the voice of a goddess, she said, "I agree."

I was taken by her large brown eyes, and enunciated with charming brilliance: "It enables two people to cut through the misconceptions and false assumptions, and to experience each other fully in this society of ours which usually militates against genuine contact or communication. Eros helps us to communicate forthrightly."

"That's an interesting insight ..."

I was ready to ask her out for dinner, ready to buy the book for her with a special suggestive inscription of my own, when I noticed her left hand: *married!* Pulchritudinous middle-classness. Wife, mother, paragon of respectability. There was no time now to initiate an affair, to woo and captivate, to steal her from some prominent Island doctor or dentist or lawyer with good connections. I cursed my lackadaisical Muse.

"Why don't you purchase the book? I guarantee it will be educational. Eros is an astute teacher." I again pointed to the book on the shelf and read out loud from the cover: "A Gourmet Guide to Love Making." Then, with the most solemn expression I could fashion under the circumstances, I added, "We should keep *The Joy of Sex* with the cookbooks."

The woman smiled resplendently and said, "I think I might as well buy a copy of your *cookbook*. How much is it?"

I glanced at the back cover and quoted the price, then continued earnestly, underlining with my pointer/cane. "Complete and unabridged ... the *illustrated* edition." I suppressed the urge to give a lewd cackle, unwilling to sabotage my performance so far into the play.

"A bargain," the woman said, at last relaxing, and bringing her purse and the book forward. She looked intently at the nondescript and unerotic cover.

"But I like you so much I'm going to break some rules and give you my employee's discount. You can have *The Joy of Sex* for twenty dollars even, tax included."

"How generous. I can't believe how nice you are."

"Shhhh! We mustn't allow my generosity to become

public …" I imagined every adult Islander locked in a darkened room, flashlight in hand, and reading *The Joy of Sex*, thus betraying their political affiliations and ancestors' repudiation of Eros.

The woman reached into her purse and pulled out two ten-dollar bills. I quickly but politely grabbed the money from the woman and chivalrously escorted her to the door leading to Queen Street, not past the front cash register into the mall, all the time praising the sexual genius of Dr. Alex Comfort. Through the store window I watched her walk out of my life, the most beautiful specimen of middle-classness I'd ever seen.

I returned to my reading with feelings of unrequited love and sexual unfulfilment thumping at my heart. The damn middle-class woman had aroused me to afternoon fantasy. The transporting fantasy subsided as I read the beginning of a biography of Sarah Bernhardt and contrasted the great actress's triumphs with my own abject, play-less state. *Oh the vicissitudes and burlesques of life.*

I eventually decided on two fairly inexpensive paperbacks – plays by Ibsen and Sophocles, I like to dip into different centuries occasionally – and handed a salesclerk the twenty dollars, my grease-painted face happy testimony to my conquest and talents. Briefly I realized that I was a thief, and how simple it had been. I believed I could now play either Bonnie Parker or Clyde Barrow effortlessly and truly. I handed the change to a little boy crouched nearby, patted him on his dishevelled head, and said in a voice befitting a reformed Ebenezer Scrooge, "Here, my precious urchin, the residue from my spoils." He gripped the coins and ran to his mother, now a matronly woman, but perhaps once the most beautiful specimen of middle-classness that someone had ever seen.

After leaving the mall, I walked down Queen Street and joyfully strolled past the Confederation Centre of the Arts, scene of a few of my more memorable minor roles. I tapped my cane on the sidewalk as if to frighten away guilt pangs or evil spirits, smiling at people I knew who passed but didn't recognize me. Then I pranced up the stately steps to the Confederation Centre Public Library, the next leg of my afternoon odyssey. Into the hallowed building, into the vault of knowledge, into the city's glorious bibliotheca.

I sauntered around the first floor, not looking at books or magazines, but at people. Several of the old regulars were there, two of them dozing in chairs, newspapers on their laps, the events of the world as distant from them as hope. I walked toward the non-fiction section, pursuing a bobbling head of yellowish hair that had riveted my attention. I instantly fell in love with that magnificent head of hair, still not having seen the face that rested beneath the flaxen tresses. Love, chaste and sincere, surged into me, Eros stumbling about in search of firm footing.

The object of my affection pulled two thick volumes from the stacks and sat down at a long wooden table. Immediately she began to read one of the books, her head bent in concentration, her back to me. I moved next to her table and stood poised opposite her for several romantic seconds, finally sitting down with gestures worthy of an Old Vic actor. With precise timing, I placed my leading-man's cane lengthwise on the table, and then opened my Ibsen paperback to the first act of *Peer Gynt*, beginning to relive another play I had never starred in. I looked up but the girl was still buried in her book. After removing the blue silk handkerchief from my breast pocket, I coughed softly twice into the prop I had used so dashingly in my one attempt at Noël Coward, followed by one loud cough, the handkerchief fluttering defiantly. Success ... although limited. She resumed her reading with a scholar's diligence.

I couldn't call the girl attractive – she was seventeen or eighteen at the most – but my love would not abate; there was that flowing hair and the irrationality of Eros. I coughed again and she looked quizzically at me. Back to her damn book. Cough, cough ... I returned the handkerchief dramatically to my breast pocket.

An angry look, Joan Crawford at her most ferocious. "Is there something bothering you?" the object of my affection asked.

"No, I simply wanted to get your attention," I informed her with a bewildered innocence only the most sensitive actor could convey.

"You've succeeded in disturbing me. I have a paper to write," the girl said as if she were auditioning for the role of Katherina the Shrew.

The flash of braces, the metallic shine of wired teeth. The demise of love, but my passion still persisted. Eros is a prankster at heart.

"I love you ..." I was speaking to every gracious leading lady that ever glided over a stage, even if I might have been sounding more like Marlon Brando in *The Godfather* than Rex Harrison in *My Fair Lady*.

"You're crazy ..." God, the world was full of eager psychiatrists, quick-label artists.

"Please be kind. I'm tottering on the precipice of oblivion, on the verge of falling into a dark abyss." I wanted to do those lines over but frowned sadly instead.

"You don't impress me," she said with unbecoming antagonism, unnerving her Petruchio.

Through a simple transformation, my expression over-flowed with love and longing, Petruchio becoming the young Romeo: "I still love you ... 'O, she doth teach the torches to burn bright! / It seems she hangs upon the cheek of night / Like a rich jewel in an Ethiop's ear; / Beauty too rich for use, for earth too dear! / So shows a snowy dove trooping with crows / As yonder lady o'er her fellows shows.'"

"Hey, wow, that's from *Romeo and Juliet*. We just studied that in school last week," the unpredictable object of my affection gushed forth.

Serendipity! Blessed fortuity! My love to Fortuna. "There aren't many people outside of the theatre who would have known that. Now that *is* impressive, young lady."

Katherina turned into Juliet with a wide, artless smile, and once more I was blinded by a mouth filled with hardware, but gamely I confessed my earthly sins: "I'm sorry I was so flippant before, but I wanted to meet you. I'm terribly maladroit around strangers."

"That's okay. I kinda understand." What a tremendous delivery; she could have eclipsed a young Judy Garland in *The Wizard of Oz*.

"You have very understanding eyes ..." *Like two dead moons ... but that hair, strands that would enchant Eros himself.*

"Thanks for the compliment." She played with her magical hair, becoming younger by the moment. I thought she would reach the fetal stage before my eyes.

"You like Scottish and Irish traditional music?" I asked her, trying to keep our play from becoming total farce.

"I guess so," she mumbled indifferently.

"If you're in the mood sometime, a good friend of mine plays in the best traditional music band on the Island. Fine old jigs and reels to set the heaviest foot a-tappin'."

"I'm sort of partial to rock 'n' roll, if you understand what I mean."

"I live for rock music," I said with a touch too much enthusiasm. I coughed my apologies to Stanislavsky.

"I think some theatre might be more appropriate for us to see together," I went on as the girl continued to play with her beautiful hair. "I hear a new theatre group might put on *Romeo and Juliet* next month and we could see it."

"I'd like that, honest."

"I know I should have asked before, but what's your name?"

"Mary."

I became sick, as if I had forgotten my lines on stage. Why did it have to be Mary? Why do some parents forfeit their creativity? My father told me I would have been named Mary had I been born a girl. I smiled the smile of sincerity at the planet's ten millionth Mary.

"And yours?" Mary asked.

"Enrico," I blurted out. What else could I say, I had to compensate. I should have been more creative myself, but Enrico was pushing the Island's limit on names. I handed Mary my Ibsen paperback and asked her to write her phone number in it. *Sacrilege!*

Standing up and looking down at Mary, I became every bit the wise, charming, older lover, a combination of Olivier and Gielgud in their primes. I squeezed my cane as if I were slaying a disobedient dragon that was annoying my maiden fair, and said, "Please forgive me for my earlier behaviour."

"Not to worry," she told me. "It was cool."

Abhorrent word! "You're so kind. I'll call you soon." Suddenly my performance was crushed somewhere between Fredric March in *Dr. Jekyll and Mr. Hyde* and Anthony Perkins in *Psycho*. Smiling to conceal my true thoughts, I hid the desecrated Ibsen paperback in a pocket of my suit coat.

Mary was still playing with her hair, trying to give a sophisticated, womanly look, but failing miserably. "I'll walk you to the door, if you want," she offered, a natural ingénue not aware of her real calling.

"I would appreciate that very much, Mary ..." I was now what Mary wanted: cool, cool, cool.

Gently I took Mary's hand, and we walked quietly and romantically to the door, passing through the metal detector that shrieked insanely if you attempted to remove unchecked-out books from the library. I thought her braces would trigger the alarm, but we were spared. At the exit I took Mary's face in my left hand, extending my arm and stepping back like an artist viewing his creation from another perspective, at the same time lifting my right hand and cane heavenward in an invocation to humorous and, I hoped, unvindictive gods.

"You know something, Mary?"

"What, Enrico?"

I could no longer bear it; I had created a fanciful and farcical creature: a slobbering, sighing teenager, a Tess of the *Dummy*villes. Henry Higgins would have been flogged unmercifully for doing what I had done.

"You're sexier than a boiling lobster," I whispered like Rhett Butler distressed by the smoke of a burning Atlanta, and walked unhurriedly out of the library, abandoning one teenager paralyzed by incredulity, her mouth having fallen open to exhibit the wonder of modern technology. *O hail to thee, holy orthodontists, may you continue to save our children.*

Out on the Confederation Centre Public Library's concrete courtyard, I felt I had made a successful escape. In a world and century where there is no place to hide, where the climate change is threatening to envelope the entire Island population, somehow my mind had convinced me I had eluded all the threats to my existence. Four local alcoholics were crammed on one of the outdoor benches and openly passing the liquid treasure back and forth, celebrating their exemption. I sat along at a bench not far away, recuperating and studying the men, acquiring more emotions and mannerisms for my acting repertoire. I could not determine if these men were fragile or invulnerable, mad or safely insulated. All I knew was that I never wanted to be like them, unless it was on the stage. Jimmy Stewart as a pixilated Elwood P. Dowd in *Harvey* was lovable, a dreamer, but these men appeared to be dreamless. I couldn't help comparing them to my overly sober father.

As I began to daydream, embracing with my iconoclastic arms the beautiful woman I had earlier converted to the pursuit of Eros, a large, handsome Indigenous man sat down next to me; he sank onto the bench like a rag doll dropped to the ground by unsympathetic fate. I had often seen him around the library, or wandering the downtown streets weaponless in the midst of others who no longer saw him.

"You not feeling well?" I asked, all of a sudden talkative again, curious about the man. The Indigenous troubled men in town usually stayed out of sight but this one was different.

"Not the best, not today, no," he said, closing his sorrowful eyes, or rather his eyes falling shut. "You be my brother, man? You with me, ain't you?"

I was about to tell him of my friendship with several Mi'kmaw Elders, about my wondrous meeting years ago with Buffy Sainte-Marie, my collection of Aboriginal art, when the man opened his reddened eyes and hoisted his head toward me, forced breaths accompanying his movements.

"If you my brother you got to lend me some money. You got to help me, brother …"

I told him about the proud heritage of Poundmaker and Big Bear – all I recalled from a first-year Canadian History essay I had written on the 1885 Saskatchewan Rebellion. I was going to recite some lines from a play about Grey Owl I didn't get a part in, but I was caught by the pain in the large man's eyes.

"Please, I need money bad," the man said, trying not to plead.

"Sure, brother," I said. I took out a five-dollar bill from my wallet and pushed it into his palm. Then I handed the man my copy of two of Sophocles' plays, telling him it would be nourishment for his soul.

"I can't read too good, brother," he told me.

Feeling like a callous idiot, I apologized, placed the book back in my suit coat pocket with the other book, and handed the man the rest of what I had in my wallet, twenty dollars, thinking what the hell, this down-on-his-luck guy needs the money a lot more than I do. My mind was trying to convince me, but my emotions had control.

After I put my wallet away, the man started to maunder on about his kids and woman and the things he was going to buy for them. Sure, my new friend, proud warrior, sure, I thought. Buy your little kids all those toys Mrs. Middle-Class Beautiful gets hers. For an instant, looking at the man and listening to him, drawn into a history and hopelessness I did not understand, I felt I really knew why he drank. How I wanted to break my cane in half, but didn't. What the hell do I *really* know?

The man fell asleep next to me. The whole afternoon seemed horrid, wasted; I panned my own performances. I wanted to blame the script, to fault the scenery or lighting, to ridicule my co-stars, but it was me. Nothing could have pleased me more than to stay with this suffering man, to stop my acting for once, yet nothing was less possible for me. As I quietly left my twenty-five-dollar-richer new friend, not wanting to disturb him from his slumber, I started to prepare for my next role, another character already forming

Flowers for the Vases

(A Story of Love and Dependency)

The woman, wearing an old bathrobe, was sitting in bed against the headboard as she spoke, staring at the thin, shirtless man at the foot of the bed. His radiant, blue eyes seemed to be the only calm light in the overly bright bedroom. He listened to the twenty-seven-year-old woman speak in her child-voice, talking of death and how she couldn't function day-to-day without barbiturates as though she were reciting children's verse. The voice was innocent, immune from the pathos and effortless morbidity of her words.

The man, three years older than the woman, pulled roughly at his beard as he listened, nervously kicking with an unconscious rhythm at a wooden bed leg; he wished he had never known her history. The woman, appearing too weak to move, was a tireless confessor, possessing a true genius for emptying the contents of her soul, seeming to have an internal device for digging into the deepest recesses of her soul and depositing the matter all around him until he was nearly buried in her past and secrets. Just the voice, broadcasting sounds from some remote station, wordless as air, just that voice going straight to his heart and bypassing his mind and he would never have any doubts or regrets about her. Only words threatened their relationship, their longstanding dependency. The pain and former lovers, the institutions of restraint, she remembered them with a longing in the same way as the rudely awakened long for sleep, for that stolen, truncated dream that exceeded any of the dreamless benefits of waking. Her words seemed to say, "Give me back my dream." He tried to focus on the voice but her words jumped at him like a hungry jungle animal from a tree. He unresistingly allowed the animal to prey upon him, the man an accomplice to his own mauling.

Her long brown hair, the soft strands he used to kiss and wrap around his face as though they were a mask, was scattered in patches over the bedspread when he had come home to their two-room apartment over the laundromat, in Charlottetown. He had automatically asked, "Why'd you cut your hair?" but did not want to know the answer, any more than he was interested in knowing the exact time of his death, trying to reconcile the romance of the hair-sacrificing woman in O. Henry's story "The Gift of the Magi" and the woman on the bed. Della, he recalled with effort, was the character's name ... *Della.*

"I cut it myself. How do you like it?" she said inconsequentially, sounding as though she had performed the most unexceptional and predictable act. Sitting up on the bed she looked like a child surrounded by broken toys, yet still enthusiastic about the pieces. She turned her head to allow him a clear view of her handiwork.

"You could have gone to a hairdresser," the man said, attempting to be reasonable, knowing that she cried or screamed or curled up into an inaccessible fetal ball if she was scolded.

"I so prefer the satisfaction of doing things myself. Am I still beautiful?" she asked. There was a mixed look of anticipation and apprehension on her face, her eyes large and unclouded by any of her past, flawless green globes sentenced to exile on her troubled, gaunt face.

"You're still beautiful. You're blessed with exquisite features," the man said confidently, without any hesitation, but with an undercurrent sound not unlike a long sigh or moan of despair. He began to gather up some of her cut hair, expecting to find bits of flesh. Despite his fastidious movements, he was making an even bigger mess. In his mind he could still see her with the long hair that never failed to draw attention and stares on the street. When they first met at an audition for a local play five years ago, she had told him by way of introduction that she hadn't even trimmed her hair in three years, the last time being after she had gotten out of the hospital: "When I was in the hospital all the other patients loved my hair. They'd follow me around and fight over who would hold it. They thought my hair was magical. Not the nurses though. The nurses hated my hair," she had told him during their first meeting. Later he found out the nature of that hospital.

Her waitress outfit – white blouse, dark blue skirt, black stockings – was on the bed and he attempted to brush off her stray hairs, trying to restore some muddy icons to glistening perfection. She hated waiting on people, even in the city's most elegant dining room, but they lived primarily on her income. Their every economic decision was based on her tips and the generosity of tourists in summer. In summer she earned the most money and they bought expensive wines and pretended to be rich and successful. Whenever she became too depressed about being a waitress – it was five years now – she didn't talk about finding another job or quitting, but of the days when she lived in wealthy splendour with her parents in Montreal. Then, as if to explain the inescapable incongruity of her two-room existence, she told the story of how she had tried to kill her father even though it was her shrewish mother she hated: "He was good to me, he loved me, but he just couldn't deal with my moods. Daddy calmed down, he only needed a few stitches, but a few weeks later he disinherited me all nice and legal and ordered me to leave the house. He gave me $7300 in cash, why that exact amount don't ask me, my father listened to his own drummer. I have a lot of my dad in me ..." She spent the money within a month, long before she had come to Prince Edward Island to be an actress and met the writer she lived with now.

"You're going to be late for work," the writer said and walked away from the bed with two handfuls of hair, looking as though he were some awkward farmhand burdened with the abundance of the crop.

"You use me," she accused, with an accelerated change of mood. "You don't care if I hate my job, only that I bring in money, big tips. I have to smile and stick out my tits and be polite to all the tourists even if they wear polyester shorts or cowboy hats or have cheap jewellery around their necks."

"I love you," he said, the only effective way he knew to stop her from going on about her work, courting hysteria.

"*Love?* Yes, love," she said, mollified, a tender and devotional look waving over her face.

"Take a quick shower and get dressed. You look great in short hair. It could be a little neater, that's all. Hey, maybe you'll be the style setter and every fashionable woman on the Island will shear off her hair in homage to your impeccable tastes," he said with forced cheerfulness.

"I wish I were ugly and bald," she snapped back.

"And I wish I was so rich that I could buy you 365 wigs, one for each day, every colour in the rainbow. You'd be glamorous beyond comprehension."

She laughed without enthusiasm, nervously. He felt relieved, even by her tentative laughter. For an instant he had thought that he might have said something that provoked her.

"Do we still love each other?" she asked.

"More than life itself," he told her gently.

"Do I have to go to work?"

"If you want to eat and enjoy the basic amenities of life," he relied, sweeping his right hand across the bedroom, pointing to some of her large collections of vases displayed throughout the room: on the windowsill, dresser, small refrigerator, on top of an old, battered portmanteau, almost everywhere in the room. "If you want to keep buying your vases. Besides, work is your … sanity."

"Oh, what would I do without my sanity," she said as if sanity was a material object that could be held or observed.

"I think I'll write a great love story about your indestructible beauty and sanity and hair."

"You'll just get another rejection slip."

He ignored her cruel jab, and dropped the two handfuls of hair into a wicker wastebasket by the dresser. The vases, pill bottles, and cosmetics on the dresser caught his attention. She had enough cosmetics for five women, he thought, even though she rarely used makeup. She liked the security of all those beauty aids, like someone stocking a bomb shelter just in case.

The man moved closer to the dresser and clapped his hands together in an effort to get the remaining hairs off. While doing this he accidentally knocked over one of the woman's small vases but it did not break. She gasped and appeared horrified, as if he had struck her. He held up the vase to show her that it was intact, and asked, "Why do you have so many vases around here?"

"Vases are beautiful. A vase is to hold flowers and what in Nature is more perfect than a flower?"

"Sure, but you never have any flowers in your vases."

"My vases are there if I ever want to put flowers in them."

He gazed at her through the large dresser mirror, watching the woman wave at him as if he were about to leave on a trip. She seemed to be more real through the glass, closer not more remote, anything but an illusion.

"Do you feel okay?" he said into the mirror. He touched the glass as if he could reach her skin and she appeared to blush.

"I love you, I love you," she called at him.

He tapped out a code on the mirror's surface, a message to a distant and despondent consciousness stranded on a far-off mountain, but he didn't say anything for a few moments, seeming to wait for intervention. He could see her face tighten into a pale, taut mask, like a mime's powdered white visage. Then she began to message her scalp, rubbing what was left of her hair with a steadily increasing pressure. Her fingers worked as if propelled by strong springs.

"Do you think we're like Zelda and F. Scott Fitzgerald used to be?" she said, lifting her head into a mock sophisticated pose, fluttering her eyelashes.

"No, I hardly think so," he said, and laughed uncomfortably as if surprised on the street by a dear friend aged too much since their last encounter. "I write like shit."

"You're a marvellous writer," she protested.

"Who collects rejection slips."

"I was just teasing you, darling,"

"I'd call it taunting," he said with a stern look into the mirror, "or if you allow me to be a trifle less generous ... *torturing.*"

"You're much too serious."

"You're not serious enough."

"Then why do we love each other?"

"Desperation, exasperation, emotional combustion, blind faith, blindness, two rudderless ships colliding in the night? Take your pick."

"Oh good, a test. None of the before mentioned. I love failing tests. It was always the best schools and the worst grades for me. Nothing used to get my mother angrier than when I failed a test, except when I first became an actress. I took off all my clothes in my very first play," the woman, using dramatic stage gestures as she spoke, said from her seated position on the bed.

"You haven't gone out for a play in quite a while. That's what you really need, a role you can lose yourself in."

"It would distract me from my waitressing," she said with bitter sarcasm.

"You're going to be late for work," he said harshly.

"Put on a record, please, if our old stereo still works."

"Our ancient stereo seems to be better than ever, defying time and modernity."

"Then crank it up, darling. I dress better to music. Billie Holiday or Judy Garland, you choose."

"I prefer Joni Mitchell or Gordon Lightfoot."

"You're so safe, darling."

"I adore sanctuaries," he said angrily into the mirror, as if she were challenging an essential belief of his, perhaps even challenging the whole course and entirety of his life.

"Asylums for me," she said cheerfully.

"It's four-thirty," he announced even though the malfunctioning clock radio he was looking at stood at one-thirty, had for the last three days.

"I've paid for that laptop and fancy laser printer with the most up-to-date features, for our internet and cellphones, for your roll-top desk that takes up half of this room, for all your old vinyl records because you long for a past time, for your books that you insist be hardback because paperbacks are so temporary, for your copious supply of printer paper. I've paid for your clothes, you peacock," she said, pointing to the objects cited, as though pointing to culprits in a police lineup, each one more guilty than the other, then to the open clothes closet in which was hiding an even larger gathering of criminals.

"You're hardly the breadwinner, are you?" she concluded, breathing like someone who had stumbled after a long run.

The man went to the small stereo set in the room without looking at the woman. He had heard her accusations and berating catalogue too many times. He used to say that when he became famous he would pay her back, double what she had spent, but he had long ago stopped with his painful verbal IOUs.

"How about some early Marianne Faithfull?" he said, holding up the record album *Broken English*.

"No! Billie Holiday or Judy Garland."

"What's wrong, Marianne Faithfull not heartbreaking or depressing enough for you anymore?"

"She's still alive. The living depress me. They still make excuses. You know how excuses plunge me into the darkest moods," she said with unstinting melancholia and sadness, with the keenest instincts of the tragedienne, her gestures and tone declaring that to live untragically was the greatest crime.

Reluctantly the man put on one of the woman's favourite record albums. When Billie Holiday began to philosophize that "They Can't Take That Away From Me," the woman stood up and stretched as if she was warming up for a strenuous dance class.

"That's better," she said, swaying to the music, her body rippling in a new mood. "I wish you'd get that glum look off your face when Billie's singing to me."

"Bad memories," the man said sadly.

"Oh, come on, that was years ago. My first month on the Island after all those suffocating years in Montreal," the woman countered jovially.

"I can't forget. Billie Holiday was singing when I came home and found you on the floor."

"Stomach pumps are marvellous contraptions," she said, rubbing her stomach as she danced slowly around the room.

"You could have died," he whispered and moved away from the dancing woman.

"You wrote a lovely story about my tragic brush with the Angel of Death. Fifty scrumptious dollars you got for it, if my memory captures the past correctly."

The man went back to the mirror and continued to watch the woman. He thought she was too thin and so pale as to be almost spectral. Once he had adored her slenderness and paleness, the eye-catching long brown hair. Once he had worshipped her because she seemed to be fragile and vulnerable, severed from conventional beauty. He used to adore how she appeared to be from a different, less threatening century.

When she had finished putting on her waitress outfit, the woman moved over to the man and put her thin arms on his shoulders, as though balancing on a delicately constructed footbridge, and he quivered, as though a gust of cold air had penetrated him to the bone.

"Don't touch me," he said, with fainthearted uncertainty.

"So I'm contaminated now," she said, removing her arms from his shoulders and pressing her hands against his face, the hands shaped into fists.

"I'm just tense. I've been drawing too many blanks lately. I feel like I'm trying to create in a dismal corner of Hell."

"What do you think Hell will be like?" she said, wrapping her arms around his waist and murmuring affectionately. In the mirror he could see only her arms, as if they belonged to a thin statue without a body. At that moment, nothing but the world in the mirror seemed to exist for the man.

"This room," he said, his eyes narrowing in conviction, and then opening widely as their blueness reflected the topography of Hell.

"Is that what Hell is, being in a room with a lover forever?" she said, peeking around his side and making a distorted face into the mirror, a mischievous child's imitation of a wicked witch.

"It's not having choice."

"Heaven has choices?"

"No, it's probably worse. Except you lie to yourself and think having no choice is good, supernal, *heavenly.*"

"What was it Sartre called Hell?"

"Hell is people. It's spelled out beautifully in *No Exit,*" the man said excitedly. "That's always been my favourite play, even when I messed up acting in it at university. Garcin says to Estelle and Inez, 'Hell is … other people.' I wish I could remember the French. I used to know that line in French. What a line: 'Hell is … other people.'"

"Hell is other people," the woman repeated, behaving as if she had just fallen upon a ponderous insight by herself. "Sartre must have been a *pleasant* man. Or one of those guys who drive the tourists around the Island in double-decker buses all summer. Those drivers couldn't possibly stay fond of people, exactly like Sartre. Sartre must have driven one of those infernal double-decker buses."

"He didn't lie to himself," the man said calmly.

"We're in Hell now?" the woman asked, peeking into the mirror again, squinting as if against some dazzling light.

"More or less. But so is everybody else. There are billions of little comp-artments of Hell, *billions and billions.*" The man leaned forward, nearer to the mirror, but the woman did not release her hold of him. Then he said, his breath inscribing a design on the glass, "There wasn't a single mirror in *No Exit.* I remember that now. There was a statue of Cupid. That was one of the props. I knocked the horny little Cupid over on opening night, much like your vase earlier this afternoon. But unlike your precious vase, the Cupid statue cracked in half, symbolic of my acting career. *That was Hell.*"

"You should work as a waitress if you want to get a good definition of Hell. When the tourists pile in by the busload and you have to smile at them," she said with a ludicrous smile, "even if they're demanding and rude."

"The tourists will love your hair," he said without compassion or even a mitigating glimmer of irony, as though he were giving familiar directions for the hundredth time.

"My choice," she rebutted his annoying tone.

"*Was it?*"

The man disengaged himself from the woman and started to reset the clock radio, setting it at the five o'clock he was certain it now was.

"It's five on the dot," he announced, pointing emphatically to the clock radio, laughing at the foolishness of his action and remark.

"I'll be called if they're busy or worried. I'm so very indispensable," she said carefreely, and then rushed to the stereo set and turned the record over. Even before Billie Holiday's voice returned, the short-haired woman began to sing "My Man," soon joined by the recording's mournful, unconquerable voice.

The man went over to the phone on his desk and lifted the receiver toward the woman. He pointed it like a gun at her.

"You know I don't like to talk on the phone, darling."

"How can I forget? You need to see a person's eyes when you have a conversation," he said, attempting to imitate her innocent voice, but sounding more like an insecure adolescent male.

"Don't mock me, parasite," she said in her child-voice, but with undisguised retaliatory fury.

"Are you going to work or not?"

"When Hell freezes over," she responded and gave a schoolgirl's giggle. "When this room freezes over," she added seriously in her child-voice.

The man went to the stereo set and lifted the needle arm in the middle of Billie Holiday singing "Don't Explain." He put on a Gordon Lightfoot album and turned up the volume so those in the laundromat below could hear the singer begin "Sit Down Young Stranger."

"Please put on something else, darling. He's still alive."

"My heart belongs to the living."

"Go to Hell!"

"It's five-fifteen."

The woman hurried to the dresser and turned the clock radio down on its face, as if that act could purify her life or save her from disaster.

"Do you think my hair will grow back?" she asked the man.

"Most certainly," he told her. "You'll be like Rapunzel in no time."

"Then I'll cut my hair again."

"A little shorter and you'll look like the women who were shaved bald to punish them for collaborating with the enemy."

"In which country? For which cause? Is that justice?" the woman shouted, demanding an accurate history lesson.

The man ignored her outburst, as though she had interrupted the most profound lecture with irrelevant questions. When the short-haired woman went to the door, he returned to the dresser. She turned to look back at him and saw that he was observing her in the mirror and at the same time touching one of her vases.

"When are you going to put flowers in your vases?" he asked.

"When I want to," she said defiantly.

"You don't have to go to work if you don't feel up to it," the man said. The woman ran to the dresser and embraced him, kissing his shoulders and neck. He turned around and began to kiss the top of her head, as if attempting to seal wounds with his lips.

"What an entanglement we have," she said, on the verge of tears.

"God, I love you," he said, kissing all of her face now. "Next story I sell I'm going to take the money and buy you flowers for every vase in this room."

The woman watched the man in the mirror, and said, "You would be better off if you didn't need me so much."

"I couldn't live without you," he said with a sadness that made her remember how it felt to want to die.

She kissed him and said slowly and pityingly, "You are in Hell, my poor darling, aren't you?"

In the Mind of Love

*T*he Toronto psychiatrist, after his last patient of the afternoon had left, sat at his desk looking at the woman's file and scratching his bald head. He was pondering two questions: First, Why was he completely bald at forty-three – had been balding since his early twenties – and his father, at sixty-eight, had an impressive head of silver hair? And second, Was he falling in love with this patient? He was contemplating asking the woman he was so enamoured of to cease being his patient, so they could see each other outside his office in a more personal manner. He might have done some foolish things in his life – neither of his two failed marriages had been a textbook case on fidelity or durability – but he would never date anyone undergoing therapy with him. He caught himself drawing Cupid-arrowed hearts with their initials in the centre on the cover of her file folder, and he shook his head in an effort to banish still another erotic daydream about his patient.

After drawing a few dozen Cupid-arrowed hearts, the psychiatrist decided to call a colleague he had gone to school with – his best friend since undergraduate days and all through medical school, internship, and psychiatric residency

– and who now lived in Chicago, and was one of the tallest psychiatrists, if not the tallest, in the world. Since the days of his incredible pubescent sprouting, the man has steadfastly refused to be measured or even to give his height, but most of the estimates, over the years, have ranged from six-foot-ten to seven-foot-five, depending on the estimator's perspective.

His friend estimated that he was exactly seven feet in height, and had actually made an alcohol-fortified attempt to measure him as he slept in a hotel bed on Prince Edward Island, but as he was drunkenly moving a hand-held shoe of his, which he calculated at twelve inches in length – he didn't want to think of his friend as 213-plus centimetres, it just sounded too grotesquely gargantuan – along the side of the equally drunk sleeping man's body, he awoke, and rushed several long, wobbly strides to the bathroom, arriving not a second too soon. The friend had measured five shoe lengths, and was certain two more would have done the trick.

He recalled how the two of them, having taken a break from their gruelling medical school studies, had visited Prince Edward Island two decades ago, one of those throw-a-dart-at-the-map larks. Had the dart hit Nova Scotia or New Brunswick, or New Zealand or New Guinea, for that matter, their lives certainly would have been different. But the dart, thrown, at the time, by one of the tallest medical students, if not the tallest, on Earth, hit the world map in his friend's room directly above the third *T* in Charlottetown, Prince Edward Island. "You couldn't have hit that tiny spot, even if you had tried," the then balding medical student said to his best friend. It had been a three-day drunk, and despite having tickets to see the musical *Anne of Green Gables*, both were too hungover to go.

"How's Big Shrink doing?" the Toronto psychiatrist said over the telephone.

"Are you ever going to stop calling me that?" the Chicago psychiatrist responded, pleased to hear his friend's voice.

"You'll always be Big Shrink to me."

"Assuming you haven't gotten a hair transplant since I last gazed on your delightful cranium, you'll always be Glabrous to me."

"Ah, if your friends can't humiliate you, who can?" During a tense, exciting game of *Scrabble*, the young medical school giant had affixed vertically the letters G-L-A-B-R-O-U to the S of the horizontal word S-O-O-T-H-E, for 98 points – including a 50-point bonus for using all seven of his letter tiles – and yelled triumphantly "Glabrous! Glabrous!" but one of the other players challenged the word's existence. While another player was looking up the challenged word in a dictionary, Big Shrink, who was not to get his nickname for another few years, rubbed his friend's balding head in definition, and the nickname Glabrous was born.

After a brief long-distance reminiscing session – they hadn't spoken in six months, hadn't seen each other in more than two years – Glabrous burst out in emotional confession: "I'm in love with one of my patients."

"You're in trouble now," Big Shrink said to his friend.

"She's absolutely convinced she's Anne of Green Gables."

"There are worse delusions."

"I can't even describe how beautiful she is. Beautiful and intelligent and charmingly witty … a marvellous woman … but she dresses like the teenage Anne character, and she's thirty-eight … a sensational thirty-eight, but thirty-eight nonetheless."

"Isn't there anything you can do?"

"I'm not certain I want to do anything."

Big Shrink reacted in shock to his friend's remark.

"I'm in love with her," Glabrous said again, and drew a series of tiny Cupid-arrowed hearts in his appointment book.

"Think about what you're saying. The implications."

"You're the only one I can talk to openly about this."

"Do you love the thirty-eight-year-old woman or the teenage Anne she thinks she is?"

"I could say both. But it's her as Anne. When she's not Anne she's not as attractive to me," Glabrous confessed, drawing a particularly large Cupid-arrowed heart, and continuing to draw hearts during the rest of the hour conversation with his friend.

"I invited her to go to Prince Edward Island with me," Glabrous revealed to his friend during a late-night telephone call, a week after the previous call. As he sat in the dark in the living room of his nineteenth-floor Toronto apartment, talking to his friend lying in the custom-made, oversize bed of his twenty-sixth-floor Chicago apartment, he continued: "She was elated with the idea of going with me to Prince Edward Island. But she wants to stay my patient, believes I'm helping her. She's frightened that the Anne persona will take her over and wants to be free of that persona."

"Visiting the physical setting for the Anne books might create a new set of problems."

"I promised to be a gentleman. Separate rooms. Platonic. I had to promise all those things."

"You going to leave your libido in Toronto?"

"I will win her over. It will be a courtship. Where better to court a woman than on Prince Edward Island, in summer."

"Twice married not enough for you?"

"I think this is the one that will last."

"The bachelor life has been good to me."

"You must be the tallest bachelor in the world."

"That is a preposterous assumption. I bet, right at this moment, somewhere in the world there is a convention of towering bachelors, many of the colossal lads dwarfing me."

"Your imagination is as fanciful as Anne's."

"Your Anne's or the character Anne's?"

"Take your pick, Big Shrink ..."

After three more therapeutic long-distance calls to his friend, each time revealing more and more about his love – longing, craving, desire, *obsession* – for the thirty-eight-year-old woman who was convinced she was Anne of Green Gables, the Toronto psychiatrist announced that he had booked a flight for the two of them to Charlottetown. For therapy. To see the musical. She had read all of Lucy Maud Montgomery's Anne books, listened to a recording of the musical countless times, had seen the musical numerous times when it had toured, but had never seen it performed live on Anne's Island, something she considered an unfulfilled dream. Big Shrink, worried about the career-threatening love affair his friend might be embarking upon, said that the dates of his Charlottetown visit happened to coincide with his own vacation, which he had originally planned for northern California. There was a brief but intensely emotional discussion of the ethics of even travelling with a patient and, after his friend invited him to join them, as a psychiatric chaperone of sorts, Big Shrink agreed to meet them in Charlottetown. Glabrous wanted his best friend to meet his best girl, he said over the telephone. "You're sounding like an infatuated schoolboy," Big Shrink said to his friend, but resisted voicing his professional opinion aloud.

Glabrous and the woman, having arrived much earlier in the day, were waiting at the Charlottetown Airport when Big Shrink's flight arrived. As much as he had described his best friend to the woman, she couldn't get over how tall he was. And a very lovely smile, she commented. A smile that is simply gloriously, enchantingly ambrosial. Big Shrink hugged his friend, and then bent down to kiss the woman – "You shouldn't be afraid to call me Anne ..." – on the cheek. She had her red hair in braids, and radiated an exuberant, youthful energy. He immediately felt an attraction for the woman, and by the time the taxi was halfway to their hotel, he had fallen in love with her also.

Glabrous had rented two adjacent rooms on the top floor – the tenth – in the largest hotel in the city – only appropriate for Big Shrink, Glabrous remarked. "I remember the last time we shared a room in Charlottetown, in that little dollhouse of a motel where I nearly put my head through the low ceiling," Big Shrink said to his friend as they walked toward the front desk, and they quickly related to their curious companion an expurgated version of their three-day stay in the Cradle of Confederation, two decades ago.

After checking in and freshening up – the two men in the luxurious room they were sharing all the time talking about the woman – the three decided it was too sunny an afternoon to remain in their rooms, and decided to explore the city. The three walked buoyantly around downtown Charlottetown, exhilarated, doing the tourist walk with the abandon of big-city people temporarily freed from the big city. They spent the longest time in a store – Big Shrink called it a shrine, Glabrous an exotic emporium of Anne goodies, the woman a segment of paradise brought to Earth – dedicated to Anne of Green Gables and all things Anne. Big Shrink purchased a half-dozen different Anne dolls, which he intended to give to the woman later; Glabrous chose Anne T-shirts for the three of them, and an Anne jigsaw puzzle and three Anne-decorated collector's dinner plates, for his sweetheart; and the woman, along with two *Anne of Green Gables* songbooks and a meticulously detailed model of Green Gables house, chose the largest two Anne of Green Gables wig-and-hat sets in the store, but they were still much too small for the two men, more so for Big Shrink, but the men were good sports and tried on their gifts – "Instant hair," Big Shrink said, poking his straw-hat-and-red-braided friend; "The cutesy bonnet adds much needed stature to you," Glabrous poked back.

After some more bantering, the two men took their wig-and-hat sets off and handed them back to the woman, and the three happy customers left with shopping bags full of Anne-related purchases. The two friends enjoyed themselves, felt relieved from the pressures of their big-city psychiatric practices. The woman, admiring the warm friendship and boyish playfulness of the two psychiatrists, told them they were true kindred spirits, like Diana Barry and Anne Shirley.

Big Shrink and Glabrous and Anne, after a long, leisurely, pleasurable meal, and the joy that only bonhomie and love and exquisite wine can bring, walked up Queen Street – "Not quite as dazzling as Toronto's Queen Street," Glabrous commented – toward the Confederation Centre of the Arts, looking forward to the culmination of a wonderful evening. They still had their shopping bags full of Anne-related gifts, which they had exchanged amiably during dinner. Big Shrink had a lifetime of people staring at him, but the other two were not as accustomed to the attention. Well, Anne, when she was dressed as the famous Anne, did attract more than her share of stares, but was not self-conscious about it. The only reason she had sought out a psychiatrist was that as she assumed her Anne persona more often, it was becoming increasingly difficult for her to hold on to employment. Losing her job in a travel agency – the third job she had been fired from in four months – had brought her desire to support herself and the comfort of her Anne persona into tormenting conflict. Glabrous, long troubled about his early balding, had battled hard not to be self-conscious, not to worry if people were staring at him. He had learned to accept the hand that life had dealt him, and while he often wore hats outside, he refused to consider a hairpiece. At her first session, Anne claimed she always associated baldness in men with virility – "scrumptiously, delectably, lusciously virile, I find you" – and the psychiatrist had to employ his utmost professionalism to deal with the exultation he felt surge through him.

"We are going to see the real Anne, the real stage Anne, and you will be freed from your obsession," Glabrous declared to the woman as they entered the theatre.

During the first act of *Anne of Green Gables*, both psychiatrists tried not to look at the woman sitting between them, but they both periodically glanced at her, to see if she was enjoying the play, to see how it was affecting her, and because both of them loved her. Big Shrink, sitting in an aisle seat, his legs stretched far into the aisle but his body leaning against the woman, wanted to confess to his best friend that he had fallen in love with Anne, but didn't have the heart. And for the first time in years, he started to entertain the idea of settling down with a woman, perhaps marrying. He had believed his thoughts about marriage were far behind him.

During the intermission, Big Shrink and Glabrous discussed the play, as friends, as men in love, as psychiatrists, and the woman they loved stood animatedly between them and lifted the discussion to an exalted realm. They were the centre of attention in the crowded theatre lobby, but they were in their own world. After the enjoyable, delightful first act, they settled into their seats, and liked the second act even more than the first. All three of them had tears in their eyes when Matthew died. After suppressing the urge during the first act, Anne started to very quietly sing along with the songs in the musical. An irate tourist sitting behind them grumbled a few times, and the two psychiatrists were able to keep their cherished darling – denial be damned, that's what she was in both of their eyes – from bursting out in song, or more alarming yet, jumping on stage and attempting to dethrone the stage-acting Anne. Each man held one of Anne's hands and kept her in her seat. At the end of the play, they stood and clapped, totally enthralled with the musical, deciding to see it again before they left Prince Edward Island, and both men more in love with Anne than before.

Big Shrink and Glabrous, as they were leaving the theatre, their minds on the woman with them, almost at the same time professed their adoration for Anne Shirley.

"It's Gilbert Blythe I love," the woman said, in a

transported, theatrical style that perplexed both of the psychiatrists.

They went to a nearby local bar, and again were the centre of attention, but the two psychiatrists were in love, and thirsty, and drank and talked about the musical, and Glabrous only worried a little that Anne was releasing her persona. He hoped to have a lifetime to treat her. He had never known anyone so beautiful, or so free from the burdens of the world. He harboured a thought that he dared not say: Why would she not want to be Anne? Anne, however, as a mature woman. The best qualities of a loveable character ripened into maturity.

The two psychiatrists had a beer-chugging contest, much to Anne's amusement. "We haven't done that since med school," Big Shrink said.

"I seldom drink these days. I'm too health conscious," Glabrous boasted.

"I do concede I have a taste for the old Devil brew. After a day at the office, I need a beer or two. Three if it's been a particularly anguish-laden, dysfunctional-ridden day," Big Shrink described, part happy performance, part sad confession.

Both the woman and Glabrous laughed, not knowing if Big Shrink was being serious or humorous. If his friend had a drinking problem, Glabrous was certain he would have known.

The woman was keeping up with the two men, drink for drink, even though she refused to engage in the beer-chugging contest. "I'd throw up if I tried to drink *that* fast," she said.

"Let me tell you about regurgitation," Big Shrink said, and related the story of the time he and Glabrous had shared a tiny, low-ceilinged room on Prince Edward Island, and he had the worst hangover of his life.

The woman, the alcohol stimulating her sense of mischief, took the wig-and-hat sets out of her shopping bag and placed them precariously on the men's heads. "With some glue, they might stay on," she speculated, grinning impishly.

"I'd never do this in Toronto," Glabrous said, and his friend proclaimed with mock seriousness, "I doubt if anyone would notice if I wore this in Chicago."

"You'd be the tallest psychiatrist wearing an Anne wig and hat in the universe," Glabrous said. "People would have to notice. You are noticeable. The personification of noticeability ..."

The more the woman drank, the less she was like Anne. She undid her braids and wiped off the freckles and makeup she had on to create her Anne persona. By the time they had decided it was time to leave – actually, the bartender told them the bar was closing— she had only the remotest attachment to Anne. Yet despite the Anne persona's near evaporation, both psychiatrists had throughout the evening of drinking and merriment done various imitations of Gilbert Blythe, primarily in an attempt to woo their companion.

"I implore you to consider giving a kiss-kiss to Gilbert," Glabrous said, and she kissed him lightly on the lips.

"This Gilbert is in need of affection, too. Lack of affection will take an inch off my height," Big Shrink said, showing a smile that was perched between the lustful and the befuddledly innocent.

She leaned over their table and kissed Big Shrink all around his face, but not directly on the lips.

"Give the tall Gilbert some tongue action," Glabrous said drunkenly.

"I will do what I wish," the woman said in the best spirit of Anne of Green Gables, even if she was slipping out of the persona. Then she kissed Big Shrink on the chin, but passionately, and he said he had grown three or four inches.

"But where?" his friend said, and the woman and Big Shrink both playfully slapped Glabrous on the back for his lasciviousness.

Out on the street, a pleasant, clear summer night, they walked back to their hotel, the two men singing an improvised rendition of "Gee, I'm Glad I'm No One Else But Me," but Anne not joining in with their tuneful frolicking.

It was Anne who suggested that they have a nightcap in her room, and the two love-smitten men enthusiastically endorsed the suggestion, Glabrous attempting to give Big Shrink the high-fives but not able to reach his skyward-extended hands.

Within an hour, they had drained the room's mini-bar, and went to the men's adjacent room and began to empty its mini-bar. The more the men continued to drink, the more they attempted to imitate Gilbert Blythe, and the less restrained either one of them was with his ribaldry. They were undergraduates again, in love with life ... and the same woman.

"Is Annesy-wannsy going to invite Gilbert to her roomsy tonight?" Glabrous asked, more drunk than he could remember being in years.

"I'm not interested in Gilbert," the woman said, her Anne voice completely gone.

Both Gilberts were amazed by the transformation. Big Shrink turned to his friend and said with slurred profundity, "You have effected a miraculous cure ..."

"I do not want to sleep alone tonight," the woman said.

"I am in Heaven," Glabrous said.

"You are in a hotel room on Prince Edward Island," Big Shrink shouted into his friend's ear.

"Same thing … identical," Glabrous said, pressing a hand against his ear to indicate his discomfort with Big Shrink's sudden, thunderous statement.

"Sorry, old friend," the chastened psychiatrist whispered.

After a voluptuous geography lesson on her body's desires, the woman started to give an impassioned recitation, but neither Gilbert understood what she was reciting.

"What are you saying?" the first Gilbert Blythe/Glabrous asked.

"You sounded exquisite, but I did not understand a word," the second Gilbert Blythe/Big Shrink acknowledged rather sheepishly.

"It was 'The Ode to Aphrodite,'" the woman said, seeming to make her declaration to a gallery of observers in a celestial theatre. "You have been privileged to hear the poetry of Sappho … in the original Greek."

"I see before me a goddess more radiant than Aphrodite," the first Gilbert Blythe/Glabrous sang out in loving praise.

"Aphrodite, my kind of gal," the second Gilbert Blythe/Big Shrink said, then, doing a cautious swirling dance, went on, "I didn't know Anne Shirley could recite Sappho."

"Anne Shirley might not be able to, but I can," the woman said. "I am a scholar of Sappho."

"You never told me," the first Gilbert Blythe/Glabrous said, hurt evident in his voice.

"It was not relevant to our sessions," she said with a haughty contempt.

116 – J. J. Steinfeld

"A rare ability it is to recite Sappho's poetry in the original Greek," the second Gilbert Blythe/Big Shrink said.

"I am writing my doctoral dissertation on Sappho."

Amazement and bewilderment flushed both men's faces.

The scholar of Sappho closed her eyes and uttered another line of Greek, then said, "How I would love to wrap my arms around a woman."

The first Gilbert Blythe/Glabrous admitted, "I have had this fantasy of being a woman ..."

And the second Gilbert Blythe/Big Shrink admitted, "I've had the fantasy longer than you."

They started to criticize each other for never mentioning their being-a-woman fantasy during their earlier days, throwing psychiatric jargon back and forth at each other, as though they were having a duel between jealous rivals.

"The one with the best fantasy will be my companion tonight," the woman said, her voice taking on a new melodious texture.

The two Gilberts looked puzzled but hopeful.

"Wait here," she instructed the men, and went to her room, returning in less than a minute.

She threw two pairs of black pantyhose onto the first bed, and said, "To help you with the mood ..."

Giggling and egging each other on, the two men, throwing modesty to the wind, or at least to the air conditioning, each put on a pair of black pantyhose, Big Shrink having to rip his pair of pantyhose in order to get them partially up his long legs. The woman once more placed the wig-and-hat sets on their heads, and said, "Oh my, we're like triplets now: black pantyhose ... red hair ... defiance of convention emanating from all our intoxicated pores ..."

For the next few minutes the two uninhibited psychiatrists attempted to outdo themselves with their impersonations of a woman, and the woman, former Anne, gushed forth her admiration, and desire, for two such alluring, imaginative ladies, whom she lightheartedly christened "Josephine" and "Daphne," after the characters played by Tony Curtis and Jack Lemmon in *Some Like It Hot*, and exclaimed, "Some certainly do like it hot … very hot …"

"Who will be the lucky woman?" Josephine/Big Shrink asked.

"Choose the fairest one of us," Daphne/Glabrous said.

"I'm going to my room, and after I've made my decision, I will call this room and invite the fairest one to join me for a night of ecstasy."

The woman left the room and the two psychiatrists hurried at the same time to the bathroom, excitedly washing up, brushing their teeth, applying fresh deodorant, and going on about the unlimited horizons of the imagination. Their too small Anne wig-and-hat sets had fallen off, but they kept on their black pantyhose.

After their anticipatory ablutions, the two sat down on opposite sides of one of the beds in the room and stared at the telephone. They stared and stared, but it failed to ring. Then they called the woman's room but there was no answer. Fearing she may have fallen asleep or passed out, Daphne/Glabrous and Josephine/Big Shrink went to the woman's door and knocked and knocked, not getting a response. Unable to open the door, they went back into their room and called the front desk, expressing their concern that something might be wrong.

"A different woman from that room checked out a few minutes ago. Said she was a friend of the red-headed woman in whose name the room had been booked, and her friend had to leave earlier," the voice on the telephone informed them.

The two men quickly put on their pants over their black pantyhose, and, in confusion and fright, took the elevator down to the lobby, looking at their dishevelled, inebriated selves in the elevator's mirrors. At the front desk, a clerk with a keen eye for detail and fashion described the glamorous woman – "I couldn't believe it, she was looking *so* Marilyn Monroe" – who had dropped off the red-headed woman's key, and they realized that it had been the dear precious Anne they both loved, wearing a blond wig. Josephine/Big Shrink and Daphne/Glabrous fought through their beer-filled night to reclaim the psychiatrist in them.

"She didn't give her name, but I sure wanted to call her Marilyn," the front-desk clerk explained. "All she said was that she was going to take a double-decker bus all the way back to Toronto. I told her those tourist buses don't go *that* far, and Marilyn said she begged to differ ..."

Josephine/Big Shrink and Daphne/Glabrous both stepped out into the summer night, and knew that their Anne was gone, perhaps forever. As they stood there and consoled themselves, they were thankful no one could see they were each wearing black pantyhose that formerly belonged to a woman who had been the most desirable Anne of Green Gables ever.

The Führer's Halloween

*T*he husband and wife had been arguing for several days over the Halloween party. Muni shouted that he would go, but he wouldn't dress up like an idiot. Dvora argued that he would be the only one not in costume, a real oddball.

"Have a good time for once, Muni," Dvora said in a pleading voice, pointing out still another time that he was working himself into an early grave. "You don't celebrate anything," she scolded as she paced back and forth behind her husband's desk in the bedroom, "at least you can make an effort to enjoy Halloween – it's pagan enough for you."

"I used to celebrate Hanukkah," Muni argued, continuing to make more revisions to his latest academic paper. In his mind he saw himself as a little boy lighting the candles in the menorah, spinning the *draydl*, eating too many *latkes*, filling his hands with Hanukkah *gelt*. He had always bought books with that gift money.

"That was before you met me," Dvora said, and started to dress in her costume. "Before you decided that being a practising Jew was an encumbrance. You don't have to pray or put on a prayer shawl at a Halloween party, so don't give me a hard time, Muni. Think of it, you don't have to be your serious self for a night …" The woman loved to dress up, to go to parties and dance until she was exhausted.

"We deal with our personal demons differently," Muni grumbled, and wrote in his paper that the Nazis were adept at masquerading their true intentions behind sinister euphemisms and an elaborate apparatus of lies.

During their six years of marriage Muni and Dvora had often argued about "recreational" outings, about dragging him away from his work. She loved him, even when he was stubborn and worked long hours after coming home from the university, sometimes all night, falling asleep at his cluttered desk. She had loved him from the moment they had met as undergraduates at the University of Toronto, he an eighteen-year-old fresh from Montreal and already certain he wanted to be a history professor, she the same age but not having the slightest idea then of what she wanted to be. She loved him so much that she followed him to Prince Edward Island a year ago, away from her family and Toronto for the first time. "There's no synagogue on the whole Island. I won't go, Muni," she had protested when he first announced the job offer. She couldn't believe that after twenty-eight years she would live in a corner of the world where there actually was no synagogue.

"God forbid, a Jew shouldn't have a bricks-and-mortar synagogue," Muni had said without a great deal of sympathy. "Living on PEI will test your faith. How can you measure your devotion accurately when life's spiritually easy and God's right in your backyard?" Then, when Dvora had started to push him into a corner with her tears, he told his favourite story again: how he had vomited during his bar mitzvah in Montreal, narrowly missing the Torah but soiling the rabbi's shoes.

"I promised Joanne and Keith we were coming in costume," she said, appealing to her husband's sense of fair play.

"Tell them I have a new strain of venereal disease and I want to enjoy my latest affliction in solitude," he responded, scratching playfully at his crotch.

"We're going in costume, *both of us*," she said firmly, raising her arms as if making an invocation to some Halloween deity.

"Only if I can go as a Charlottetown *dybbuk* or maybe a cute little Island *goldem*, how's that?" he said, without interrupting his writing.

"You'll go as a pirate, Muni. We decided on pirates three weeks ago," she said, moving toward the bed and pointing at the costumes she had sewed for the two of them. "You were born to be Long John Silver," she continued, trying not to lose her temper.

"An Orthodox Jewish pimp and his princess of a hooker would have been better," he growled unconvincingly, unable to recall which writer had used the argument he was paraphrasing, Hannah Arendt or Joachim Fest. He made a note to look it up tomorrow; he would prefer, however, to go to his office at the university now.

"It's for a good cause, Muni. You brought me to this island and told me to get involved, so I got involved," she said with a seriousness that was undiminished by previous repetition. The woman did volunteer work at a shelter for battered women and their children. The Halloween party benefit dance was to raise much-needed money for the Prince Edward Island Transition Association. She had not been able to get a social-work job here, Dvora reminded her husband. *"You'll find a good job in no time; they'll be dazzled by your MSW from the University of Toronto,"* she mimicked her husband over his year-old words, and made him feel guilty.

Muni fought his guilt by pointing to the sixteen-volume set of *Encyclopaedia Judaica* – a wedding present from Dvora's parents – in the two-shelf bookcase next to his desk, and saying, "Look up if there's an entry on Jewish pimps and hookers."

"Why don't you see if there's an entry for Jewish workaholics," Dvora snapped back at her husband.

After dressing in her pirate costume, Dvora stepped into the adjacent bathroom. "Let me put makeup on you," she called to Muni, applying the finishing touches to her own face. Viewing her gaudy and ferocious pirate face in the mirror, she thought that it was good her worrying mother wouldn't see her like this. Her mother's first words after finding out about the move east had been, "What kind of Jew goes to live in a foreign land, Dvora?" … "Charlottetown, is part of Canada." … "Where will your kids go to school? How will they learn Hebrew?" … "We don't have kids yet, Mama. Muni doesn't want to start a family for another two years, when we're both thirty, remember?" …

"Jewish pirates don't make sense," Muni said, standing up from his desk after two and a half hours of work, bent over without rising once.

"Neither do Jews on this island," Dvora retaliated. "No synagogue. We can't get Hanukkah candles here …" Her mother had promised to send Hanukkah candles this year, ten boxes. "We're only staying two more years, Mama."

"There are a few dozen or so Jews on the Island, the cream of the Diaspora," Muni said defensively, stripping to his undershorts. He stretched and did several deep-knee bends, his self-mocking parody of callisthenics.

"I'll bet there are more Jews in Tasmania than here," she said.

"I didn't know the world wasn't Jewish until I was thirteen, when I started to subscribe to *Sports Illustrated* and my parents finally bought their first TV set," he said.

"You learned too well," she said sadly, coming back into the bedroom and helping him dress, then massaging his sore shoulders and neck. Dvora gently touched the scars on her husband's back, from the time he had single-handedly attempted to break up a meeting of neo-Nazis in Toronto.

"My regurgitating in temple must have been an omen about the Gentile world, my baptism into reality," he said. "I didn't have my first dream about a *shiksa* until I was fourteen, but God, that nocturnal emission could have made any record book of sex."

"You'll be a handsome pirate, Muni," Dvora said lovingly, and led her husband into the bathroom. "Just think of all the *shiksas* who will gladly walk the plank for an irresistible pirate."

"You think we'll win first prize and get our picture in the newspaper, so I can send it to my parents?" he asked.

"As long as no couple goes as a rabbi and rebbitsin," she answered, adjusting his purple eye patch and then straightening his cardboard sword. "But fortunately, not too many people on the Island know what a rabbi or rebbitsin is."

Muni laughed and sat down on the toilet seat in order that Dvora could better apply his pirate makeup.

Joanne and Keith, a most convincing pair of boiling red lobsters, were already at the church hall, sitting at one of the roomful of long metal tables, when Dvora and Muni arrived. In the front of the church hall an Island rock band was playing loudly.

"I hope voracious lobsters don't eat tasty pirates," Dvora said, after she and her husband had sat down across from their costumed friends. The four joked for a while, then the lobsters went to the dance floor as Dvora pestered Muni to dance with her.

"I'm not comfortable dancing," he complained, as if she had asked him to dive into shark-infested waters.

"You need the exercise, Muni. When was the last time you got any regular exercise?" she said, poking only half-playfully at his biceps and stomach.

"I used to jog three times a week at graduate school," he said, trying to firm his stomach muscles.

"That was ages ago, Muni."

An aluminium-foil-coated robot, a dial on its shiny chest spinning erratically, walked up to Dvora and Muni's table, and said in a sputtering voice, "Hello, Professor Herschkovitch."

"Yes?" Muni replied, unable to guess the identity of the robot.

"It's me, Vicky," the robot said, and Muni nodded in recognition.

A second young woman, dressed as a native woman, stood next to the robot. "Barb, from the same class as Vicky," she said, even though the professor recognized the other student.

"Excellent symbol of modern technology you got there, Vicky," Muni commented, finding her costume even more ludicrous than his own.

"I'm Kateri Tekakwitha," the second young woman revealed. "She was an Indian saint," she added as if speaking to a dense schoolboy.

"I know that quite well, Barb," Muni said, narrowing his one exposed eye.

"For sure, you're a professor," the student said, then laughed uneasily.

That's not the reason, Muni wanted to say, but smiled indulgently at his two costumed students. Suffering appealed to him intellectually, even the suffering of long-dead saints. He had once considered writing his master's thesis on seventeenth-century Jesuit martyrs, before his interest in suffering Catholics lessened and he decided to switch his academic research to Germany, writing his master's thesis on Hitler's pre-1933 attitudes toward Jews. Muni's PhD thesis, "The Dark Image: Anti-Semitism in Nazi Cinema, 1933-1945," had already been published as a book.

"Have you ever read *Beautiful Losers* by Leonard Cohen?" the professor asked Kateri Tekakwitha.

"Not yet," she said.

"You should, Barb. Leonard Cohen has Kateri Tekakwitha in his novel ..."

"No kiddin'?"

"No *kidding*," Muni said with only mild derision. "And perhaps you should have given a little more thought to the cultural appropriation, Barb."

"I'm sorry about that, professor," the student said, not certain why her history teacher was criticizing her.

If Dvora wasn't sitting next to him, he would tell his student how erotic *Beautiful Losers* is, and suggest that they discuss the book after she's read it.

The aluminium-foil-coated robot and Kateri Tekakwitha walked away, and Dvora resumed her attempt to get her husband to dance. "As compensation, Muni, for bringing me to this island … for one year of confinement in the *goyisheh* land of Anne of Green Gables."

"Her real name was Anne Herschkovitch before she changed it to Anne Shirley," Muni said. "She's a distant relative of mine."

"Very distant, Muni," Dvora said, not appreciating her husband's comical remark.

Muni withdrew his cardboard sword from its cloth sheath when two Wild West outlaws, large crucifixes dangling around their necks, strolled past with guns drawn and together drawled, "Howdy, Muni and Debby." Dvora jabbed a finger into her husband's ribs and Muni knew exactly what had irritated his wife. He exaggerated a pained expression for her and put his sword back into its cloth sheath.

Dvora believed that Jews needed the company and protection of other Jews to survive in a hostile world; Muni argued nearly the opposite: for a Jew to get strong, to become a modern-world survivor, he or she needed to get along without the aid or reinforcement of other Jews. Dvora wanted to move to Israel, where, she said without a trace of irony, even the police were Jewish. In 1981, Muni had jumped at the teaching job at the University of Prince Edward Island; he wanted to get away from Toronto and the sanctioned lunacy he had grown to despise. The compromise was for three years on the Island and then, in 1984 – that will be an auspicious Orwellian year, Muni taunted his wife – immigrating to Israel, to be, as Dvora liked to remark, in a land where you didn't have to worry about your heritage or name. Here nearly everyone called her either Debby or Deb, Dvora never sounding right from the lips of Islanders, if it was attempted at all.

"You folks from away?" people invariably asked when

Dvora and Muni were introduced. "Herschkovitch, that's not an Island name," people often commented. "We're the lost tribe of Charlottetown," Muni would joke, but Dvora hated to hear such concern over their surname and wished someone would pronounce her first name properly.

"They can pronounce Muni passably," he claimed, but was forever being asked where he had received such an unusual first name, never heard that one on the Island. "My mother loved Paul Muni, the actor. You see, Muni was his real first name, when he was Muni Weisenfreund." "I see." They would shake their heads, more perplexed than ever. "My mother loved *I am a Fugitive from a Chain Gang*," Muni would say and offer a synopsis of the 1932 movie, sometimes seriously, other times as a vehicle for mockery. Muni Herschkovitch's mother had been an actress in Yiddish theatre and English theatre until her nervous breakdown. Even in Montreal the Second World War reached her again with an accuracy that the son could never comprehend.

After the rock band took its first break, the emcee, a prominent city businesswoman dressed as a ballerina, began to talk about the commendable work of the Transition House Association and also about the prizes to be given away later for the best costumes. She leaned over a small card table, which displayed the prizes donated by a local women's service club: first prize, an eiderdown quilt; second prize, an ornate wall clock; third prize, a magnum of champagne; and fourth prize, a huge teddy bear. There was one prize for each winning couple, and a duplicate prize for winning individuals. More people were arriving and the church hall was filling up.

"I wish this wasn't a church hall," Dvora said to her husband.

"Why?" Muni said mischievously. "I never throw up in churches."

"Don't hold back your supper on my account," she said.

Muni was watching the succession of costumed people, mentally evaluating the costumes and grading them the way he graded his students' essays. He thought of his mother's detailed and fond descriptions of the roles played by Paul Muni: Louis Pasteur, Émile Zola, Wang the Chinese farmer in *The Good Earth*, the gangster Tony Camonte in *Scarface*, Benito Pablo Jurez, Professor Joseph Elsner in *A Song to Remember*, character after character, movie after movie, he knew them all, and he imagined an entire Halloween party of Paul Muni impersonators, his mother the happy judge. For almost a year, while she was institutionalized, Paul Muni was all that Muni Herschkovitch's mother talked about.

"Any predictions on the winners?" Dvora asked her friends sitting at the table.

"It's got to be the rainbow-coloured unicorn and the green rooster. They clash delightfully," Joanne said.

"No, no, look at the androgynous mummy," Keith exclaimed and waved at the staggering, enwrapped creature nearby.

"You lobsters ought to win it. You're the sexiest things here," Muni said.

"Have you ever slept with a lobster, Muni?" Keith asked, giving Joanne two little kisses on her antennas.

"Lobsters aren't kosher," Muni told his friend, "but I can make an exception." He started to stroke one of Joanne's papier-mâché claws and asked the female lobster, "What's your favourite position, Madame Femme Fatale Lobster?"

"Aren't lobsters a bit too obvious and corny?" Dvora,

upset by Muni's flirting with their friend, said to Joanne and Keith.

"Should we have come as potatoes?" Joanne said, enjoying the attention she was receiving from Muni.

"Potatoes are too asexual," Muni said, and licked both of Joanne's claws.

When the rock band resumed playing, even louder than before, Muni gave in and went to the dance floor with Dvora. He moved unrhythmically and self-consciously while he danced. Then, in the middle of a song, he stopped dancing and stood rigid, his body directed at the entrance to the church hall.

"What is it?" Dvora asked, gripping her husband by the wrists, sensing that he was extremely distressed. Muni broke away from his wife's grasp and walked off the dance floor, she only a step behind.

"Who do you think you're being?" Muni said as he stood over the table at which a recently arrived couple sat. Dvora tried to pull her husband away, before there was trouble. She thought of his scarred back.

"Shiver m'timbers, who do you thinks, m'pirate friend?" the seated man said, smiling widely and tapping his fingers on the tabletop to the beat of the song the band was playing.

"You better not be Adolf Hitler and Eva Braun," Muni said in a voice that was harsh and threatening.

"My, you're observant, for a one-eyed pirate," the seated man said, without modifying his friendly tone.

Muni stood silent, his fists clenched and pressed against his hips, a tense and angry expression on his face.

"What's the problem?" the seated woman said to Dvora.

"He's a historian and your costumes have upset his historical sensibilities," she tried to say calmly, without anger.

Dvora believed that only rational and dispassionate behaviour could settle arguments or defuse volatile situations. Her years of doing social work in Toronto had taught Dvora that.

"Our costumes have nothing to do with you," the seated woman said in a severe manner that made Muni bite down on his lip.

"I happen to be Jewish," Muni shouted as if Dvora was nowhere near, as if only he and the seated couple existed in some vast desert in which all words needed to be shouted in order for only the barest echoes to be heard.

"That's fascinating," the costumed man said ingenuously, offering Muni a brown-gloved hand to shake; he was genuinely pleased – and surprised – to meet a Jew on the Island. The hand remained suspended and untouched until the man lowered it.

"They are just costumes," the seated woman said. "You two are pirates, right, and we're just Hitler and his lady." She pressed two of her fingers against Hitler's moustache, as if anticipating it was about to fall off. That action made Muni quiver.

"My parents were in concentration camps," Muni declared in an unraised voice, beginning an incomprehensible history lesson. Dvora began to pull Muni by his pirate shirt. Keith came over and she asked him for help, the two of them managing to get Muni back to their table. Joanne, who had gone to the cash bar earlier, returned with four beers in large plastic cups. Dvora kept her arms around Muni, as Keith told him not to look at the two costumed jerks, there could be ignorant people anywhere, including on the Island. Keith was an Islander, and often defended the Island way of life when

Dvora complained about what was lacking on Prince Edward Island.

The costumed Hitler and the costumed Eva Braun stood to dance, and Muni watched them. For the rest of the evening he did not take his eyes off the couple. Disconnected lines from *Mein Kampf* pounded at Muni's mind, seeming to emanate from the lips of the costumed Hitler. Dvora suggested that they go out and get something to eat, but Muni refused to move; he barely seemed to be breathing.

Dvora prayed that the couple dressed as Hitler and Eva Braun would not win a prize when the emcee began her announcements. They won fourth prize for couples – the huge teddy bear – a result that evoked laughter and cheering from the people in the crowded church hall. Joanne and Keith won the magnum of champagne, third prize for couples.

Keith carried the bottle to the table and made a lively attempt to get his friends to go back to his house for a celebration. Muni refused to budge or speak. Joanne and Keith had never seen Muni this way; Dvora had: whenever he watched a movie or television program about Nazism or the Holocaust; whenever he read or heard there had been an attack against Jews somewhere in the world; whenever he heard his father describe how happy and carefree his wife had been as a young girl before the Second World War.

Keith popped open the magnum of champagne and said they might as well celebrate here if they were leaving. The band began to play their last rollicking number but Dvora made no effort to get her husband to dance. After pouring the champagne into the four plastic cups that had previously been used for beer, Keith offered a toast to the continued success of the Transition House Association. As the others lifted their cups, Muni picked up the bottle and rushed to Hitler and Eva Braun's table.

"Why don't you get lost, pirate man?" the costumed Hitler said.

"Leave us alone. We're here to enjoy ourselves," the costumed Eva Braun added angrily.

"I need to know what your motives are for wearing those costumes, nothing more," Muni said, his friends and wife now standing cautiously behind him. He appeared, outwardly at least, to have calmed down.

"We've got to be able to laugh at ourselves," the costumed Hitler said. "Haven't you ever seen movies that made fun of the Führer?"

Before anyone could react, Muni poured the remainder of the champagne over the clothing of Hitler and Eva Braun, poured until Keith wrenched the bottle away, but the magnum of champagne was already empty.

"You're fuckin' out of your mind," the costumed Hitler, jumping to his feet, yelled. The costumed Eva Braun, remaining seated, tried to dry her companion and herself with a handkerchief, and also loudly accused Muni of being crazy.

The band continued to play even though a crowd had gathered around the table with the disturbance, leaving the dance floor nearly empty, most people seeming to sense the start of a simple barroom brawl.

"You're probably right about the state of my mental health, Adolf and Eva," Muni said, removing his eye patch and throwing it high into the air. "My craziness is a gift from God," he intoned, as if he were a Hasidic Jew praying. The eye patch, like a miniature parachute, floated down. Muni walked quietly away, Dvora following.

The Heart

"Your sketch has more than a tinge of malevolency, my burdened friend," the old man said in perfect English but with a German accent, speaking without cruelty or malice, like a concerned father telling his reckless son to drive more carefully after a bad accident.

"Truth in art!" came the reply like a shotgun blast in the dark, like a still worse car crash. The artist, Isaac, ripped the sketch from his thick pad and placed it before the man he was sitting across from and had just drawn with scrupulous care. The artist took a messy, drooling sip of beer and watched the man's face as he studied the almost photographic drawing. The artist was not waiting for approval or praise, but for a betraying twitch, a flicker of recognition for the precise irony of his painting's lines.

"Bitterness destroys art," the sketched man uttered with a strained detachment, crushing his previous solicitude. "If we must converse in aphorisms."

"Now can I see what's inside your precious box?" Isaac said, unable to quell the urgency in his voice, angry that he might be giving the old man an advantage in combat.

The old man touched the jewellery box on the table, stroking some wild animal whose wildness was in the most tentative abeyance. The wooden box appeared large enough to hold bracelets or necklaces and was adorned with symmetrical designs suggesting tranquillity and remoteness. Then he lifted the box off the table and held it under his chin, appearing to dare the artist to grab it from him.

"Why are you so eager to open my little Pandora's box?"

"Because I've heard rumours about the *contents.*"

The man with the jewellery box allowed a smile to engrave his features, as if opening the box in his mind and being intoxicated by the aroma of its contents.

"What exactly is it you hear is in this box," the man said, brushing the box against his cheek, "which has been in my family for two centuries?"

As if a direct answer would mean unexpected death, the artist quickly said, "I will do you a sketch without malevolency, no bitterness whatsoever, if you give me a peek." With a flowing wave of his arm, Isaac signalled to the bartender for another beer, even before finishing the one he had.

"I do confess I have a fondness for your work. Your studies of the human body are rich in vitality and a delicious artifice rare in Canadian art, but such a bargain I cannot strike. Mystery is important to me and my well-being." The old man also offered a silent signal to the bartender, but with a much more restrained gesture, a slight poke into the air. "Why are you so desperate to see the contents of my heirloom?" he asked with words slowly measured out, the ideal speed for taunting or seduction, like a woman removing her stockings slowly before her impatient lover.

"Because, Herr Wilhelm, if the rumours are true, I will kill you."

The bartender placed the drinks before the two men, the clatter of glasses seeming to echo, "kill you ... kill you ..."

The old man laughed heartily, without affection or contrivance, and gave the jewellery box an emotionless kiss. The tip of his faded purple tongue did a languid dance upon the box's ornate surface.

The artist stood up, tipped over his fresh beer, with bold unapologetic clumsiness, then bent over to sign the now drenched sketch of the old man: "With malevolent love, Isaac Katzman."

The bartender's words, "You've become quite the regular," ripped through Isaac's thoughts. *I'm part of nothing, an outsider, safe on the periphery, an artist, severed from attachment,* he wanted to shout at the bartender and the others in the lounge, the real regulars. *They* were embedded here, not him; he was free to come and go, to live in his mind and art, away, far away from them. He recalled the first time he had wandered into the lounge, four months ago, having just settled into a small rented room in a large house overlooking the frozen river a few blocks away.

"You're new, aren't you?" the bartender said, his large hands deftly concocting three Irish coffees as he spoke.

"New as can be." Isaac felt good that cold night, knowing no one, miles from his last residency and slag heap of regrets, loving the incorruptibility of January 1988, barely three weeks old then. "Isaac Katzman," he added with the vigour of a famous man dispensing the magic of his name, then suddenly realizing his fame had vanished upon waking.

"That's not an Island name," the bartender said and placed a beer before Isaac on the bar, then went to deliver the three Irish coffees. Isaac had been on Prince Edward Island less than a day and already he had heard the comment three times: from an elderly woman at a downtown Charlottetown coffee shop who told him where he could look for rooms, from his new landlord, and now the bartender. He was to hear it a dozen more times before he became used to it and abandoned any search for sinister import.

The narrow-eyed man on the stool to his left asked, "Visiting?"

In the jovial, almost mocking tone that afforded him the most protection, Isaac said, "Nope. I'm here to plant my roots." Then, to confuse the questioner even more: "Deeply, beyond the ability of even the sturdiest hands to extirpate." Isaac's smooth, uncluttered hands went through planting motions, finally patting the imaginary soil down hard. "Your red soil is incredible, I've been told. Can't wait for the snow to melt. Red is the Devil's second favourite hue."

Another customer at the bar asked the routine questions about job, family, and background, and Isaac supplied the witty answers that alienated some, intrigued others: "I'm here to captivate your women. To paint the dark apparitions in the Island sky. Because I don't have a criminal record on the Island …"

"Where your people originally from?"

"Germany, the heart of Deutschland. We had Germany is our back pockets once," Isaac revealed, giving his backside a slap.

"Mr. Wilhelm, he's also from Germany," the bartender said, pointing to a corner table for four, occupied by a single old man with tired-looking eyes, dressed as if for a formal affair. Isaac turned and saw the German lift a glass in toast and invitation to the newcomer. Before him was an ornate jewellery box.

"German Jews are not the same as Germans!" Isaac declared, as if affirming or denying the existence of God before a sleepy jury intent on not listening.

"Sorry, what do I know," the bartender quickly apologized. "We don't have many Jewish people on the Island. To tell you the truth, I don't remember ever serving one."

"We're lucky to have twenty-five on the whole Island," the man on Isaac's left offered with a head shake of authority, appearing to count Jews in the air.

"Maybe forty, forty-five tops," the bartender added.

"At least you got a *minyan*," Isaac said to everyone's confusion. Without explaining the Hebrew word, he turned around on the bar stool and stared at the German over the rim of his beer glass, getting him into his sights. As a debate began over the number of Jews on the Island, estimates ranging anywhere from ten to a hundred and fifty, Isaac walked over to the German and stood silently over him, a bird of prey uncertain as to the exact composition of the feast below.

"Care to join me?" the German added with unforced refinement.

"What's in the box, Herr Wilhelm?"

"Allow me to purchase you a drink."

"A Löwenbräu?"

"If you wish."

Whenever Isaac came into the lounge, the imperturbable German was always there, at the same table, dependable as the tides. His two sons raised Ayrshires twenty miles outside Charlottetown but the old widower kept an apartment in the city, on the waterfront near the marina so, as he liked to say, he could watch the boats.

"Six days in a row," the bartender said to Isaac, as if offering irrefutable evidence for his assertion that his customer was a regular. People came in and waved or called "hello" to Isaac, already a local celebrity, an eccentric, a fresh wind from away, not quite a threat. He thought, his emotions contradictory, *I know too many people here.* But Isaac Katzman had no desire to move on, not again.

"A present for you," Isaac said and tossed the thin, rectangular package onto the German's table. Isaac had used the brown, stiff paper of a grocery bag to wrap the gift. The German picked up the package and ran his fingers over both surfaces before carefully unwrapping it.

The German offered his distinctive, vigorous laugh when he saw the metal licence plate with MEA CULPA embossed on the surface. Since only rear-end licence plates were required on the Island, some drivers either had customized front plates or novelty plates purchased at local stores, proclaiming such phrases as TAXED TO DEATH, SMILE YOU'RE ON RADAR, I LOVE PEI POTATOES, I'D RATHER BE FISHING, I'D RATHER BE SQUARE DANCING, I'M SPENDING MY GRANDCHILDREN'S INHERITANCE …

"Put it on the front of your Mercedes, Herr Wilhelm."

"How do you know I drive such an automobile?"

"The bartender is a fount of valuable information."

"*Ach*, our bartender, our omniscient man."

"Will you put it on your car?"

"If you become my lover for one night, one hour only, one sincere embrace, I will affix your lovely gift to my automobile for eternity," the German said, modifying his offer as Isaac's grimace grew more infuriated.

His harsh expression dissolving into fixed deliberation, Isaac sat down and began sketching the German, not responding to his offer. He had nearly a hundred sketches of the man and could draw him perfectly from memory.

"Why do you draw me so much? There are so many attractive ladies here who I am certain could fill you with infinitely more inspiration."

"Because, my dear Herr Wilhelm, I don't have the nerve yet to use bullets."

As the two customers at the bar held their arms side by side, comparing multicoloured tattoos, Isaac slowly rolled up his sleeve and held his slender forearm up to the men and the bartender. A familiar anguish flooded him without warning, unavoidable as night, inescapable as decay, yet welcomed because it made more sense than merriment or contentment or the anaesthesia of triviality, because it fit in unobtrusively with the cruelty and stupidity that jutted out most prominently when Isaac stood back and looked over history, when he reached for explanations and unlacerating reasons.

"I go for artistic pictures myself," the man with an armful of nautical tattoos said. "Fucking numbers don't mean lobster tits to me," he added with the gruff gusto of a passionate critic sinking his teeth into an unusual *objet d'art*.

Then Isaac stood up, as if in a daze and pulled along by wires, and stumbled over to the German in the corner.

"You're much too young," the German greeted him, having observed the tattoo-comparing episode at the bar. "You look no more than twenty-eight."

"Thirty-five. Failure keeps me youthful," Isaac said, with a forced cheerfulness. He sat down at the German's table as if pushed.

"You are precisely half my age."

"Kiss the number and I'll explain how I got it, if you'd like to know," Isaac said, raising his voice so everyone in the lounge could hear, pretending to blow dust off his tattoo. "I offer you veracity for once ... if you can handle it, Herr Wilhelm."

The old man blew a kiss at Isaac and Isaac kissed his own tattoo, with the intensity of a lover fearful this would be his final kiss. After a pause in which he seemed to search for resilience or additional strength, Isaac explained unhurriedly and articulately, despite his drunkenness, how he had paid fifteen dollars and a small oil painting to bridge the gap between dead relatives, tormented parents, and his privileged, sheltered self.

"I thought I could expel my ghosts and demons," Isaac said, placing his head on the table, gasping as if exhausted from being chased for a considerable distance through history.

"Your exorcism, was it a success?"

"They grew stronger, more muscular, the indefatigable ghosts and demons. I'd need a million tattoos."

"Six million, perhaps," the German said with satisfaction, as if he had been waiting hours to deliver a noteworthy pun. He removed his tie, folded it neatly, then opened his shirt and exhibited a series of scars along his shoulder and chest. "Three bullets, operation after operation, and I have no bitterness, no muscular, indefatigable ghosts, no demons. I had forgiven all my enemies before you were even born."

"Some scars, Herr Wilhelm, are more worthy than others," Isaac said in a long groan, not lifting his head, unable to lift his head, the words burrowing into the table. Then, after abruptly banging his head once against the table, sounding a warning to the dead, he begged, "Open the box, please."

"What exactly is it you think I have in my heirloom?"

"The bartender told me you have the petrified heart of a Jew in there. A souvenir from the Second World War."

"What an unpleasant, unbelievable rumour."

"Like human-skin lampshades and shrunken heads and oven chimneys all the way to the sky?"

"I envy your youthfulness, your artistic talent ... but I also pity you. So much bile, so much weakness."

Isaac's tears poured over the table as the bartender approached to tell him he had had enough for tonight. Tomorrow was another day for drinking and having a good time.

"I'm not going home with you, Isaac, unless you tell me the truth about yourself," the short-haired woman who sat between Isaac and the German said, an arm around each man, swaying back and forth in time to the lounge's incessant conversation.

"You go home with him," Isaac accused, pointing without shame at the German.

"He's not a deceitful man," the woman said with genuine affection. "Mr. Wilhelm is a gentleman, and he's always honest with me."

Isaac began another fanciful story, so needing the short-haired woman's company tonight, determined not to leave unescorted. Even as her soft face showed displeasure, Isaac elaborated and embellished his story, the absolutely true story of Isaac Katzman, greeting-card artist and former secret agent. He could have told her the truth and had the forty-year-old woman in bed forever. He could have confessed that he had inherited painful memories from his parents, who had rarely spoken to him of their pasts, had nightmares often that he was a concentration camp inmate alongside his suffering parents, and moved from city to city to create new, safe identities, always without success, his painting providing the only thread of a lifeline. Twelve cities in the last nine years, straight across Canada like a blind messageless carrier pigeon. Selling paintings, telling far-fetched stories, engaging in bruising memory dances, more faceless women than he cared to recount, and always the need to move, to uproot, not to leave a forwarding address, only the Isaac Katzman originals with the thin, doleful faces and anguished eyes and nostrils filled to nausea with the smoke of history.

Until nine years ago, Isaac had dealt with the memories and recurrent nightmares without the need to flee, content with the thought of painting, the belief that he was going to be the next Marc Chagall. Then his father died twenty years before the actuaries promised, the concentration camp number unerased, leaving Isaac the last male in his family, the end of the line, the Zion Express to the Promised Land about to be derailed. He had studied his father's body for a full three hours before his mother came home and began her Auschwitz screams. He would have studied the body endlessly, defying putrefaction, had not the screams made the corpse seem dreamlike and unreal. Less than a hundred days later, when he found his mother's body and suicide note, he kissed the number on her forearm, then left the house with a single suitcase of clothing and some art supplies. That was nine years ago. He could have spelled out his past clearly, given the chronological details with just the proper moisture in his sad, seductive, brown eyes, mapped the sadness and decay in his heart so even the most hard-hearted woman would have pressed him unselfishly to her bosom. But he had learned the futility of his confessions long ago. Besides, after a few more elaborate stories, this woman, Herr Wilhelm's friend, would go home with him also. He would make love to her, paint her portrait, then offer a few more essential lies as if his life depended on it.

"You're such a bullshitter, Isaac. But how can I resist those beautiful brown eyes," the woman said, pinching his cheeks with a drunken ferocity. "Sometimes I think your stories keep the Island afloat."

"Rubens, impeccable big-peckered Rubens, would have loved to paint you," Isaac said drunkenly and kissed the lips that had kissed Herr Wilhelm.

Isaac came into the lounge amidst the Friday night revelry and was greeted with drunken affection, but he went straight to the German's table and placed down the armload of books he had been carrying.

"The complete and unexpurgated works of Elie Wiesel, Herr Wilhelm, for your edification and enlightenment."

"I do like your gifts. My apartment is now filled with them."

The next night, Isaac entered the lounge with a large, framed oil portrait of Herr Wilhelm is an SS uniform, the starry sky full of the coruscating hearts of Jews. The artist awkwardly held the larger-than-life painting and walked between tables, making sure everyone was witness to his creativity, explaining his use of colour and light, declaring in his loudest voice that he was entitling the painting *Faust in Drag*.

"Most humorous, most humorous," the subject of the large portrait said, as Isaac walked about conducting his art lesson. "Humour, of course, is our salvation," the German added good-heartedly, offering an occasional dainty clap with upraised hands.

The bartender led Isaac out of the lounge, trying to reason with him. Several of Isaac's less severe paintings were hanging in the lounge and adjacent restaurant, and more than a few customers had voiced their admiration for the additions to the décor. Nonetheless, the bartender made sure Isaac and his painting went outside, as if an annoying dog had wandered in and threatened to befoul the premises.

"What's wrong, you afraid the liquor inspectors might cancel your licence on account of displaying the truth?"

"You're a good guy, a great tipper, I love most of your paintings, but Mr. Wilhelm is a good customer too. He's been a regular ever since I started working here and that was six years ago. I know he doesn't mind your shenanigans, and he did take that unflattering painting you did of him in a Nazi uniform home, but some of the other customers aren't so tolerant. And tourist season is going to start soon. The regulars sort of understand, but what about the tourists?"

"Show them the gas chambers," Isaac said and ran off into the night, leaving the bartender to hold the larger-than-life painting.

"First drink is on me, Isaac, old friend," the bartender said gently, intercepting the artist at the lounge's entrance. "In fact, all of tonight's drinks are on me. As many as you want. No cut-off tonight."

Isaac smiled but quickly detected the foreboding in the bartender's lowered tone.

"I have to tell you," the bartender said, as if delivering a rehearsed funeral oration, "the owner thinks it best if you don't come in here anymore – you know, the tourists. There are plenty of other bars in town."

Isaac expanded his smile and lifted his arms upward in a strenuous stretch, then let them rest on the bartender's broad shoulders.

"I sometimes feel I'm standing in the centre of Semyonovsky Square," he said to the perplexed bartender. "Waiting for the firing squad to do their duty. Just like Dostoevsky. I feel a lot like Dostoevsky, when I don't feel like Van Gogh or Nijinsky. Then I find out that it was all staged, a grand hoax, I'm not going to be executed, only sent to Siberia, and for the rest of my life I never really leave Semyonovsky Square ..."

Isaac was speaking as if he had already had five or six beers, but he was fully sober. The bartender kept patting him on the back and offering consoling words, but Isaac was impervious to the bartender's touch and effort at consolation. He was trapped in the middle of Semyonovsky Square.

Inside the lounge, Isaac continued with his rambling stories, pretending to be Prince Myshkin or mumbling some lines from William Blake or having his fingers across the bar counter like a still healthy Nijinsky or sketching bizarre parodies of Van Gogh's *Starry Night* and *Sunflowers* on napkins. He sang "Hatikvah," "The Battle Hymn of the Republic," and "Edelweiss" in mutilated and slurred succession. Before Isaac had finished his first beer of the evening, he walked over to the German and said, "I must see what's inside your box. I can't wait anymore. No more vulgar games."

"Isaac, Isaac, concentrate on your painting and leave the world alone. It just agonizes you. You may find this difficult to believe, but I have grown fond of you over the last few months. You are like a son –"

Isaac grabbed the German's jewellery box and tried to open it, but it was locked. The old man leapt up and attempted to retrieve his treasured heirloom. Before others could reach the two struggling men, Isaac smashed the jewellery box several times over the German's head and he fell to the floor like a dropped bottle. Isaac continued smashing the box against his own chest, coughing in triumph as the cracks in the wood widened. A drunken patron wrapped his tattooed arms around Isaac and tackled him to the floor, the artist landing on top of the fallen German. The lounge was ensnarled in shouts and confusion, like a carnival suddenly swirled into true madness by a dreadful accident.

"It's empty!" Isaac shouted, as the box dropped and the lid broke completely off.

"I fooled you! I fooled you!" the German cried in exaltation, trying vainly to spit at Isaac, to drown him.

With the same suddenness as his rage began, Isaac's mood turned calm, the only one in the lounge then with any vestige of equanimity. The bartender, like the handler at a cockfight, started to help the three fallen men up, careful to keep them apart.

As the lights from a police cruiser flashed into the lounge through slatted window shutters, Isaac looked into the old German's tired-looking eyes and said without a trace of bitterness or disappointment, "Well, you can never be too careful. If not a petrified heart, you could have had a dangerous device for forgetfulness."

Estimating Distances

*E*ileen looks out her eleventh-floor bedroom window and can see the smoke of a distant fire. How many kilometres away? How long would it take me to drive that far? A small fire or a large fire? she wonders, realizing that it depends on the distance. She is terrible at estimating distances.

In the living room of her apartment are several of her friends, invited over to celebrate the fifth anniversary of her divorce. "Any reason to celebrate," her ex-husband said to everyone in the room. They weren't even friends any longer, but he is married to a close friend of hers – *Of course you are both invited; I have no phobia about former husbands.* "If you want to live in a high-rise, this is a good building, great view," her close friend had said, remembering when her husband, then Eileen's husband, lived in this building. That remark was after the argument over Eileen's treatise on guerrilla warfare, as her ex-husband called it.

"Guerrilla warfare is as old as belligerency. If you're at all interested in guerrilla warfare, read von Clasewitz. Read Vo Nguyen Giap and I'd strongly recommend Che Guevara," she had told everyone in the room.

"Eileen used guerrilla warfare in our marriage," her ex-husband explained.

"Only out of necessity. However, the conditions were not conducive to employing the strategies of guerrilla warfare."

"When are you going to write the history of guerrilla warfare in Canada? You might as well tell them your silly story of how you were a guerrilla in the hills of Prince Edward Island."

"You are twisting my personal history all out of shape."

"Eileen, when she was a teenager on Prince Edward Island, wanted to stop some cottage development. Preserve the pristine shoreline."

"Nothing's pristine anymore, even back then …"

She had needed to get away from the friends, her ex-husband, the drinking, the accusations and insults and belittlements disguised as banter. The bedroom had seemed as safe as anywhere.

Eileen is looking at the flames. Brian. She thinks of Brian. The birthday card is on the dresser. She had bought it two weeks ago, a full month before his birthday. Bought it on her own birthday. Over the years she often thought of her childhood sweetheart, of the man she would have married had she stayed on Prince Edward Island. Brian is twenty in her mind's eye – the last photograph she had of him, of them together, a piece of chocolate birthday cake on a fork she was holding, about to enter his mouth. His birthday or hers? She laughs sardonically: maybe Brian had set this fire. That was a lifetime ago.

What would Brian say if she called him? She could be anyone, he wouldn't be able to tell. She couldn't sound the same – years of smoking, heavy smoking now. Or she could say right away, "It's Eileen. I hope you haven't forgotten me ..." She did send him a birthday card every year. A few words, best wishes, a hint of their youths together, an invitation to visit if he ever came to Vancouver. He would get updates on her life from her parents, who lived in rural Prince Edward Island – hardly satisfying information, as superficial as gossip – and there would be his birthday card to her, usually something oversized and ostentatious, a letter every few years, lists of the books he had read since the last letter, but she would never answer, only the yearly birthday card, no telephone calls, no e-mails, an understanding that distance had to be respected, hiding places not disturbed.

She goes to the dresser and signs the birthday card. It is a bland card, *Best wishes on your birthday. Like a fine wine you improve with age* ... She writes: *The old 4-H'er is 43. How's your head ... your heart ... your hands ... your health? I had to strain my memory to remember what the H's stood for. I'm sure you haven't forgotten the 4-H pledge.* Back home, in the weekly community newspaper, if she was feeling mischievous, she might have taken out an ad, with his picture as a teenager or younger, the caption, *The old 4-H'er is 43.* What picture would he have used of her? She had turned forty-three two weeks ago. The detritus of the years, she thinks, shakes her head, remembers Marvin, her paternal grandmother's second husband, talking about the detritus of his life. She traces out Brian's name on the window, a nervous, questioning calligraphy. Then she goes to the bed, sits down, lights a cigarette, and picks up the telephone from the night table.

"It's Eileen. I hope you haven't forgotten me ..."

"I need some hope," Brian said, as he and Eileen walked back toward her parents' house.

"You know the answer to that," said Eileen, hardly wanting to respond to his familiar complaint. She thought of it as a complaint or a plea, had been unsympathetic to him only because he had squeezed all life out of the words, was wallowing, not swimming. At the time she was in her first year at the University of Prince Edward Island, unhappy, stifled, wanting to move to a larger centre. She had made the decision to transfer to Dalhousie University in Halifax, would tell him later, it wasn't like she was going to the end of the world. *There is little for you here, Brian. Your horizons are limited. I'm not staying here forever ... Eileen, this is our home ... Listen to yourself, Brian. No hope, our home ... My whole family is here. I could start a business. I know I could run a good business. I could take business courses here as well as anywhere else ... Not as well as anywhere else, Brian ...*

"Your cancer sticks enjoyable?" Eileen's father said as she and Brian approached the dining-room table.

"We wish we could stop," Brian said.

"There has to be some scuff in our perfection," said Eileen, and her parents and Brian's parents looked at her as if she had made a rude noise. "Where do you come up with these expressions?" Brian's father said.

The seventh person at the table, a thin, fashionably dressed man – "He looks like a dandy, a fop, our very own Sir Percy from the *Scarlet Pimpernel*," Eileen whispered to Brian – detected the mild disruption only through the reactions of the others. This was his first visit back in twelve years, last seeing Eileen when she was eight, and he was thirty, back on the Island, in those days, for his wedding to Eileen's grandmother, a woman only two years from being twice his age, the family members were saying, until someone pointed out that she had lied about her age and was more than twice the age of her new husband. The publisher of the weekly community newspaper, a family friend, at the wedding said he wanted to run their photograph on the front page. And young Eileen suggested a caption: *Love is blind to age ...*

Eileen told the newspaper publisher at the wedding that she wanted to be a writer, and he offered her a job when she grew up, and Eileen made the publisher put it in writing. Years later, Eileen wrote a reminiscence of her grandmother, first married to a much older man, then to a much younger man, which won a high-school literary prize – third prize. "Marital Convolutions," she called it. She argued that she hadn't won first or second prize because she used certain words. Words about her grandmother's sexual vigour, the vitality of her libido, into her eighties. In the reminiscence she described Marvin as a fluttering, flamboyant, uninhibited Scarlet Pimpernel, a man it was hard to believe was born and had grown up in rural Prince Edward Island, characterizing the marriage as better suited to being a quirky, idiosyncratic film. Marvin and her grandmother were their own ongoing film. It wasn't until a decade later, sitting with his wife and watching television, that Brian saw the *Scarlet Pimpernel*, realized what Eileen had meant. A few years ago she had noted on a birthday card that the *Scarlet Pimpernel* had been made into a stage play and she had seen it in New York.

There had always been debate whether Marvin was part of the family, especially when Eileen's grandmother had died. Died in a small town in California, her ashes sent home with a friend who was going to vacation on the Island, no Marvin to accompany them. Mix the grey ashes with the red soil, Eileen had said when the ashes arrived on the Island. Speculation as to why he was back after twelve years: "I bet he's dying" ... "Wants to rub our faces in it" ... "Returning to the scene of the crime" ... But Eileen's mother said there was no crime, Marvin had not done anything wrong. Getting married and moving to another country is not criminal. It might have been smart. "You never moved, Mom," the daughter said. "People in our family did not like to leave the area, Eileen. Six generations have lived here. You know that ..."

"I want to clean up the detritus of my life," Marvin said, sounding more like the Scarlet Pimpernel than Sir Percy.

Eileen knew what detritus meant, said she preferred to use the word *debris, the debris of my life.* Brian said *junk* wasn't a bad word, *the junk of my life,* and the family gathering turned into a search for the proper word to describe a less than adequate life. *Rubble, discards, castoffs, slag* ...

Saturday afternoon. Her parents' house – pancake lunch. Next Saturday afternoon, his parents' house – rancher's brunch, even though they lived on a farm and not a ranch. The week before they had attempted to determine how many of these Saturday-afternoon meals they had gone to. He said it had been over 750 and she laughed at his number, accused him of wild exaggeration. "We've missed weeks, come on ..." The two families. Then Eileen and Brian got engaged and became part of it. "We knew you two would get married," each parent said, one after the other. "When Brian's mom and I were pregnant," Eileen's mother said, "we used to talk about what if one of us had a boy and the other a girl." Eileen had once interrupted a version of the story by saying, "Like two royal families trying to solidify their fortunes and consolidate their power."

"Name a Saturday we've missed," Brian said and stuck his forefinger close to Eileen's nose, and she snapped at it. She would have bitten it hard; had another time, during an argument over her academic plans, that living on the Island was stifling her creativity.

As she was doing a mental calculation of Saturday-afternoon meals, he described a few of the more severe storms they had gone through to make it to one family's home or the other's. When they got their driver's licences they would go somewhere afterward, but no squirming out of Saturday lunch – Sunday-morning church they might be able to skip, but not Saturday-afternoon lunch, holy, entrenched, ritualistic. The cigarette ... the walk past the barn ... or into the barn ... It was after one of the Saturday-afternoon meals, during the middle of winter, that they first made love.

"Those are the two most in love teenagers I've ever seen," Marvin said.

"I'm not a teenager," Eileen said.

"I'm only a teenager for another two weeks," Brian said.

– Eileen? ... I can't believe it ...

His first thoughts are of the argument they had when she told him she was definitely transferring to Dalhousie University. He looked at the finger she had bitten. The slightest scar, if you looked closely.

She had gone a year ;to the University of Prince Edward Island, transferred to Dalhousie University – Brian angry at her decision, but she saying she had to experience more of life – graduate school at Queen's University, then moved to Toronto

– We'll keep in touch, this doesn't mean I won't eventually move back; not a thing keeping you tied to the Island – Regina, Calgary, back to Toronto, to Vancouver. Married, divorced …

He thinks of them walking into the house, after they had made love, being criticized for their "smoke break," of her desire to write a book that would scandalize the family, the entire community, that would make her a pariah – an accomplishment she would be proud of. "Why would you want to be a pariah?" he had asked, not knowing yet what the word meant. He had accused her more than once of using words to make him feel inadequate, though she said she wanted to help him improve himself. She went to university on the Island, he worked at a gas station, saved his money, wanted his own gas station, maybe own a big company one day. The publisher of the weekly community newspaper hired her as a reporter, said he would never violate a binding contract. She lasted a month, quit after writing a story on the use of pesticides in potato farming. "Barely twenty years here and I feel ossified," she explained to the publisher.

– I thought I'd call and wish you a happy birthday. I wasn't ecstatic about hitting forty-three. But what can you do?

– I was waiting for your card, Eileen.

– You'll still get a card. It's right on my dresser. This year I'm adding a little substance to the celebration, if you want to call the sound of my voice substance.

– Only thing I like about birthdays is getting your card.

– I don't like anything about birthdays.

– I've kept all your cards. I thought if you ever became famous, they'd be worth something.

– Famous at what?

– A famous journalist.

– I am a freelance editor, a word caresser for hire. I like to think of myself as a literary factotum, a jack-of-all-trades. Should I say jacqueline-of-all-trades? A few might think jackass-of-all-trades more accurate.

– My service station hasn't become famous either. I added a convenience store. We have a fair-sized video section. I'm in debt up to my eyeballs …

Teenagers again. The time when he told her his plans to burn down an abandoned house at Halloween, she accusing him of having warped fantasies. The next morning she heard on the radio news that the abandoned house had been burned down, and the next day his friend was arrested, but not him. The friend never betrayed him. "What kind of loyalty is that, over a malicious act?" Eileen said. Brian did not attempt to defend what they had done, only that his friend was a good friend.

"Hadn't you ever wanted to do something like that, Eileen?"

"No, not like that. It's too mindless and stupid."

"You calling me mindless?" he said.

"What you did. The mindless, stupid thing you did …"

She heard him mention the friend's name: Noel. Said she didn't know he had died.

– They said he had so much alcohol in his system that night it was amazing he could find and start his car. What a lie. He knew what he was doing. He killed himself. He told me he wanted to kill himself. I never told anyone that, Eileen.

– He used to show me what he wrote. He wanted to go out with me, but I said I'd need your written permission.

– I remember how happy he was when he won that story contest at school. But he never wanted to be a writer. It was a story about a parallel high school on another planet. Except where the teachers were so tiny as to be almost invisible and the students could belch out huge, colourful bubbles and capture the teachers inside. Strangest thing I ever read …

Brian remembers the time Eileen handed him something under the dinner table. Felt the foil, realized it was a condom. "Lambskin," she whispered. "Costs a lot more." He dropped the foil packet and it hit her mother's shoe. Eileen's mother reached under the table before he could. "For a school project," Eileen had said quickly. "A history of contraception. Did you know that use of the condom goes back hundreds of years?" "Never liked using those things," Brian's father said, taking the foil packet from Eileen's mother, and held it up, as if displaying a rare insect he was attempting to identify.

– We were so careful. Had I gotten pregnant …

– I wanted to get you pregnant, Eileen. If we would have started a family …

– We were much too young.

– Our lives sure would have been different … Why did you laugh? How much have you had to drink?

– I had a picture of the day you used two rubbers, you were so scared. Wanted to put on three, but I told you that was ludicrous, not to mention expensive. You were going to suffocate your penis.

– You can't suffocate a penis. I only used two at a time a few times. After Noel got Marcy pregnant. That scared me.

– How did Marcy take the accident?

– She wasn't living with him when it happened. James comes in to get videos every so often.

– Who's James?

– Noel and Marcy's son …

Brian starts talking about his two children, both teenage boys.

– They're both readers. That's your influence, Eileen.

– I read much more when I was younger.

– I've read all of Lucy Maud Montgomery's books.

– Would you believe it, Brian, I still haven't even read *Anne of Green Gables*.

– You never had kids, did you?

– My ex-husband and his wife are trying to have a child. He must be popping potency pills like candy. She showed me a book on motherhood after forty, autographed by the author. I wish I'd edited that book, I said, then had to emphasize I was joking. She got cranky with me. If I have another drink, I'll do a fertility dance for my ex-hubby.

– I'd like to see you do a fertility dance.

– I have a spare room. Come here for a visit.

– When have I ever travelled? Why don't you come home for a visit, Eileen? How about Old Home Week? You've never come back for Old Home Week.

– Not going to happen, Brian. I would like to see you. You won't believe Vancouver.

– I like it so much here on the Island.

– I live on the eleventh floor. I bet you've never been on the eleventh floor of anything.

– You've never been over the Bridge.

– Not that bridge, Brian …

How they would argue about connecting the Island to the mainland, Brian recalls. He said he never wanted to live to see a bridge built. But the Confederation Bridge was built and his sons have driven over it, but not him. Eileen always thought that a bridge was a good idea. Wrote an essay at university on the history of the schemes and plans to connect the Island to the mainland.

– The house we bought, it's just down the road from that abandoned house Noel and I burned down. I'm still here but the wife isn't.

– Got your wedding invitation. That was a long time ago, wasn't it?

– Time flies when you're having a crisis.

– I contemplated coming to the wedding.

– Not a match made in Heaven. That's what I get for marrying my second choice.

– I should have invited you to my wedding.

– Your parents told me all about it … showed me pictures. Your husband was shorter than you.

– I don't remember Jennifer too well.

– Not much to remember.

– She was a good singer in high school, I remember that. She won some amateur talent contest, didn't she?

– That was her sister. I think I should have married her sister. Since you weren't available …

– No invitations for crumbled marriages.

Eileen thinks about her marriage, the years compressed into a few memory images. She knew from the beginning that the marriage wouldn't last, even said it to her husband at the wedding but he laughed. He wanted to go to Prince Edward Island for their honeymoon. She thought the idea of a honeymoon was silly. She was editing a very difficult book and didn't need a honeymoon disrupting her work. Besides, she had said, I've burned all my bridges. That was long before the Confederation Bridge.

– I stay in touch with my parents. They've been out here for visits. Once every year or two.

– I know. When they come into the gas station, they always let me know something about your life.

– They think I'm crazy living here. Dad goes to a strip club each time he visits. I cover for him. Don't tell Mom he goes. I went with him once. Real father and daughter bonding ...

Eileen thinks about the time she and Brian got drunk and he begged her to act raunchy, to put on nylon stockings and a garter belt. He begged and pleaded but she refused. She told him to go find a prostitute and through his drunkenness he asked where would he find one on the Island. "You poor, deprived, horny little boy," she had said. She lights another cigarette, apologizes for coughing into the phone.

– I haven't had a cigarette in about ten years, Eileen.

– I'm still smoking away.

– I remember how we used to enjoy smoking together. A beer and a cigarette together. What fond memories.

– Tonight I've had brandy and I've had wine.

– No beer?

– I haven't had a beer since I left the Island. Do you believe that?

– I had a beer with lunch.

They both remember how they shared a beer, drinking out of each other's mouths. Noel and Marcy also used to do that. Eileen remembers how Marcy asked her if she had ever kissed another girl, on the lips, you know, like with a boy. It wasn't until years later.

– I was really naïve and foolish, Brian, wasn't I?

– Your heart was in the right place. Every so often, something reminds me of your little crusade. Small-town life ...

She had read a book on Che Guevara, written a school report on guerrilla warfare, and he had bought her a poster of the revolutionary leader – she had used that poster to try to stop the sale of some farmland for tourist cottages. That got her publicity, and a big article and photograph in the weekly community newspaper. The same newspaper that had the article on the Halloween burning of the abandoned house. "We approached the military objective in the dead of night, under cover of darkness ..." The same newspaper that ran the photograph of Eileen's grandmother and Marvin. The same newspaper that had reported Noel's fatal car accident. The same newspaper to which she wrote letters to the editor and where she eventually got her first writing job. The same newspaper ... "Brian, what would have happened if the house hadn't been abandoned?" she had asked him when they were looking at the newspaper article together. "What would have happened if two teenagers were screwing inside? ... "

– Saw a documentary on Che a few nights ago. I wanted to call your parents, Brian, tell them to watch it. It was too late at night. Four hours difference in time ...

– I would have liked to have seen it. Every time I hear anything about Che Guevera, I think of you.

"Che," Eileen said at the dinner table, "helped to change the world."

"Never heard tell of him," Brian's father said.

Eileen wore a beret to one of the dinners. Her mother grabbed the beret during an argument over revolutionary politics and put it on her husband's head. Then he put the beret on Brian's mother's head, and she put it on her husband's head. Brian and Eileen chanted Che Guevara's name while the beret was making its way around the table ... several times around the table.

– I think Che is more popular now than ever. That was a big story several years ago when his remains were returned to Cuba.

– Funny, I was talking to your parents about Cuba on their forty-fifth wedding anniversary. They celebrated by driving completely around the Island. It's something they had always wanted to do, they told me, tears in your dad's eyes when he said that. They had to have their brakes fixed that day so they could go on the drive. That was my anniversary present to them ... a free brake job ...

Eileen thinks of the time she wanted to take a trip to Cuba, had the money saved, but Brian wouldn't go with her. She spent a lot of time unsuccessfully trying to convince him to take his first plane trip. She wanted him to see a psychologist about his aversion to flying, and he told her he had no desire to get on a plane, or to leave the Island. Instead of going to Cuba, she took her first trip to Toronto, and slept with her first man other than Brian.

– Maybe you were wise to stay on the Island.

– Maybe you were wiser to leave.

– I don't think I had all that much choice.

– Both my boys have been to hockey tournaments in Ontario and in Quebec. They've already travelled more than I have. You think not going farther than New Brunswick is a problem?

– That's right, you did fly once …

She thinks of Brian at the hospital in Moncton. Her visits. First and only time he flew on a plane was after a fall from a barn roof, having to be airlifted to a Moncton hospital. He recovered and was driven home by his father.

– A psychiatrist I went to a couple of years ago said I personified the Island, and it became something of a lover. A lover I loved too much or loved not enough … or even despised. The psychiatrist said I was repressing feelings about wanting to move back to PEI. Maybe he was right.

– Why were you going to a psychiatrist?

– Business and pleasure. I was commissioned to write an article on the psychiatric profession, and my life was in a minor shambles at the time …

Brian thinks about his plans to enter politics. His uncle wants him to run for office. Thinks he isn't cut out to be a politician. He wants to ask Eileen's advice. His grandfather ran for election twice, but lost badly both times.

– I'm considering running provincially in the next election. If I get the nomination.

– You're going to have to wear a beret, Brian. I'll lend you my old one. I still have it.

– I don't believe you.

– I haven't put it on in years, but it is in a closet somewhere. You still have the poster?

– My mother ripped it down when I still lived at home. Don't you remember, Eileen?

– No, I don't. Use that photograph of us in front of the Che Guevara poster in your campaign.

– Who took that?

– Marvin. Marvin wanted to immortalize us. Where in the world is he now?

– Marvin visited about two years ago. No advance notice. Brought his then new wife. That caused a stir, believe me.

– How old was *she*?

– About his age. They held hands the whole time they were in the house. Not that they stayed long. Mom didn't invite them to stay for dinner. Never saw Mom rude like that. Marvin came into the gas station, and I invited him and his wife to have a meal with me. When Marvin went to the bathroom, she told me she was pregnant and it scared her, being forty-seven. I thought she was more like fifty or fifty-five.

– I'm editing a book on teenage mothers. It's a sociological study. But I'm starting to write fiction. Working on a short story about Che Guevara. He wasn't killed but escaped to Prince Edward Island. Lived in seclusion. I, or rather, a character based on me, meets him ... We go back in time, Che and I, and use his guerrilla tactics to fight the rent collectors in nineteenth-century Prince Edward Island ...

– Why don't you set your story in Vancouver? That's where you live.

– I have a harder time imagining Che in Vancouver. Now, Prince Edward Island ...

Her close friend comes into the bedroom and says, "We're getting drunk, drunker, without you, Eileen. The flirting is getting disgraceful ..."

Eileen cups the receiver, and says, "This is important. I'll catch up."

– I have a drunk in my bedroom. She's married to my ex ... There, she's gone.

– Do we act like we did when we were kids, if I visit?

– Oh, yes.

– We were always getting into trouble, Eileen.

– You could use three condoms.

– We might not like each other.

– We used to like each other. I'm willing to take the chance.

– Maybe I should visit around Halloween.

– Don't burn any houses around here.

– I was eighteen. I can't remember how many beers ...

– Mindless ...

– Just because I've never been as far as Vancouver.

– I do still have the beret, Brian. I swear to God, I still have the beret ...

Still holding the telephone, Eileen goes back to the window and sees the smoke of the distant fire again.

– I'm looking out my bedroom window now, and I can see a fire. It's far away, but I can see it, Brian. I was thinking of when you had me drive us past that burning abandoned house.

– You'll never let me forget that, will you?

– If you get on a plane tomorrow, and fly here, I'll put on the sexiest outfit you've ever seen. I have these sheer black stockings that will really excite you. You can help me put them on.

   – You never did that when we were young.

   – I've matured.

   – You know I can't fly.

   – You flew to Moncton.

   – I was unconscious.

   – Close your eyes and pretend you are unconscious. I'll pay for your ticket.

   – I can pay for my own ticket.

   – I thought you were badly in debt.

   – I have a line of credit.

   – It would be a big change in your life.

   – The idea of going on an airplane …

Eileen begins to chant Che Guevara's name, interrupting Brian's excuses, and he joins her, and together they become revolutionaries against time and unfulfilled dreams.

The Poetry of the Long Ball

*F*or this entire 2001 baseball season – the season Barry Bonds broke the single-season home-run record; the season during which the horrifying terrorist attacks on the United States caused even baseball to pause and reassess the deepest, most essential aspects of life – I've been contemplating the most important question of my life: *Stay on Prince Edward Island or move to Toronto?* I promised myself that I would make the decision today, Saturday, the day before the final day of the extended 2001 season, no more procrastinating. Nothing like an approaching forty-eighth birthday, spent on your own, marriage in tatters, to get the old philosophical fires burning. Eighteen years ago, my mother, a third-generation Islander, had no trouble making the decision to uproot and move to Toronto.

As if it were a religious rite to help me in thinking about my future, I take out a shoebox of baseball cards, remove my prized set of 1977 Toronto Blue Jays, and spread the vintage cards out on the kitchen table, the players frozen in time but eager in my imaginary dugout to run out onto the field and play ball. From where I am sitting at the kitchen table, facing the patio door, I can see two fidgety blue jays at the backyard feeder, a common enough sight where I live, but I think how appropriate, as I'm rearranging the baseball cards and anticipating the Saturday-afternoon Blue Jays game on TV.

Born, raised, my entire life on Prince Edward Island, a fourth-generation Islander, and now I'm considering the big move. Planning on selling my business and starting fresh in Toronto. A new life at forty-eight, hardly like a rookie anticipating his first season in the majors. I'm not one to put any store in prophetic signs from above, or earthly portents, but I do find it oddly significant that the Toronto Blue Jays made their snowy major-league debut in 1977 at old Exhibition Stadium and Prince Edward Island officially adopted the blue jay as its provincial bird in 1977; not only that, but 1977 was my first year in business and the birth of my oldest child, who now plays with his brother and two pals in a local band that can recreate so exactly the sounds of groups like the Hollies, Cream, Dave Clark Five, Gerry and the Pacemakers, Herman's Hermits, and the Beatles that you'd think the British Invasion was still going on. They're in their twenties, but all the songs they perform are from the 1960s, long before any of them were born. Their sixties British pop-music repertoire is amazing.

My daughter, who has a beautiful voice but no desire to be a performer like her brothers, was born the day the Blue Jays won their eighty-second game of 1985, ensuring that the team I had devotedly suffered with through eight losing seasons would have its first winning season. In fact, she came into the world at virtually the same instant that the final out was made. I know, I was listening to the game on the radio, much to my wife's displeasure. She never did understand my passion for baseball or the Blue Jays.

Too restless to be alone with my indoor baseball-card heroes or outdoor ornithological companions, but needing to watch my beloved Blue Jays, even if they have had a lacklustre season, I get up from the kitchen table. Where do I go when I have to think about a critical life-changing decision? Where else: a sports bar.

"Last summer, it was during August, I was sitting along the third-base line in SkyDome, and watching the Blue Jays play," I say to the man seated at the table next to mine, in my favourite Charlottetown sports bar. "Everything in my life has changed because of that trip to Toronto." I finish writing the lineups on my scorecard. I chart as many games a season as I can, either while listening on the radio or watching TV. My enjoyment isn't complete unless I keep track of every pitch.

"I've been to Toronto a few times, and it sure didn't change my life. I was always real happy to get back to the Island," he says, and bangs his coffee cup down as if the solidness of the tabletop embodied everything worthwhile about the Island. The man's eyes go from the baseball game on the large screen above our tables to the newspaper he was reading.

"My marriage has ended, I'm contemplating selling my business, I don't drive a car anymore, and you know, I'm really, seriously considering moving to Toronto," I say, noting a line-drive single to left field, on the fourth pitch, a one-ball and two-strikes count, on my scorecard. If I don't get every pitch, an accurate count, scoring a game feels like a wasted effort. "If I could arrange it, I wouldn't mind going to every Blue Jays home game."

"Was the roof closed or open when you were there?" the man asks, looking at a full-page car ad in the newspaper. God, I realize, that is the same model of the car that hit the pedestrian when I was driving to the Blue Jays game in Toronto.

I rub my chin in thought, and look up at the sports bar's high ceiling: "For the life of me, I can't remember that. I remember the batting orders and lots of the plays, but I can't remember if the roof was open or closed ..."

My trip to Toronto last summer was the first time I had flown. Or even left the Island. Wouldn't get on a ferry, and later, when the Confederation Bridge was built, wouldn't drive on that either, not for love or for money. Maybe it was some type of psychological disorder, I don't know. No one else in my family has an aversion to flying. But I had changed things in my life before. Went through three months of therapy before my big trip to Toronto. Hypnosis. Breathing exercises, positive thinking, prayers. Had given up smoking and drinking earlier in my life, without therapy or hypnosis. Fist-clenching determination. Pure resolve. Utter willpower. But despite everything the psychologist had told me, all the techniques for coping, his soothing suggestions, I started to imagine several huge, muscular, half-human, half-mythological creatures holding the airplane in the palms of their hands, gently floating the jet from Charlottetown to Toronto. That worked better than any medication or psychological magic.

Impetus, my dad likes to emphasize, is as big a factor in sports as in everyday life. I think it's his favourite word, going by how many times he uses it. The impetus that was behind my big life-change was a simple enough event: I went to Toronto for my mother's wedding. She divorced my father and moved off the Island when I was thirty. She hadn't been back for a visit and I wasn't able to leave, until she called and pleaded with me to come to the wedding, the biggest, most important event of her life, except for when I was born. "What about when you married Dad?" I asked, a little gentle teasing, but she took the question quite seriously. "At the time it did seem very important," she explained, "but I was so young, barely twenty. Now I have the perspective of almost seven decades lived ..."

She sent me a plane ticket, and told me she would have a baseball ticket to see a Sunday-afternoon game waiting for me, the final game of a Blue Jays home stand, after the Saturday wedding. I thought I would go my entire life without ever seeing a Blue Jays game in person, and was there a bigger baseball fan on all of Prince Edward Island? Without using the words *astounding* or *inexplicable*, all I can say is that the flight was wonderful and I loved the experience. Couldn't understand why I had avoided planes for so many years. (Remember, this was before the terrorists forever changed how we view aircraft, not to mention everyday existence.) Before the plane had landed in Toronto, I foolishly thought of learning to pilot my own small plane, flying to baseball games all over North America, maybe even to Japan. A month after my first flight, I had a dream about being a stunt pilot, performing daring manoeuvres, trailing a flowing sign that urged people to believe in the unbelievable, whatever that meant.

In Toronto, my mother met me at the airport, and after our first embrace in seventeen years, and an introduction to the man who was going to be my stepfather, she waved a baseball ticket in front of my face and her fiancé waved a Blue Jays T-shirt, and all three of us did a joyous little dance like baseball players at home plate after the winning run was scored in a crucial game.

My mother and freshly minted stepfather were on their honeymoon cruise, and I was on the way to see my first major-league baseball game live, after a lifetime of following the sport. My scorecards and notebook of statistics on the Blue Jays were on the passenger seat. First time off the Island. First time I had flown. First time I had gone to my mother's wedding. So many firsts. At forty-seven, I felt like a new man. I was driving in the city, my stepfather's car, luxury like I've never known. I had never driven in the big city, though I have a passion for driving. On the Island, once a week, on Sunday, I would drive to one end or the other, down east or up west, as they say on the Island, and back home to the middle of Charlottetown.

But my drive to SkyDome was not to be smooth. I was enfolded in my stepfather's luxurious automobile, the pre-game show on the radio, and the little car next to me hit a pedestrian, the man hurled into the air and landing in front of my car. I slammed on the brakes, then got out of the car and tried to help. I talked to the man until the police arrived. Saw a shoe, with blood on it, on the hood of my car. Didn't immediately realize what it was. Reached to touch it, but the blood startled me. Wondered if it was a left shoe or a right shoe.

The driver of the car that struck the pedestrian was hitting himself in the chest repeatedly. But he didn't bend down to the injured man the way I did, and he didn't get the stranger's blood all over his jacket. I threw away the jacket before I got back into the car. I had difficulty describing the accident to the police, even though it was half the distance from the pitcher's mound to home plate away from me. My mind had not been fully on the driving. Anticipating the ball game and listening to the pre-game on the radio, an imaginary game entered my thoughts – and I was playing. Two outs, and I was up with runners on first and third. How could I tell the police officer that? My first trip to Toronto. Never flown before. I wonder if Yonge Street is as long as the Island, as the crow flies. I actually said that to one of the police officers. He told me that he and his wife had gone to Nova Scotia for their honeymoon, seven years ago, but they didn't make it over to the Island. Maybe another time, he said. He had a little girl who would love to see the musical *Anne of Green Gables*, and he wouldn't mind doing a little golfing on the Island.

I called home to Charlottetown in the morning. "The Blue Jays won," I told my wife, and went on to describe some of the exciting plays. As if she wanted to hear about the game. "What's wrong with you?" she asked, and I told her I was feeling great. She had never heard me speak so fast, and I told her I had never been to Toronto before. First time I had been the one to be away in our twenty-four years of marriage. My wife liked to travel, but I never went with her off Island.

I went to the game after the accident, but I missed the first two innings, so the official scorecard I purchased was incomplete, as far as the pitch count was concerned. After the game, I drove around a great deal. Until nearly three in the morning, when I decided to get some coffee. As soon as I sat down at the counter in the all-night restaurant, I saw this woman. She was wearing a Blue Jays cap. I wanted to tell her I was wearing a Blue Jays T-shirt. That I had seen a man hit by a car, and I had seen the Blue Jays squeak out a victory. The woman looked exactly like one of the salesclerks at the mall where I have my store. A woman I found attractive, sometimes fantasized about. But I would never be unfaithful to my wife. I moved closer, thinking it was her, the salesclerk from the mall. Put my notebook on the counter. She had a larger notebook. "You write?" she asked, pointing her pen at my notebook. "Baseball statistics," I said, like confessing an obsession for chocolate or fine foreign wines. "I'm wearing a Blue Jays T-shirt underneath my sweater," I said. And then I lifted my sweater up, something I would never have done in Charlottetown.

"My father was a hermit, my mother was a recluse," she read from her notebook. "A poem I'm working on," she said, and continued reading: "I would live in a cave. I would live in a cavern. I would live alone on an island, but I won't live on Toronto Island." While reciting her poem, she laughed, smiled, pouted – her face changed expression every line or two. Thought she was acting in a play, trying out various emotions until she got it right. "I live on an island, Prince Edward Island," I told her. "Tiny insular world," she said. "I'm fascinated by the concept of being a hermit, even though I'm a sociable, gregarious person," she said, smiling contradictorily.

"Herman's Hermits," I said. "I've heard of them," she said, "but they're way before my time." "I liked them when I was a kid," I explained, and told her, "My two sons, amazingly, know the lyrics to every Herman's Hermits song. 'Mrs. Brown, You've Got a Lovely Daughter.' 'I'm Henry the VIII, I Am.' My sons are in a band that sings British pop songs from the sixties." She asked me to sing a little. Yeah, sure, me sing in public. Doesn't have to be loud. Not like I had to jump on a table and belt out a song. Sing it softly to her, and I did, parts of several songs. By the time I got to "Leaning on a Lamp Post" I almost could have jumped up on a table. And we had the most wonderful conversation. Music, baseball, the seriousness and silliness of life, I was using her expressions.

But most of all we talked about baseball, especially home runs. She told me that nothing made her heart soar higher than watching a home run: the pitch, the contact with the bat, the flight of the ball. We discussed the history of the home run and how many home runs were being hit these days. I guess records are made to be broken, as the old expression goes, I said. We discussed the theoretical limit for home runs in a 162-game season, wondering if some future power hitter could accomplish eighty or ninety or even a hundred home runs. "I could almost make the majors, they're so desperate for quality hurlers," she said, going through the motions of pitching, she a southpaw.

I had three cups of coffee, she four cups of tea, and then I drove her home. She claimed it was the most expensive car she'd ever been in. My stepfather's car, I told her, wanting to be completely truthful with the amazing woman I had met. Then I told her what had happened that night, and I almost cried telling her the sad story. She invited me up, to see a video she had made. What, no etchings, I joked. She wanted me to see *The Poetry of the Long Ball*. Two hours of home runs, the hitters running the bases, fan reaction, taped from her television or the televisions of friends. Joe Carter's mammoth 1993 World Series blast … talk about poetry. Sound of the ball on wood, the flight of the sphere, the fans cheering, the ball reaching its out-of-the-ballpark destination like a wordless rendezvous with the eternal. Even a couple of inside-the-park homers. She said she wished she had either of Doug Ault's two 1977 Opening Day round-trippers, and I said I had his baseball card in perfect condition …

The effort in taping and editing, the selection of background music, no commentary, just the poetry of the long ball. She gave me a copy of the video as a gift. Told me her plans for the video, and I offered to help her with marketing in the Maritimes. I mentioned about copyright and trademark, and suggested that she would need permission from Major League Baseball to use the home-run footage, and she assured me that she was going to contact the proper officials. That's all I came back with, a video. I gave her my incomplete scorecard from the game and bought her twenty packs of baseball cards in the morning, as a goodbye present. I told my wife I forgot my scorecard in Toronto. The one and only time I go to a major-league baseball game and I forget my scorecard. I had the Toronto woman's phone number. If I'm ever lonely or bored. She knew her baseball stats. And those theoretical discussions.

After I returned to the Island, sometimes I would call her, when I was lonely. To talk about baseball. About life. She said I could stay at her place, if I didn't mind a couch, when I visited Toronto again. She promised to take me to the opening game next year. Told her I wanted to give a big city a try. I have never lived in a big city. A big city with a major-league team, she said. And I laughed. That goes without saying. We fell into e-mailing each other every day. Several times a day. During and after baseball season. Looking forward to the next season. When I watch the video she gave me, it feels like being next to her in the stands. Watching the home runs is ... is so ... so erotic.

The injured pedestrian seemed to rest there for the longest time. I didn't recoil or scream or say anything. There were screams in the street. Was about to sound my horn. What good would that have done? Got out of the car. As if comforting someone I loved, yet I had never seen this man before. I could hear him mumbling a few words, but they weren't directed at me. Didn't want to describe to my wife what had happened. One night I am going to dream about that man, that man whose shoe landed on the hood of the luxury car I was driving, whose hand touched my arm, whose blood was on my jacket, a jacket I had to throw away. What the dream will be like, I don't know. But it will be unlike any dream I've ever had. I don't know why I sense this, but I do. Yes, I anticipate that dream. Maybe soon, maybe in years, maybe when I am very old and nearing death. *Nearing death.* Isn't that an awkward way to describe dying? But all ways, it seems to me, are awkward when attempting to deal with death, to describe it. Then again, I am not the cleverest in describing life. Death and life, life and death. I'd rather keep score during a baseball game. If I have to analyze why I do it, have done it since I was a young man, all I can say is that keeping score makes sense to me. I like to chart baseball games, whether on the radio or on television or if I go to the game itself, which has been only once so far.

When I think of everything that has been going on lately, the changes, the possibility of even more rearrangement of my existence, I can't help but see that baseball is interwoven into my life. It's not that I ever was a very good ballplayer, though I did enjoy playing and I had some memorable moments, but somehow baseball has become psychologically significant to my very being. Following baseball and its statistics gives me enjoyment, real pleasure. I remember that instant when my domestic life changed irrevocably, and that certainly was connected to baseball. My wife was in the living room, watching the video of *The Poetry of the Long Ball*. I had already watched the video ten or eleven times since returning from Toronto two weeks before. I had told her what an incredible achievement the putting together of *The Poetry of the Long Ball* was, called it artistic and brilliant.

"Did you have an affair with her?"

"Who?"

"The woman who gave you this silly video."

Before I could explain the bond the Toronto woman and I had, the mutual passion for baseball, my wife told me she was going to move in with a friend, that we needed a break from each other. Stale, she said, as if she were talking about an old loaf of bread, our marriage has grown painfully stale.

When I called my dad, to tell him about my wife moving out, he asked about the wedding. Told him about the small, tasteful wedding, the trip to Toronto, meeting a woman who appreciated baseball as much as I did. My father asked me to describe my mother's new husband. I compared the two men, father and stepfather. He's like a little undernourished second baseman, you're like a burly first sacker, I told my father, and he said that I think about baseball too much.

"So, you going to Toronto …?" I hear the man in the sports bar ask, as the batter makes solid contact with a fastball – *going, going, gone for a home run* … Did she get this beautiful, poetic homer on tape? I couldn't help but think. Unfortunately, it was a Baltimore Oriole who had hit the homer, not a Toronto Blue Jay, in what could be characterized as a battle of the baseball birds.

"I'm having such a hard time deciding. Not like deciding to order either a bottle of beer or a glass of wine."

"You have Hamlet's problem. He was wishy-washy, couldn't make a firm decision."

"Did Hamlet ever hit a home run?" I say, imagining Hamlet swinging at an outside fastball and missing, strike three. Then I imagine myself stepping up to the plate, bat in hand, and there is one of those half-human, half-mythological creatures on the mound, waiting to pitch to me.

Yes, I think, I will move to Toronto, hit my home run. A new life ... a life as new and fresh as the start of a baseball season ... the pennant race about to begin. But first I want to finish scoring the game, then I will go home and watch *The Poetry of the Long Ball* one more time, just to make sure I am making the right decision.

Conception

Sunday, August 19, 2001, an ordinary, tranquil afternoon in rural Prince Edward Island. Except ...

At the dinner table, a small family gathering, Jeremy, nineteen and bursting with youthful desire to change the world, was showing his younger brother, Gavin, sixteen and deeply absorbed in pop culture, the gas mask he had worn when he was in Quebec City a few months before. When Gavin put on the gas mask, his mother said, "Get that dirty thing away from the table" as his father reached to pull it off his face.

Jeremy's grandmother pushed her son's hand away from her grandson's face and said, "It's beautiful ... a historical artifact."

Amidst the argument over the gas mask, the oldest person at the table, Jeremy's grandfather, casually mentioned that they should commemorate the sixty-first anniversary of Trotsky's assassination on August 20, 1940.

"No one commemorates anything about Trotsky on Prince Edward Island," Jeremy's father said. "Besides, today is August 19."

Jeremy claimed to have the coolest grandparents on all of Prince Edward Island. Growing up, the terms he had heard the most in describing them were "Old Lefties" and "Former Radicals." His grandfather had long white hair that he sometimes wore in a ponytail; his grandmother had short white hair, but in old photographs her hair was as long as Jeremy had ever seen, at least until he went to Quebec City in late April. They were his fairly conservative father's parents. It was his mother, also fairly conservative, who first told Jeremy that his grandpa and grandma would be arrested on the spot if they ever returned to the United States, but it was never clear what their crimes had been except deploring "the system." While Jeremy was at Quebec City protesting what his grandfather called the ills and injustices of globalization and his grandmother called the corporate crap in the world, his grandparents were in his thoughts, and they were what he first talked about to the long-haired young woman he met, and she fell in love with his passion and he fell in love with her idealism. Then they put their gas masks on together, like two ballet dancers attempting to synchronize their steps.

Jeremy's parents didn't want him to go to Quebec City. His grandparents had said in unison, "Right on!" to which his father said, "Strange phrase from Old Lefties."

Gavin removed the gas mask and handed it to his grandmother, as if for safekeeping, and she quickly put the gas mask on. "Anti-globalization," she said, making it sound like the first line of a beautiful old protest song. Her son, waving a fork in anger, tapped at the gas mask.

"Like the ice pick that killed Trotsky," the grandfather said.

"A fork is not an ice pick!" the father said.

"I would loved to have slept with Trotsky," the grandmother said. "Frida Kahlo, my favourite artist, slept with him."

"Madonna too," Gavin said cheerfully.

"Madonna slept with Trotsky?"

"No, one of Madonna's favourite artists is Frida Kahlo."

"Ah, the young, they need to have a revolutionary spirit," the grandmother said, looking lovingly through the gas mask at her oldest grandson.

"The young, they need to understand the past and maintain an orderly society," her son said, still waving his fork/ ice pick.

"What did the tear gas smell like?" Gavin asked.

"Like the Devil farting," Jeremy said.

"If we didn't believe in changing the world, you would never have been born," the grandfather, giving his wife a romantic hug, said to his son. It was an accusation as much as a historical statement.

"Old Lefties …," the father said contemptuously.

Jeremy and Gavin had heard the story many times: Their grandparents had married and moved from the United States to the Island … to the woods, to start an alternative school and retreat. They did not like the word *commune*.

"Trotsky made it to Halifax," the grandfather said. "Too bad he didn't make it to the Island."

"If we hadn't been protesting …"

"Over what?"

"We were protesting nuclear testing. That's when we met. It was the time I felt most alive. We fell in love."

Jeremy's father shook his head derisively, as if to say, *I know, I know*, and then Jeremy's grandfather joyously made the revelation: "That's when you were conceived. In the glorious intensity of protest, passion, and idealism."

Jeremy ran from the room, ready to phone the long-haired young woman he had met in Quebec City. Already, in his mind, he was telling the story of this dinner and the gas mask to his young child.

Should the Word Hell Be Capitalized?

*I*n a Toronto synagogue, during my stepson Bradley's bar mitzvah, I thought about the first time my parents and I talked about Jews. I was fourteen, growing up in Charlottetown, and we were sitting at the kitchen table having Saturday morning breakfast. My mother had the newspaper open and my parents were selecting the movie they would be going to that night. *Sophie's Choice,* my mother suggested, justifying her decision by saying she had read an excellent review of the movie, and went on to explain that Meryl Streep plays a Polish woman who had been in Auschwitz, but the character isn't Jewish. My father said he wasn't all that interested in seeing *Sophie's Choice,* but grumbled that there wasn't anything better playing in town. He stood up from the table and said, "I have three Jewish families on my route. They're all on automatic fill-up."

My mother and I both looked at my dad, who had been delivering home heating oil for more than twenty years on Prince Edward Island, as if he had made the most startling revelation about his work.

"Living on the Island," he said, stretching as he did whenever he stood up from sitting, "three Jewish families on one driver's route is extraordinary." Then my father sat back down and said the words that angered my mother. "Tell me, what are the realistic percentages of that happening?"

My mother folded the newspaper, and kept hitting it against the kitchen table as she spoke: "How many damn lottery tickets did you buy this week …?"

I never had a Jewish friend, I recall telling my parents, attempting to get them away from the latest argument about my father's lottery-purchasing habits. But the argument had a life of its own, and nothing I could say could dampen its intensity. During the rest of breakfast, my parents quarrelled, about the movie, about the history of the Jews, about their married life, but most angrily about my father's unshakable belief that he would one day win big and our lives would be completely changed. They argued and argued until my mother left the house with the announcement that she was taking a long drive. That was the way arguments ended in our house, with my mother taking another long drive.

That time, I remember, she returned a few hours later, after a calming drive along the Island's north shore and a visit to a secondhand bookstore in downtown Charlottetown; she returned with a hardback copy of William Styron's *Sophie's Choice* and two paperbacks: an anthology of essays on Jewish art and *Anne Frank: Diary of a Young Girl*. I recall the books so well because I still have them. My father looked at the three books, said I was too young to read *Sophie's Choice*, and made a comment about Anne Frank being spelled with an *e*, just like Anne of Green Gables, before saying to my mother, "You want one of my Jewish customers to adopt the boy? Then he could really learn about Jews." Another argument started, when my mother accused my father of having made an anti-Semitic remark and my father said that she reminded him of the character Bette Davis played in *What Ever Happened to Baby Jane?* – the crazy one.

I told the rabbi who had officiated at the bar mitzvah, and who had helped my wife convert to Judaism a few years before, about the three books my mother had bought me when I was fourteen and I had reread several times over the years. Then the conversation shifted to hockey. The rabbi was a big hockey fan and we were discussing the current season and my stepson's hockey abilities – Bradley has incredible hockey talent and I have already started fantasizing pro hockey success for him – and wouldn't it be something if Bradley eventually made the NHL and the rabbi was interviewed one day between periods of a nationally televised game as the rabbi who had officiated at the goaltending sensation's bar mitzvah. The rabbi told me he had been no good at sports but – and this was a big theological but – if he had to choose between one season with the Montreal Canadiens – his favourite team since childhood – and being a rabbi ... He did have a hearty laugh, but a part of me thought he was being sincere, that the laugh was trying to disguise his heartfelt desire.

"No Biblical injunction against a rabbi in the NHL. However, I will have to check with the Talmudic scholars, just to make sure," he said, and went through the motions of shooting a puck at a goal. He shot so hard on goal that his skullcap fell off. "Who's the imaginary goalie?" I asked, as I picked up the rabbi's skullcap.

"My main man Moses, winner of the 1280 BC Vezina Trophy for goaltending excellence ..."

After he had scored two more goals against the Old Testament's heroic lawgiver yet suddenly porous goalie, the rabbi wanted to know how Robyn and I had met.

"I have always been fascinated by how people who marry first meet. Chance? Fate? Matchmaker?" At this point, a smile crinkled his face and he said a good friend of his used a matchmaker to find him the woman of his dreams. Got the idea after he had seen the play *Fiddler on the Roof* in New York, Herschel Bernardi was starring. The rabbi pointed out that he himself had seen the play in Winnipeg, Montreal, Toronto, New York, with Topol starring, and a high-school production in Halifax, of all places.

I told him I grew up in Charlottetown, and the first time I went to Halifax, when I was eight, I got lost, and my parents called the police to find me. We were staying at a motel, my first trip off the Island, and I wandered away on my own in the evening and went to see a movie a couple miles from where we were staying. On the drive over I had seen Paul Newman's name on a movie marquee and remembered the hockey movie *Slap Shot* my father raved about months before, said was funny as can be, but had said I was too young to see because there were more swear words than he could count, even if he was counting real fast; nonetheless in my youthful rebelliousness I found the movie theatre on my own hoping to see *Slap Shot*, but it was a different Paul Newman movie altogether, and I kept on dozing off.

"Never been to Prince Edward Island," the rabbi said, "but I hear it is a delightfully romantic spot. What a place for two young lovers to meet."

"My parents were both in their forties and met during a convenience-store robbery. They weren't the robbers," I hastened to add, as if I might be accused of being an accessory after the fact. "The two robbers instructed everyone to get on the floor. My mother and my father were on the floor together and afterwards they met. The robbers were caught about an hour later trying to get on a ferry boat."

"That is fascinating, my friend. All the makings for a movie. And how did you and Robyn meet? She's a bit older than you."

"It hasn't been an issue that she's a decade ahead of me. Robyn says we're half a generation apart."

"A lot can go on in a half a generation."

"My first year teaching, I rented a room from her. It was an old house she had inherited from her mother. We realized our parents had had us later in life – her mother was forty-six and her dad was in his late sixties, while my mother was forty-three and my dad was forty-seven. We hit it off quickly. Within a week I had moved in with Robyn, and she rented out the room again. The next tenant was a woman who had published her first book of poetry and had a substantial grant to work on her second book. She looked remarkably like a dear cousin of mine on the Island and I told her that. A few months later the writer published a poem with a line, 'I live in a dreary room, in a dreary house where my landlady's lover's red-soiled Island cousin is the identical sister I never had ...' Dedicated the poem to me and my cousin. Never told her my dear cousin had died before her thirtieth birthday."

"The present is in the past. The past is in the present," the rabbi said. Then he asked me who I thought the greatest goaltender to lace on skates had been, besides his main man

Moses. We each compiled a list of our top five netminders and wound up in a heated, almost theological, argument over two Canadiens goalies, Jacques Plante and Bill Durnan, who the rabbi knew had each won the Vezina Trophy six times – and Plante a seventh time, when he played with the St. Louis Blues and shared the award with Glenn Hall. I told the rabbi he knew his hockey history the way my father knew about movies, and he took that as a big compliment.

I was at my desk, grading papers, when I received the phone call from my mother, calmly requesting that I come home as soon as possible.

"He's been asking 'Should the word *hell* be capitalized,'" my mother told me. There was a pause, and she described how my father had been asking the question all day, an agonizing inquisition.

I knew right away that it was her way of letting me know my father was gravely ill. I put down the receiver, and finished grading the paper I had been reading when my mother called: a clever book report by an exceptionally bright student comparing the movie versions to the novels of Shields' *Swann*, Atwood's *The Handmaid's Tale*, and Ondaatje's *The English Patient*. I often used movies as a way of getting my students interested in literature. An influence of my father. Then I found myself crying and thinking of a drawing of my father I did, when I was in elementary school. He was standing in front of his home heating oil delivery truck, smiling; my caption read: To keep customers cosy warm, toasty warm – the remedy for inclement weather is a phone call away. The phone number was on the truck, in my mind. The caption was from a television commercial for the company my father had worked for. I dialled the number, long-distance, and my tears trickled away, told the woman who answered the phone, "I want a million litres of fuel oil delivered snappy, my gonads are freezing –"

"Your gonads are freezing?" Robyn said, standing at the door.

"Isn't eavesdropping against the law?" I said, embarrassed.

"It is also my bedroom," she said.

"My father is dying," I told her, and she came in and embraced me, almost choked me with compassion.

After we met, and fell in love, Robyn told me she was born one-fourth Jewish. A grandfather who was divorced from her grandmother. We discussed genealogy and fractions that night. What would that make her son? The problem was solved when Robyn converted to Judaism. She worked on me a little but there was no way I was going to become any religion. I was born Presbyterian, I revealed, but I never even learned to spell it correctly. I had to tell her I was kidding, that I am an excellent speller. She was pregnant with our child when her son was being bar mitzvahed. The child would be Jewish, she said, because she was Jewish. Every thirteen years you can have a child, I said, and if the child is a male, you can have a bar mitzvah every thirteen years. My comment had gotten me a half-playful shove.

If I ever write a novel about growing up on the Island and my family, I know what my first line will be: *My father drove a home heating oil delivery truck, but got it into his head he had been a dermatologist.* Then I would write: *My father wanted to write a novel, but he could never get past the question of whether the word* hell *should be capitalized. My mother loved my father, except when he purchased lottery tickets, which was quite often …*

My father wanted to be a writer but he got hung up over the strangest little spelling problems, such as whether he should use *toward* or *towards*. I told him it didn't matter, as long as he spelled the word consistently. It did matter, he shouted at me. It matters if you are going *toward hell*, without an s, or *towards hell*, with an s. Then he told me, not shouting, that he never could decide if *hell* should be capitalized or not.

When I think about my father, I can't help think about lottery tickets. A definite motif in my childhood and growing up.

"One complete wall," my father said. He was looking at that wall in the garage and I was standing next to him. He was smiling – smiling with pride, with satisfaction. I looked for some weakness or regret, a sign of frailty, even an involuntary cringe on the absurdity of having all those losing lottery tickets taped on the wall, already a few tickets on a second wall. He wasn't far off from retirement then.

"One big winner and our lives would have been different, son." He looked upwards, attempting to locate whatever deity was responsible for lottery wins – big lottery wins.

I reminded him that he had won $1,000, ten years before.

"On your birthday," he said, and the way he muttered those words scared me. That had been his biggest lottery win and I still remember the celebration we had, Dad spending nearly half the winnings on a party. All during the party he said that my birthday was lucky and after that each year on my birthday he bought more than the usual number of lottery tickets. But no big wins, not even close to a $1,000. He could remember each and every little win, but considering how many tickets he bought over the years, he was not a man with very much luck. And the losing tickets would wind up on a wall of our garage, like some people put up tools or old licence plates. "One big winner …"

My mother has, on occasion, attempted to calculate how much my father has spent in their married life on lottery tickets. The thought sickens her, she says. She works in the accounts department of a fuel oil company, a different fuel oil company from where my father used to work. A competitor. She is frugal, level-headed. My cousin, who was immortalized in that poem along with me, when we went to visit her in the hospital, said that it was a strange coincidence that they both worked for fuel oil companies. The Island is small and that makes for all sorts of noticeable coincidences, my mother explained. The son of one of the punks who had robbed the convenience store that day, my cousin said, just about the last thing she said to us, had been a student of hers and had written a touching essay on visiting his father in jail. But on that occasion he had been in jail for passing bad cheques. Why had she never told us that before, my father wanted to know, and my cousin said she had not made the connection until she was in hospital.

My mother's phone call has triggered so many memories, and not all of them seem very important, but memories can exert their own voice. I hadn't thought about our neighbour from across the street in Charlottetown in a long time, but now he seems to be banging away at my memory's door. Every Wednesday our neighbour would go out with a shovel and bury the feces of his dog in his yard. We called it "Poop-Shovel Wednesday." We knew little about him. One day he invited my father to play golf – a Sunday – and my father turned him down. Later that day, the man knocked on our door and said, "I got a hole in one." He stood at our door and repeated several times, "I got a hole in one ..."

At supper, my father said that Mr. Poop-Shovel Wednesday was lying, trying to elevate himself in our eyes.

On the local evening news the following Monday the sportscaster announced the hole in one on the par 3 hole. That was the first time I heard our neighbour's name. Same last name as a hockey player my father had seen play as a boy.

I said that winning a lottery was like getting a hole in one, and my father got angry. I told him we had studied figurative language in English class that morning. Words like *simile* and *metaphor*. I had used a simile.

Then he went off to the garage, to put his latest losing lottery tickets on a wall.

We had a large TV, yet by the time I was growing up my father rarely watched television, except for films and, later on, the videos my parents rented in great numbers. He would periodically unleash tirades against what was on TV in those days, extolling instead shows from the old days, like *The Ed Sullivan Show* and *Perry Mason* and his all-time most beloved program, *Don Messer's Jubilee*, but when he watched TV, he wanted the big screen, almost like being in a picture show.

When we got a VCR, long-established movie-going habits in our family changed. My mother told me they would go once or twice a week from the time they met, but as they got more and more into renting movies, that dwindled to once a month. But my father and mother went to the movies monthly without exception: they would get all dressed up and leave the house like on a first date, and when they got back my father never seemed to care for the movie. But he knew the tiniest little details about movies. Information like Clint Eastwood had a bit role in *Tarantula*, or James Arness, who was Marshall Dillon in TV's *Gunsmoke* had been in *The Thing from Another World*, the original 1951 version, or Raymond Burr, the star of the *Perry Mason* TV show, and who was born in New Westminster, British Columbia, way on the other side of the country from us, had been in the first *Godzilla* and before that in *Bride of the Gorilla*. When I was a kid, I admired this knowledge. By the time I went off to university I found it cumbersome, ludicrous. But I would never tell my father that.

On my last visit home, about a year ago, my father's health was already deteriorating badly. I made the big announcement that I was going to be married. My mother wanted to know when she was going to meet her future daughter-in-law, and I asked them to come to the wedding, but she didn't know if my father was well enough to travel to Toronto. She said we should get married on the Island, a church wedding, at the old Caledonia Church where they had been married and her mother had been married, but Robyn and I both wanted to have a simple city hall ceremony, and besides, Robyn was Jewish.

That night my father rented two films from the 1970s: *Marathon Man* and *The Boys from Brazil*. My mother asked why he had rented two older movies, and he said that both movies were about Jews. I told them that Robyn and I had rented *Sophie's Choice*, and we watched it together as a family.

Laurence Olivier plays a Nazi war criminal in *Marathon Man* and a Jewish Nazi-hunter in *The Boys from Brazil*, my father said, and asked me what I would do, hypothetically, if I met a Nazi, perhaps another teacher at my school.

My mother said that was the stupidest hypothetical question she had ever heard, and my father asked her if she would kiss a swastika-wearing neo-Nazi, just on the cheek, didn't have to be on the lips, say for an easy $10,000. For no amount of money, my mother said. My mother took a long ride and got into a minor accident.

I had tickets for a hockey game the night after my mother called me and I told Robyn I couldn't stay home and think about what my father was going through. She refused to go with me, but I called the rabbi and invited him to come with me. I had excellent seats. It wound up a one-sided game and the team he had cheered for, both of us had cheered for, had been crushed. It wasn't until the third period that I told the rabbi I was going home for a visit in the morning, that my father was gravely ill.

"Transmigration of souls is a powerful concept, don't you think?" the rabbi said as our team scored its only goal of the game and the fans offered a begrudging cheer.

"Haven't given it much thought," I said, even though I had been thinking about my father's dying a great deal lately. Robyn thought it wasn't right for me to go to a hockey game with my father at death's door, but I said I would be seeing him in less than twenty-four hours. It wasn't the same as Meursault going to a Fernandel comedy film soon after his mother's death, I said. I had to explain the literary allusion, and Robyn told me she had never read Camus' *The Outsider*. My father, I had thought, would be able to name five or six Fernandel films, but I couldn't recall if the film title was mentioned in the novel.

"Transmigration of souls," the rabbi said, his eyes closed, saying the words prayerfully. "I fall asleep every night thinking of large concepts. My form of counting sheep is contemplating large concepts ..."

I asked the rabbi if he had ever read *The Outsider*, and he said certainly, when he was at rabbinical school in New York, but he always called it *The Stranger*. Depends how you translate *L'Etranger*, I said. The opposing team scored their final three goals of the rout during the ten minutes we discussed Camus.

After the game, the rabbi and I went out for a coffee. I think he was trying to comfort me, and I told him that as I was growing up on the Island, my father drove a home heating oil delivery truck, but a few years before he retired he got it in his head that he was a dermatologist. In a past life, of course, he would explain, if my mother challenged him. He knew a great deal about skin diseases, but after a while it was mainly leprosy he talked about. Leprosy and leprosaria. "Why can't you call it a leper house?" my mother once yelled out at the dinner table. "I was educated to call it a leprosarium," my father yelled back, and declared that treating dermatoid afflictions had been his calling. They argued as if he had really treated lepers at a leprosarium, in a previous life.

The rabbi said his father had a few peculiarities, but nothing that shook the equilibrium of their household. His mother, on the other hand, did on occasion shake the equilibrium by refusing to light the candles on Friday night. But that would last only a few weeks at a time, the rabbi explained, and life went on as normal. Robyn would never miss lighting the *Shaw-bus* candles I said, and the rabbi gently corrected my pronunciation of *Shabbes*.

My mother claimed that when my father started writing a story about leprosy, which he would work on occasionally and wanted to turn into a novel, that was the start of his dementia.

"*Dementia*," my mother said to me, said the word as if uttering a curse.

That was around the first time I heard him ask, "Should the word *hell* be capitalized?" I hadn't decided to major in English then, but I was developing a keen interest in language and literature.

"That all depends on the context," I answered my father. Told him that I have the same problem with the word *earth*.

My dear cousin also taught high-school English. She was the one who influenced me to be an English teacher. But she stayed on the Island and I skedaddled, as she liked to characterize my departure for Toronto. On one of my visits back from going to university in Toronto, she told me she was having an affair with another teacher. She had been talking for twenty minutes before I realized the other teacher was a woman, and married to a neighbour of our parents. Mr. Poop-Shovel Wednesday.

"That's amazing," I said near the end of the conversation, but I was uncertain what I was referring to.

When I came home, my father was lying on the couch in the basement, the television on but the sound muted, a thick notebook open on the coffee table, several pens. My mother rearranged the pens as I listened to my father.

"I can't decide if *hell* should be capitalized. I'll never be able to write my novel ..."

Then he closed his eyes and started chanting "Should the word *hell* be capitalized? Should the word *hell* be capitalized? ..." He didn't get very far into the chant when he fell silent.

"You're not going to die," my mother said. "We have three videos to watch tonight."

My father called me over but he didn't seem to recognize me. I told him I was a high-school English teacher in Toronto.

He had known a woman, a lovely, talented woman with acting aspirations when she was young, who had been in the audience at *The Ed Sullivan Show* when the Beatles were on the program, he told me. When I was younger, sometimes the story had included the Rolling Stones or Elvis Presley. I asked if the woman had ever seen Wayne and Shuster on *The Ed Sullivan Show*. On several memorable occasions, my father said without hesitation. All that was going to be in the novel he was writing.

"Write in my notebook for me, please," my father said. "Notes for my novel." He looked around the room, and said, "The world is so vast," his eyes exploring his surroundings as if he was looking at an unknown land. "So much we don't know. No matter how many years we wander the continents or navigate the oceans ..." I wrote as he spoke and my mother stroked his head. Then he asked me, "Should the word *hell* be capitalized?" Just like when I was a teenager and lived at home.

"Our son is married," my mother said, trying to bring my father back from his exploration.

"As soon as you're feeling better, I want you and Mom to visit me in Toronto. You are going to love Robyn and Bradley. Bradley had the most beautiful bar mitzvah. I wish you could have been there."

"Did I tell you I had three Jewish families on my route?" my father said, and I told him, "Yes, Dad, when I was fourteen."

"You an English teacher in Toronto, you say?"

"That's what I am, Dad."

"Then you should know if the word *hell* is capitalized or not …"

My father died before either winning big in a lottery or writing a novel. As bookmarks in one of our video guides, my mother found, on the morning of the funeral, three lottery tickets for a big draw later in the week.

"Wouldn't it be something if he won big," I said, and added that I thought it would be proof that there was a God if one of the tickets was a big winner. My mother was upset, terribly upset. My father kept buying lottery tickets, my mother told me, right up to the end, that he was probably buying tickets at that very moment from St. Peter. She cut short a criticism of my dead father by saying that he didn't drink or smoke. His only worldly vice, as far as she knew, was buying lottery tickets. My father was a dependable worker, a good provider, save for the purchase of lottery tickets. But it was a big worldly vice, she said, resuming her criticism: unfulfilled dreams, unrealized ambitions. "But certainly not an uncommon malady in our world," she interrupted her teary-eyed faultfinding.

My mother threatened to rip up the three lottery tickets, but I took them from her. She was so angry that her hands were shaking. She seemed angrier about the lottery tickets than when my dad was alive.

At the funeral, his older brother, who had come all the way from Saskatoon, told me that my father was studying to be a dermatologist when he was a young man, but had dropped out of school. Lost all heart for school and studying. A woman broke his heart, an actress, who went to Hollywood but never really made it, or ever returned to Canada. Then my uncle asked me if I knew that the skin was the largest organ in the body. My father had told me that numerous times, I told my uncle.

With my father's will was a long, handwritten letter, some of the seventy-five pages written neatly and others scrawled. My mother and I sat in the living room and took turns reading the letter to each other. What we could make out of the letter described my father's love for me and my mother, how his happiest moments were when we watched videos together as a family, the names of films he liked and the names of films he disliked, a rambling philosophical section on the human condition as depicted in films, how he derived great satisfaction from his delivering home heating oil, all the people he helped to keep warm, potential characters for his novel, that life was a perplexing, unfathomable puzzlement. At the end of the letter was a single sentence P.S., which took me a minute to figure out: "It was the life I was required to live."

"Required by whom?" my mother said. "Surely God would not require the purchase of lottery tickets. Surely ..."

"You think he went to hell?"

There was a silence. We both tried not to smile.

"Capital-H or little-h, it doesn't really matter. Hell is hell," my mother said.

Robyn and Bradley came to the funeral. It was the first time they had met any of my family. Bradley told me he needed to write a paper for school about a disease and someone famous who had suffered from it. He told me he had asked his rabbi, and he had suggested epilepsy and Julius Caesar. I suggested leprosy but couldn't think of anyone famous who had suffered from it. "But my father would have known," I told Bradley. Robyn told me she had read *The Outsider* on the flight over, but intended to read something lighter on the flight back. I told my mother she was going to be a grandma and she did a little dance of joy right there at the cemetery. And your grandchild is going to be Jewish, I told her, and she told Robyn the story about my father having three Jewish families on his home heating oil delivery route, all on automatic fill-up.

On the day of the big lottery draw, I checked the winning numbers. One of the tickets won $1,000.

"Part of our inheritance," I said to my mother, holding the winning ticket in the air.

"You can have it all," she said, tears and anger battling for control of her emotions.

"His second thousand-dollar win in a lifetime. What are the realistic percentages of that happening?" I asked.

My mother grabbed the winning ticket from me and ripped it in half. But it was a clean rip and I knew I could easily tape the winning ticket back together.

Hanukkah / Godot / Christmas

*T*he house was already full of people when Joel walked through the front door, looking for Noreen. There were two mistletoes hanging over the door, to go along with the two Christmas trees he could see, a ceiling-touching one in the living room and a much smaller tree in the dining room, and he wanted to try out the under-the-mistletoe kissing tradition with Noreen. He had already told her he loved her and she had told him to cool his amorous jets. Bad enough his declaration of love had been on the first day of Hanukkah, four days ago, and he had neglected the candle-lighting observance that night, but she was engaged to be married; and adding to the unruly infatuation mix was that she was going to direct him in an amateur production of *Waiting for Godot* in the new year. At least, Joel thought, she was lukewarm about her fiancé and more than a little derogatory.

Noreen had a glass of wine in her hand when he found her in the rec room downstairs, where a group of people were dancing to "Jingle Bell Rock." He smiled at the memory of his maternal grandmother singing that song in Yiddish, one of the many Christmas songs she had translated. His grandmother, dear Bubbe, actually liked Christmas songs, especially the ones written by Jews, and she knew at least a dozen of those Jewish-penned songs. Joel remembered watching the musical *White Christmas* on TV with her one Hanukkah, she singing along merrily with Bing Crosby to Irving Berlin's "White Christmas," except in old-world Yiddish. His maternal grandfather, equally dear Zayde, had passed away by then. He was no fan of the holiday season, Joel recalled, sometimes commenting in his old left-wing Yiddish-accented way that Santa Claus was the patron saint of capitalism.

After Joel took off his winter coat, Noreen said with delight, "That T-shirt is quite different."

"I wore it especially for the occasion. Designed it myself."

"Samuel Beckett and Anne Shirley together at long last."

"Platonically posed, of course."

"Interesting literary juxtaposition, Joel."

Looking around the festively decorated rec room, with yet another Christmas tree, this one artificial, Joel said, "You and I are the only ones here under forty, I'd bet all my Hanukkah *gelt* on that," and then explained the tradition of giving small amounts of money to children during the eight days of Hanukkah. Noreen had warned him that he might not like this party; most of the people would be in their forties and fifties; her fiancé was fifty-three. She was thirty-four, though Joel, twenty-two, at first thought she was no more than two or three years older than he. Turning toward the people in the rec room, he asked, "Which one of these lucky gentlemen is your fiancé?"

"He's upstairs. Discussing some business with a friend. You two will not get along, trust me, Joel."

"Conflict is the heart of theatre."

204 – J. J. Steinfeld

"If anyone wants to know who invited you, say you're my cousin. I always wanted a cousin."

"Call me baby cousin. I can play the part, Noreen."

"Have a beer and enjoy the Christmas spirit. Up in the kitchen fridge."

"Introduce me to your fiancé, Noreen."

"Make some new friends first. Socialize, baby cousin. Tell them about your brilliant playwriting and fledgling acting career."

"I will have *two* beers and get quasi-drunk on the Christmasness of it all," he said, as he headed for the stairs. "I warn you, I can't hold my liquor, cuz …"

Noreen had met Joel a week ago, during a community theatre audition for *Waiting for Godot*. She thought he would be perfect for Lucky, although he would have preferred playing Estragon. They had gone to the same high school, a decade apart, his parents moving to the Island the year Joel started high school; they had moved back to Toronto last year, with Joel staying to finish his fourth year at UPEI. He had somehow managed to charm her and wrangle an invitation to this Christmas party, even though her fiancé would be there. Yesterday, they had spent an hour at a downtown coffee shop discussing the practical, sensible reasons they shouldn't fall in love.

Upstairs, Joel opened the refrigerator and took out a beer. He moved near to the stove and stood watching the activity in the kitchen.

"Have you been naughty or nice this year?" one of the nearby women asked the large-headed man who passed by her at the entrance to the kitchen. The woman held her glass awkwardly, choking it, and attempted to look serious. She was posing the lighthearted Christmas question to people who wandered into the kitchen's sanctuary. It was an untidy kitchen but not as crowded as the other rooms in the house.

"Naughty, naughty, naughty, sweetheart," the man said, upsetting the woman with his lewd squinting, and she chased him away with a scornful, "Get lost before Santa erases you from his gift list."

"We've never met," the woman said, offering her hand.

"Noreen's cousin. Distant cousin. Long-lost reunited cousin."

"I'm Laura. You have a name? Or should I call you long-lost cousin?"

"All my friends call me long-lost," Joel said, and the woman turned away. He wondered if any of the men who were in the kitchen or passed through getting a drink was Noreen's fiancé.

"By the way, I've been as naughty as Godot," he said, his reply helped along by a Christmas song, "Sleigh Ride," on the house's impressive sound system. "Another Christmas classic written by a Jew," he said to no one in particular.

Joel left the kitchen and went first into the living room, finishing his beer and putting the bottle down on a bookshelf, then into the dining room, attracted by the crowd of people. He wanted these people to be in the audience, watching him perform. He took a stick of celery from the ample supply of snacks, twirled it through the dip, and climbed up onto the table that was pushed into a corner of the dining room, careful not to step on the bowls of snacks.

"What are you doing?" a woman called up to Joel, his head nearly to the ceiling. Noreen came up the stairs and saw Joel on the table. She hurried through the crowd.

"Either play-acting or being exceedingly crazy. I'll leave the determination to you," he said, his hands fumbling with his belt buckle. "My grandmother would say *meshugge*, but she'd say it with affection for her grandchild." He pulled out his belt and pressed it against the ceiling. "Genuine tooled leather I have here. An unappreciated artisan toiled seven thankless weeks on it before he went mad …," Joel declaimed, speaking to the back rows of some huge theatre. When he saw Noreen, he said, "Front row centre for the elegant woman. Tell the ushers you know me."

Noreen knew Joel was being facetious, but he spoke earnestly, and his expression was grave.

"What did the artisan go mad from?" she asked, wanting to steal Joel from his performance.

"The commercialism of the modern world," he shouted.

The chattering people in the room looked at the man on the table, waiting for something terrible to happen. "Who is this guy?" a man with drinks in both hands asked.

"Godot," he enunciated slowly, dropping his belt to the floor at Noreen's feet, "and your long wait is over."

"That your first name or last?" a man wearing a fake Santa beard asked.

Joel started to smile, but altered his expression: "Middle name."

"And a fine middle name it is," Noreen said, eager to keep the conversation going, but Joel appeared to be angry, twisting his face for emphasis.

After another Christmas song, "Santa Baby," started playing, and Joel proclaimed it also written by a Jew, the owner of the house rushed into the dining room. He had been informed that someone – described hastily as a nut case and dirty drunk – was standing, and stripping, on his most valued piece of furniture, contaminating the snacks.

"Get down, you idiot!" the owner yelled as he made his way toward the man on his dining-room table.

"I claim this table in the name of sanity and all unrecognized Canadian craftspeople."

Noreen's fiancé entered the room and moved toward her.

Joel removed his T-shirt and threw it at the infuriated owner, who let it drop to the floor. "That shirt used to belong to Samuel Beckett, not that he ever saw our adorable Anne at the Confederation Centre. He wore it night and day while he was writing *Waiting for Godot*. You can have it in trade. It's worth a dozen paltry tables." Joel still had on a sleeveless white undershirt, boxer shorts, running shoes and socks, modelling his outfit without a trace of self-consciousness.

As the owner attempted to get Joel off the table, the performer continued: "What is your favourite Christmas song written by a songwriter of the Jewish persuasion?"

With people calling out the names of Christmas songs, and arguing which ones were written by Jews, Joel began to do a little dance, whistling in accompaniment.

"Don't make me call the police," the owner threatened. "Get down!"

By then everyone in the house, close to forty holiday revellers, had squeezed into the dining room to view the spectacle of the disrobing stranger. People asked each other who the man was, and the word got around that he was Noreen's cousin. Her fiancé said that he hadn't known she had a cousin, and that she told him he recently moved from Toronto and they had never been close. Despite the confusion, the crowd's mood was festive, except for the house's surly owner. Growing even more perturbed, he again threatened to call the police.

"I'll call my muscular Muses," Joel said, "to eradicate you and your nit-picking, kill-joying, sleep-inducing kind. The cops versus my Muses, hardly a fair contest." After he had spoken, Joel bowed courteously to his audience.

A few hands reached up to pull Joel off the table but he moved evasively, scattering bowls of snacks and shaking the old table, seeking balance, spraying cutting glances at those who wanted to dislodge him from his stage.

"Leave him alone!" Noreen called out, startled by her outburst in defending Joel. It was just not like her to act this way.

"If he's your friend, Noreen, take him away," the house's owner said.

"He's her cousin," Noreen's fiancé explained.

Noreen collected the discarded clothing and held it close. To her, love at first sight was so much delusive garbage, the creation of sentimental movie makers, yet she wondered if she had fallen in love with Joel the moment she had seen him at the audition.

The house's owner finally managed to get hold of Joel's leg, and pulled him roughly off the table. Joel landed on his feet, bumping into a woman who had been waiting for the boxer shorts to drop. She spilled her drink and swore at Joel. As he started to apologize, the owner punched him in the stomach, Joel grasping his abdomen with a yell of surprise and pain. He straightened up and attempted to look unhurt.

"You didn't have to hit him," Noreen said, stepping between Joel and the owner as he tried to hit Joel again, a hockey enforcer denied his calling.

"Let's get out of here. This is no place for Mr. Godot," Noreen said to Joel, the people around her losing shape, their voices indistinct and far-off.

She turned to her fiancé. "I have to make sure my cousin gets back to his room. He doesn't know Charlottetown." She grabbed her coat and bag, containing the notebook in which she had written notes about the young playwright, actor, and university student she had met less than a week ago.

"Like Lot, I will lead you from this disgusting Gomorrah." Joel took hold of Noreen's free hand. "If you look back you'll be turned into a pillar of boredom." He pulled her out of the house.

As Joel finished buckling his belt, a police car drove past them and parked in front of the Christmas party house. Joel clapped his hands in exaltation. "Our exit timing couldn't have been better."

With the cold December air caressing her, Noreen felt her mood change. Joel confused her and she wanted to ask questions, to know all about him, but she became timid, her crowded-party mask lost in the dark night.

"If you want to dare the unknown, we can read from a play, in exchange for you having helped me," Joel said. "That is, if you but venture home with me, harmless Godot, even if I will be impersonating Lucky."

"I thought you lived on stage."

"A tiny, cramped, one-bedroom apartment in an old dingy building, but with a beautiful antique menorah. You can help me light the Hanukkah candles. It has to be before midnight."

"How far is it from here?"

"Twenty minutes if we walk with rapidity. Or in a more

leisurely twenty-five minutes we can summarize our lives to each other, maybe debate the relative merits of celebrating Christmas or Hanukkah."

After unlocking the door to his third-floor apartment, in downtown Charlottetown, and grumbling that he had forgotten to buy some Hanukkah mistletoe, Joel lifted Noreen and carried her inside, she protesting only mildly. He kept holding her while he stood in the middle of the room, she looking at all the radios, not caring if her feet ever touched the ground again.

"I, as you can see, live simply. Radios and an antique menorah are my only extravagances. All of the radios work, by the way. Inherited them from my grandfather, who repaired electronic stuff for a living, a lifetime before the days of iPods and flat-screen TVs." There were extension cords and multi-plugs throughout the room. "Each radio is in the proper place. Later I will give you an audio treat unlike any you have ever heard."

He put Noreen down, and instructed her to wait, not to allow any jealous *dybbuks* or foul-breathed *golems* into the apartment. Joel complained that the *dybbuks* and *golems*, along with a few critics, were out to get him, and he disappeared into the bedroom.

He returned to the room, waving two copies of a script.

"Situate yourself comfortably on the floor," he said, and led her to the centre of the cluttered room. He handed her one script and kept the other. "My latest unproduced play. This is the one I'm working on. School keeps getting in the way … and auditions."

Joel opened the script and told her a little about it, how he imagined his grandmother as a young woman in Poland falling in love with his radio-collecting grandfather as a young man, before coming to Canada, and then they started reading lines from Joel's latest play. It did not take her long to get into the mood of the piece and they performed three scenes as though an audience was present.

"That is a poignant and intense play," Noreen said when they had finished their reading.

"I haven't felt even close to relaxed in months and it feels great," Joel said. "Catharsis à la mode. One great bowel movement of the soul ..." With an affectionate smile he kneeled next to Noreen on the floor and added, "I love a gorgeous, talented co-star, especially on Hanukkah."

"I almost forgot it was Hanukkah. Too much Christmas spirit tonight."

"We better light the candles. It's the fifth night," he said, as he took six thin candles out of a small cardboard box and put them into his menorah, explaining the significance of the five Hanukkah candles and the sixth one, the *shamus*, which was kept in the middle elevated holder in the nine-pronged candelabrum and used to light the others.

Joel lit the candles, stumbling over the blessings he used to say at Hanukkah growing up in Toronto. Lighting the Hanukkah candles was the one Jewish tradition his parents brought with them when they moved to the Island. Neither one was ever comfortable living on the Island, and after six years they returned to Toronto to get divorced, leaving the family's old menorah with their son.

"You want to read from another unproduced play of mine? Or we could improvise a play about an actor about to play Lucky in *Waiting for Godot* getting lucky with the director and singing Christmas songs in Yiddish and lighting Hanukkah candles."

Joel pulled her gently to his level, and they kneeled near each other. When Joel began to undress her, Noreen became tearful, he feeling responsible for her tears.

"You're the most beautiful human being I've ever seen," he said. "I thought if I didn't stop yapping I wouldn't have to confront that. Nothing intimidates more than beauty."

"I hate being called beautiful," she said harshly. "I hate being told how beautiful I am. So what, so what ..."

"Shut up, you ugly clump of deformity," he shouted, falling backward from his kneeling position, but regaining his balance quickly and nestling close to Noreen.

Her tears abated and she smiled, holding Joel tightly. Noreen relaxed into Joel's arms. He stroked her face, searching for a flaw, a telltale mark or small scar, but found only serene beauty despite her former disquietude.

Joel stood up and turned on some of the radios, setting them to the same classical music station. "This occasion calls for eighteen radios playing simultaneously." He rejoined her on the floor.

"I've never listened to eighteen radios simultaneously."

"Eighteen is my lucky number."

"I don't have a lucky number."

"I give you eighteen. *Chai.*"

"*Chai?*"

"The Hebrew word for life. Add the numbers of the Hebrew letters together and you get eighteen. My Christmas song-singing Bubbe right up to the day she died gave her grandchildren eighteen coins or dollars on their birthday, depending on their age. When I was young it was eighteen nickels ... then eighteen dimes ... eighteen quarters ... and when I became a man at thirteen, eighteen bucks. She died when I was fifteen, but left me eighteen hundred dollars in her will."

In the living room and with only the Hanukkah candles burning, the eighteen radios playing in symphonic harmony, Joel continued to undress Noreen. He felt unsure and more than sexually aroused. He knew that he cared for this woman, trying to block out thinking of her as a potential character for a play; so many of the people he met were just that, potential characters, material to be mined.

"I should take my engagement ring off," she said, and took off the ring.

"That's probably worth more than my writing grant from the Council of the Arts."

"All I want for Christmas is a broken engagement."

"What a wondrous present. A true gift of the Magi."

"I shouldn't do it over my clever little smartphone, should I?" she said, holding up her phone.

"That wouldn't be very Santa-like, would it? Better to get back to our romantic script."

"I need to tell you something, Joel," Noreen said, a worried tone rustling her words.

"I am not averse to using the latest in contraceptive latex," he said, taking the ring from her and balancing it on his head.

"Please, Joel. My stomach is awful-looking." She lowered her head and stared at a coffee stain in the carpet.

Joel felt saddened by Noreen's revelation but showed a wide smile. "Want to buy a diamond engagement ring?" he said, holding it up in the air. "Nothing about you, my friend, is less than pulchritudinous." He lifted her chin so that she was facing him.

"I sure hope that's an insult," she said, attempting to turn away, Joel refusing to allow the lovely face to leave his sight.

"A pretentious compliment. Pulchritude is beauty and it's you, Noreen."

Noreen closed her eyes so hard that her head throbbed. After a pause during which she heard the rasping echo of memory, she moaned, "The scars," as if it were a song of grief for what had happened many years ago.

"I fell out of a tree when I was a teenager. I fell by accident. I have to believe that. I don't want to believe a seventeen-year-old girl wanted to die. When I fell out of the tree the branches ripped up my stomach and legs."

He stood up and shut off the lights, only the Hanukkah candles illuminating the room.

She kissed him passionately, and he finished undressing her, she then helping him take off his clothes. In the dimness of the room, he could faintly see the scars along her stomach and legs, and he touched them, kissed them, as if her very beauty resided within them.

Later, while they were lying together on the floor, she said, "You never told me what your favourite Jewish-written Christmas song is."

"'White Christmas.' Just like my dear Bubbe ..."

Joel started to sing "White Christmas" in Yiddish as the Hanukkah candles burned down, and Noreen tightened her embrace of him.

The Most Remarkable Experimental
Filmmaker the World Has Ever Known

Nearly every afternoon, when the weather was agreeable,
the loving, devoted couple would meet and stroll down
to Charlottetown Harbour, less than a five-minute walk from
their workplaces – she at a gift shop where she was a salesclerk
and he at an office building where he had a janitorial job – and
sit on a wooden bench facing the boardwalk and the water,
having their simple packed lunches. They would sit close
together, holding hands, from time to time giving each other
pleasant little kisses, sometimes the kisses turning passionate
despite the openness of their noontime eating place. Both of
them believed, and said it to each other in different ways, that
had they not met, their lives would have remained dreadfully
empty, barely worth living. She, at twenty-three, had had a
drinking problem since she was fifteen, and he, at thirty-one,
had already had several close brushes with death and two stays
in jail because of his drug abuse. But she no longer drank and
he would no sooner take any drugs than thrust a knife into
himself. Yes, they loved each other greatly, and were thankful
for the hope they gave each other. They did not like being

apart, and eagerly awaited their lunch breaks so they could have another hour together.

She was the first one of the two to see the big, lumbering, burly man walking toward them, a jewel-ornamented film camera in one hand and a leather bag draped over his shoulder. "Look how huge that man is," she said, but her companion was intent on getting another kiss. "I bet he weighs more than both of us put together …" Finally the man on the bench turned and saw the large man approaching them, swinging the film camera at his side.

The large man stopped on the boardwalk, facing the couple, separated from them by a strip of greenery. He stared at them for a few seconds before lifting his camera to his face and saying, "Would you like to be in a film I am doing?"

The couple, used to seeing tourists with cameras of various sorts, thought this man might be another tourist, but with an unusual, jewel-ornamented camera, and were not pleased by the intrusion into their lunch break. They both put their hands in front of their faces, and the man with the camera said, "There's no film in my camera now. Even when I'm not filming, I never let this camera out of my sight."

They lowered their hands and glanced at each other, perplexed.

"I would never expect you to be in my film without being adequately compensated," the stranger said.

The man on the bench looked at his watch, and was about to say that they had to get back to work soon, when the large man resumed speaking, his enthusiasm evident from his first words.

"All morning I have been walking along this lovely waterfront, observing people, and you are the perfect couple I require for my film. It would not take more than three or four hours of your time ..." The large man explained that he had been working on the film for almost a year, and had shot in fifty-one different countries during fifty-one weeks. This would be the fifty-second country and the fifty-second and final week. An intense, exciting, creative year. Everything according to schedule.

"What kind of camera is that?" the man on the bench asked.

"One of a kind. A marvel. Takes pictures beneath the skin. Not X rays, don't be afraid. The inner person, let us say. It captures what the actor is."

"Sounds awfully peculiar to me."

"Peculiar, no. Unique would be a more apt description."

"Fifty-two countries, did you say? What kind of movie is this?" the woman asked, and she moved even closer to her companion.

"A grand, wondrous, exquisite film that will be unlike any other film. I require a fervently in love couple, the woman ten to twelve weeks' pregnant."

"How did you know I'm pregnant?" the woman said, certain she had not yet started to show. "We haven't told anyone." Her companion touched her belly, as if to protect the developing child from the man and his jewel-ornamented camera.

"I have an eye for these things," the large man said, lowering the camera to his side. "You are twenty-three, correct? And your gentleman is thirty-one."

"You are sure good at guessing ages," the man on the bench said.

"It is to your advantage that you have no previous acting experience. For the final scene I do not desire experienced actors," the large man clarified and pulled out two thin scripts from his shoulder bag. "If you would only read the scene, you will see the parts are ideal for you. No need for you to see the script in its entirety. The complete script is bigger than the thickest Bible," the large man went on, holding the film camera his arm's extension away from the two thin scripts to indicate how thick the actual script was.

The man and the woman each reluctantly took a script from the large man, and he smiled amiably while he spoke: "I, or my assistant, will come by here tomorrow, noonish, if it is convenient for you, and you can give your decision. You need only concern yourselves with the final scene. The other fifty-one scenes are completed. But without the final scene the film is nothing. That is why I so want you two to be in my film. You are perfect."

The woman started to skim through the titleless script, and before she reached the end, asked, "What's your movie called?"

"A title hasn't been decided upon yet. I always feel it's better to select a title after a film is completed. Until then, *Film in Progress* is the title." The large man grinned widely and looked as though he was about to laugh, but coughed instead, his jewel-ornamented camera held rigidly against his hip.

Then, returning to the beginning of the script, the woman saw the descriptions of the two characters in the final scene and she shook her head in amazement. "This describes us fairly close. It was only a week ago I got my hair cut short."

"Now you can see why I was so pleased to discover you sitting here."

"I didn't start that knife fight," the man on the bench said, rubbing the script against where he had his scar. "That sure didn't stop me from getting sent to jail," he added with a vehemence that the woman felt shake his body.

"My requirement is for a thirty-one-year old man with a long scar along his right leg. How that scar was achieved is of no concern to me," the large man said, and carefully reached into his shoulder bag and pulled out two small cloth bags, secured by drawstrings, and offered them to the couple: "For your trouble. For reading the script."

The man on the bench opened his bag first and saw the gold ingots. He held up one of the gleaming ingots to the woman, and she opened her bag.

"Tomorrow, noonish," the large man said, and started to walk away.

"These aren't real gold," the man on the bench called after him.

"As real as the precious stones adorning my camera," the large man responded, and continued to walk along the boardwalk; as he walked he spoke loudly about himself, so the couple on the bench could hear him – "I grew up in a remote, desert area, but at a young age I became a world traveller. By chance I became involved with film. It has become the driving passion of my life ..." – until he was around a corner and out of sight.

"What's in your bag?" the man asked his companion.

"Five tiny gold bars," she said, and removed an ingot.

"Mine too."

"You think the gold is real?"

"Let's go to a jeweller's right now."

"We have to get back to work."

"I'm going to take the afternoon off," the man said, but the woman told him she couldn't get anyone to replace her on such short notice. She patted her belly, reminding him that they were working for their child and its future.

Neither the woman nor the man had been able to sleep more than an hour during the night and the next morning both called in sick. By eleven they were sitting on a bench, not bothering to bring any lunch, the scripts on their laps, looking for the large man to return. They had gone to three jewellers, and the lowest appraisal for the gold ingots was $6,500, by the first jeweller. Both of the other appraisals were well over $7,000. The couple had placed their "advance" in a newly rented safety-deposit box – they had never had a need for one before – and had already decided to sell the gold, toward a down payment on a small house. As they waited they speculated further what the large, unusual filmmaker was up to. Last night they had come up with many possible explanations, from the fanciful to the sinister, but they couldn't avoid thinking there was trickery or deception involved. Only the most eccentric, wealthy person would give them gold without wanting something in return. At least expecting something much more in return than having them act – even if they had to make love, which the script called for – in the final scene of a film that made no sense to them.

A large, rapidly walking man, as big and burly as the filmmaker but athletic-looking, holding a closed umbrella and wearing a backpack, came toward them.

"Have you decided?" the athletic-looking man asked, his gestures nervous, tapping the umbrella against the boardwalk.

"Where's the guy with the weird camera?" the man on the bench asked.

"He sent me. I'm authorized to negotiate with you."

Then four brightly costumed people, their faces coated with silvery makeup, came somersaulting along the boardwalk. Achieving great height, they somersaulted to the athletic-looking man and stood behind him.

"They are rehearsing, more or less. You saw in the script about the four acrobats," the athletic-looking man said.

"Those acrobats are unbelievable to behold," the woman on the bench observed.

"The best acrobats in the world. You agree to be in the film? Another bag of gold each ..." The athletic-looking man took off his backpack, unzipped it, and removed two small cloth bags. These bags appeared to contain more than the ones they had received the previous day. "Fourteen gold ingots in each bag. We are not prepared to go higher."

The man on the bench fanned himself with his script, and said, "The script says we jump, our fingers interlocked, less than a minute after having made love, from the top floor of the tallest building in the world ..."

"You merely have to pretend to jump. The rest is done through computer technology."

"Why does the sex have to be real?" the woman on the bench asked.

"The film requires it. Fourteen gold ingots each ..."

Before the athletic-looking man had finished answering the woman's first question, she followed with another one: "Where will this filming take place?"

"We have rented an old farmhouse with a spacious bedroom, which has been transformed to look like a hotel room. Computer technology will make it seem like the top floor of the world's tallest building."

The acrobats resumed their acrobatics, moving back and forth along the boardwalk, perilously close to the water.

"Essential that the movements of the acrobats around your bed reflect the fervour of your copulation."

"I don't care for that word *copulation*," the woman said.

"I think the first draft of the script had the word *fuck*, but it got changed during a rewrite," the athletic-looking man said, holding the small, full bags not far from the faces of the couple.

"It's not the words I'm worried about," the man on the bench said, folding his script in half. "If we do agree, when would we be doing our scene?"

"Tomorrow night. Then or never. You must tell me now, so we can find another couple, woman twenty-three, ten to twelve weeks' pregnant, short hair, man, thirty-one, scar along the length of his right leg."

"How are you going to find such people that quickly?"

"He found you, didn't he?"

"Can't you use makeup for the scar? How can you tell the ages in the movie, anyway?"

"Has to be authentic. Genuine. The script is specific. He deplores falsification."

The couple on the bench looked at each other, kissed, and the man said, "This is screwy, but what the hell."

"You each get your fourteen gold ingots immediately after the scene is completed …"

The athletic-looking man, lifting his umbrella, pointed at the four acrobats: "Rehearse. Time is short …" The acrobats, achieving even greater height, somersaulted rapidly along the boardwalk, the athletic-looking man scurrying after them.

The athletic-looking man pulled up in a metallic reddish-brown van that looked like it had just been washed and polished, the four brightly costumed acrobats, silvery-faced as the day before, sitting in the back silently. The thirty-one-year-old man and the twenty-three-year-old woman, their movements cautious, got into the front seat. The man had a knife hidden in his jacket – a pocketknife with his initials on the handle. Amid their excitement and uncertainty and bafflement, the couple had argued over the knife the previous night.

– *If you think there's any danger, to you or the baby, we won't go.*

– *I don't know why we're getting paid so much. We're not actors.*

– *You heard, they don't want real actors.*

– *This is too crazy to believe.*

– *That's why I have the knife with me.*

– *But we'll be naked.*

– *The knife will be in my jacket.*

– *I don't want you to get into any knife fight.*

– *It's only a pocketknife, what are you giving me a hard time for?*

– *You know what happened that other time.*

– *I was defending myself.*

– *If something happens to us, he won't be able to get the gold back.*

– *Maybe he wouldn't want the gold back. Maybe the idiot has more gold than he knows what to do with ...*

"Doesn't your pal like showing up?" the man, fingering his hidden pocketknife, asked.

"He's waiting on the set. Many little details have to be dealt with," the driver said, looking at the road. "You are so fortunate to be able to work with him."

"We've never acted in our lives," the woman, huddled against her companion, said.

"He sees your deeper qualities and will embrace them with his camera. He is the most remarkable experimental filmmaker the world has ever known."

"What are some of his other movies?"

"You would not have had the opportunity to see them. They are not for commercial distribution."

"Then the world hasn't known him, has it?"

"We are not going to argue over attendance figures. When you work with him you will know he is the most remarkable experimental filmmaker the world has ever known ..."

It was dark, and became darker as they drove, in strained silence. "You two are an absolute godsend. We couldn't ask for two better individuals to complete the film," the driver said, breaking the silence. The four acrobats did not speak, but one of them had fallen asleep and was snoring lightly.

After an hour of steady driving, the couple, who rarely left the city, found everything completely unfamiliar.

"I can't imagine a fancy hotel room out here," the woman said.

"No expense has been spared transforming a second-floor bedroom of the farmhouse," the driver told her. "You will think it is the most splendid hotel room ..."

The couple asked questions about where they are going, and the driver repeated the directions he had committed to memory.

"I have a good sense of direction," the driver said.

"I never like driving at night," the woman said.

"Not much traffic on this road," the man said.

"No one's lived in the house for a year. We were told an elderly gentleman, a widower, owns it. Lives with his son in another city now. We rented it through a real estate agency," the driver said to the couple when they both commented on the large "For Sale" sign on the old farmhouse's overgrown front yard.

The couple followed the others into the house, and up the stairs to the second floor. "Astounding we're finally going to finish this film," the athletic-looking man said as he opened the bedroom door. The filmmaker, holding his jewel-ornamented camera, greeted them with a warm smile. The couple were amazed by the elaborately decorated bedroom on the second floor of the rundown farmhouse. "You'd think you were in a five-star hotel," the athletic-looking man said, boasting that he had been responsible for set design and lighting. After the filmmaker gave the couple a concise overview of the film, and instructed them to take their places and begin acting, the woman asked the athletic-looking man, "Will we be able to see the movie ... I mean, all of it?"

"It can be shown only once. Private showing for the person putting up the money. Then it will be destroyed."

"This gets crazier all the time."

"You are thinking in conventional terms. With money, a person can indulge themselves."

"Who's putting up the money?"

"We have a contractual agreement not to reveal the name."

"Aren't there any more people?" the man asked, taking the woman's hand and leading her to the ornate bed where the filmmaker was pointing.

"Myself, my assistant, four incomparable acrobats. And you two. They rest will be done with computer technology."

"So we've been told," the man said.

"But without the human dimension, your uniqueness, all the rest is meaningless," the filmmaker said, preparing to begin shooting the scene.

"What about costumes or makeup?"

"Your outfits are perfect. I do not want to tamper with your look whatsoever. Simply make love as though you know it will be the last time you two will ever be able to make love …"

The couple had very few lines. Despite having been ardent, imaginative lovers since the first day they had met, the man and the woman began to make love in the most awkward, uninspired manner. They performed their scene four times: the first time a ridiculous parody of lovemaking, both of them moving self-consciously, awkwardly, and giggling like schoolchildren at the silliness of what they were doing, giggling much less the second time, serious by the third, and achieving perfection, in the filmmaker's estimation, the fourth time. The acrobats performed their incredible feats of leaping and tumbling around the bed, regardless of how poorly or well the couple were performing. One of the acrobats even leaped so high that he pressed both of his palms against the ceiling. The couple stood up from the bed each time, interlocked their fingers, and went to the window. As he worked, the filmmaker, all the time dexterously adjusting his jewel-ornamented camera, talked to himself about his place in the history of cinema.

"Took less time than I thought," the filmmaker said, patting his jewel-ornamented camera in satisfaction. The couple dressed hurriedly, the man making certain his knife was still in his jacket pocket.

The athletic-looking man handed the couple the two bags of gold and led them to the van. As the filmmaker leaned out the second-floor window, praising the couple's performance again, the acrobats stood behind him and waved joyously at the occupants of the van. After a silent ride home, the couple were dropped off near their apartment, the driver saying he was feeling both nauseous and exhausted, but thanked them for their superb acting, and the van drove away.

Within a matter of days they had sold all their gold ingots and made a down payment on the rundown farmhouse with the five-star-hotel bedroom, an hour's drive to where they worked. After that night of filming, they went each afternoon, weather permitting, to a bench on the waterfront, ate their lunches, and waited for something out of the ordinary to happen, but nothing unusual occurred, and they spent their lunch hours in the same repetitious way. In the evenings they worked on their house, wallpapering and painting the walls, sanding the floors, completing the baby's room first. They did not have to do a thing to the bedroom where the filming had taken place, even keeping the handprints of one of the acrobats on the ceiling. On their days off, the couple would spend the entire noon hour sitting on a bench, waiting. They looked forward to the birth of the baby, and bringing the child to the waterfront, to sit with them on a bench. And they both knew, in their heart of hearts, though they were fearful or unable to express it, that even if they lived the longest lives, they would never see the filmmaker, his assistant, or the acrobats again.

The Semblance of Eternity
on a Hot Summer's Afternoon

In Charlottetown, the evening before, at what Julian described as a gorgeous little pub, a place to soothe an anguished big-city soul, he had a discussion about Creation and the Bible with another tourist from Ontario, a man from some little northern town Julian had never heard of. Julian, a lifelong resident of Toronto, claimed that God took an entire hour to create the Big Smoke and it was creative exertion well spent. To Julian's ear, the other tourist pronounced *To-ron-to* awfully close to *Go-mor-rah*, but with an exaggerated smile, as he continued to tell Julian about the stories in the Bible, Old and New Testaments, arguing that they had really happened. Could anyone prove otherwise?

This fervent, passionate Biblical talk on only one drink, Julian observed, and a relatively tame drink at that. He, on the other hand, was confronting these great Biblical issues after five delectable Maritime beers, about to start his sixth. "Hey, I've seen *The Ten Commandments, Sodom and Gomorrah, Samson and Delilah, King David, The Robe, The Greatest Story Ever Told, Jesus Christ Superstar, The Last Temptation of Christ, Jesus of*

Montreal, Life of Brian," Julian, ever the film buff, rattled off the titles, pleased that he was still able to think so quickly even after overindulging. Back in Toronto he was a moderate drinker, toiling away in the world of graphic design, but he was on vacation, away from comfortable surroundings and comforting routine.

"Certain things are possible, and certain things are impossible. Fairly basic observation. Except we poor mortals can't always differentiate the possible from the impossible, regardless of the insights Biblical works may provide us," he told the man, who must have thought Julian was blaspheming God, and informed him in no uncertain terms where sinners wind up, which included a sombre description of Satan's domain. Gripping a full bottle, Julian told the other tourist that the most accurate and frightful depictions of Hell were by Hieronymus Bosch, and, as he sipped his beer, proceeded to offer an intoxicated stumble through art history. "But Bosch," Julian concluded, along with his sixth beer, "in all likelihood never visited the Big Smoke or the Cradle of Confederation."

"If you don't take a vacation, you're going to have a breakdown," Julian's friend had told him a few weeks ago at a restaurant in Toronto. Actually, it was his ex-wife. The Jewish one. They were still friends, or had been so in the last two years, after her third divorce. A miracle. Not the divorce, but that they would become good friends again. Julian had two ex-wives, and liked to refer to them as the Jewish One and the Non-Jewish One. At least in his mind. Even he, with his penchant for less than wholesome comments on occasion, didn't like to be that vulgar in public, though he was tempted at times. The world, you know. How in the hell did you react to the horrible goings-on in the world sometimes?

"Don't you want to watch me have a breakdown? Front row centre. You can review it."

"Life isn't a play, Julian. And it was your first wife who did theatre reviews."

"I know, let's not quarrel. I was just playing fast and loose with chronology, like in dreams. Some of my dreams ... nightmares ... are like stage sets. I usually don't get much of an audience, but what can you do in a dream?"

"I used to think I knew when you were serious and when you were joking."

"Hey, you're still learning."

"Prince Edward Island would be perfect for you. Tranquil and calm. My two weeks there after my last divorce was a wondrous cure."

"The very thought of tranquillity and calmness makes me tense."

"The golf courses are fabulous."

"I don't play golf."

"The beaches are superb."

"I'm not drawn to sand and sun."

"Did we have *anything* in common?"

"We were both Jewish, darling."

"Yes, but your parents were European Jews and mine were safe in Canada during the war, as you liked to criticize me. *Holocaust survivors* ..."

"You don't need to make it sound like I belong to an exclusive country club."

"Julian, I don't want to get into a suffering contest with you."

"Let's face it, your Jewishness is less tormented than mine."

"Just go there. Trust me. You'll come back refreshed and rejuvenated."

"Will I still be Jewish?"

Now, while Julian is sitting alone at an outdoor table in front of a downtown Charlottetown café, the protective umbrella jutting out of the centre of the table not completely shading his face or thoughts, doodling on the glossy pages of a tourist booklet, he wonders if it was his ineloquent toast – "To all the goddamn unimaginative fraidy-cats who wind up in Hell and its décor falls way short of their sulphurous expectations" – or the six-beer loudness of his delivery that got him the boot. Quite the accomplishment to get asked to leave a quiet little Charlottetown pub, he thought, as much dismay as irony and fondness underpinning his reviewing of last evening's events. You want me to leave to the left or to the right? he had asked the bartender. He said it three times, loud, hoping someone in the bar would get his allusion to the Nazi concentration camps. He could hardly wait to tell his friends back in Toronto of his ignominious expulsion. Maybe, he considered saying, he was thrown out like a sack of potatoes. Or, heaved out. Or, two burly bouncers, world-class bodybuilders, propelled him into the street. Ah, that was the air-conditioned indoor evening. Now, a hot outdoor afternoon, but at least the air isn't as smoggy as in Toronto, Julian thinks. His beloved Toronto, warts and compromised air and all. His first visit to Prince Edward Island, and he feels like he's on another planet. "Enjoy your vacation, take in the local colour, would it hurt to nosh on a little lobster" – it was a pep talk/psychological counselling session. Maybe I should send myself a bill for the advice, he teases himself.

At a nearby table, Julian overhears a woman say to a man, "Supposed to get close to a record temperature today and it sure feels like it. I wish we didn't have to head back so soon." They are both wearing revealing tank tops, she more athletic and tanned than he. Julian wonders from where they are vacationing. From the accent, he guesses somewhere in New England, perhaps Massachusetts, wants to ask, and to inquire if they are Boston Red Sox fans.

But their tattoos, he doesn't care for tattoos, not that theirs aren't artistic. He counts three tattoos for him and four for her. Tattoos were so common now, *ordinary*. He sometimes thinks that his first visual memory was of a tattoo, even before he knew the word. As much as his mother hated her tattoo, and it was not unusual for her to strike her fist against the blue number, she would never cover her tattoo. "History," she once told her son, her Yiddish accent always a reminder of a different time and foreign world, "is on my arm, and I always want God to be able to read it." At the funeral home, the casket open, he pushed up the sleeve of his mother's dress, exposed the tattoo for the present and the past, for the living and the dead. Someone asked him to respect the dead, accused him of a disgraceful impropriety. His father had died six months earlier, and his mother had seemed to lose all her will to live. Julian was in his early twenties, receiving another lesson that the horrors of the Second World War never left the survivors. That was over thirty years ago. Memory, Julian knew, can slap viciously as easily as caress gently, sometimes both at the same time.

Julian has a glass of grape juice in front of him. How agile memory can be. Concord grape wine. Passover. His parents were still alive. One Passover Seder, maybe he was ten or eleven, the Four Questions asked like a subversive, underage professor: "Why were you in Auschwitz, Mama?" "Do you remember what you thought when you were liberated?" "Why did Hitler hate you, Daddy?" "Would Hitler have tried to kill me?" His parents didn't know what to do with their son's questions. So clever for a little boy. But some of the things he would ask, about the war, the camps, the Nazis. A little boy. Julian's agile memory was doing some serious reverse somersaults this hot afternoon.

It seemed to be getting hotter, but his hangover was just about gone. Beads of sweat like tiny galaxies on his face, and he crushed a galaxy with a straw from his cold drink, a simple masochism born of tediousness. He writes that on the glossy tourist booklet he has on the table. The heat brings out my poetic qualities, he thinks.

"Mind if I join you?" he hears a German-accented voice, thinking for a second he is hearing actual German spoken but the heat must be playing a trick. There are tourists from all over the world on the Island, why not a German-speaking one? No, an actor in a uniform, he decides, then accuses the man, who sits down at Julian's table. Plays throughout summer at the Confederation Centre of the Arts, across from where he is sitting, and at the Arts Guild, down the street a hop, skip, and a jump. In fact, plays were being performed all over the Island during the summer. He had seen several people dressed as the Fathers and Ladies of Confederation – or so his tourist booklet called them – actors giving the tourists a little living history. But Hitler was neither a Father nor a Lady of anything history has ever spewed forth. He had seen strange or odd things in Toronto also. Didn't he like to walk late at night, observe the human condition, attempt to sidestep the confinement of his everyday life? But such a frighteningly close likeness of Hitler, as convincing as any actor he had seen in film or even the Führer himself in documentary footage.

Then the bright, indescribable vision, the contours of human form, but elusive, appears at his table, joins them. Maybe another actor with talents and skills that defy category. Such astounding makeup, costume, even an aura of the transcendent Julian momentarily trembles at. There are three of us at the table, the sun plotting legendary triumphs, he jots down on the tourist booklet, as if writing a ransom note to himself, making preposterous demands. He turns to see how the others at their outdoor tables are regarding them, but they were caught in their own mid-afternoon scenarios.

Uneasy and fretful and fearful, the silence makes Julian feel even hotter, the silence makes him more afraid, and he speaks to the two as inanely as he can, inanity an amulet for safety: "If you could take on a long train journey only one book, one CD, one photograph of anything as your only memory reflection, what would they be?"

"Cattle car or bullet train?" he thinks he hears, but no, attribution to the actor's swastikaed uniform.

"This afternoon is a sweet joy of existence," the other actor comments, the voice like nothing Julian had ever heard before.

"Is it the sweetness of death, or is it the sweetness of life?" the uniformed man asks, scratching lightly at his moustache, his voice guttural.

And Julian can see the grinning trickery, the worsening tedium. Small talk, he wants to enmesh everyone in small talk, a shield, a defence, don't succumb to their trickery, traps are being set, cunning and deviousness are in the air, Julian senses, sitting there sipping his drink, thinking, I'm being hoodwinked by magical actors, why, for what reason? Is there a bored movie crew in town? Is the heat turning the pavement sentient? Is the whimper-or-bang question playing itself out before his eyes, in the heat? Do they know the lives his parents lived?

Mind-magicians, infiltrators of thoughts, prodding, tampering, rearranging. What next, rabbits with Einstein faces out of hats? Enough *mishegoss* in Toronto. Little Charlottetown, the Cradle of Confederation, and he gets *mishegoss* up to his neck. His nose, possibly. He looks down at the tourist brochure and flips through the pages, as if hoping to find an entry for these two, an explanation for the bewildering mid-afternoon conversation.

"Did you see *Judgement at Nuremberg*?" Julian says, looking at whoever and for whatever reason chose to dress like the horrendous Führer. Several films that dealt with Nazis and the Second World War or its aftermath go through Julian's thoughts, but it is this one that seems to want to replay itself in his mind. Growing up, he sometimes went with his parents on a Sunday to the picture show, a monthly treat for years, but his mother would not see anything with the remotest whiff of war or Germany; his father, however, took him to this 1961 film and afterward they went to a delicatessen and had salami sandwiches on rye, drank ginger ale, and discussed *Judgement at Nuremberg* like two scholarly detectives confronting the complex mysteries of morality and evil.

"After my time," Hitler says.

"I was a teenager when I saw it, with my father. My mother wouldn't go with us. Thanks to you."

"I never had the pleasure of making your mother's acquaintance."

"If I believed for a second that you really were –"

"Why do you not finish your threat?"

"I don't want to sound murderous on a lovely afternoon, in the proximity of so many innocent tourists."

Two tired parents, trailing their energetic twins, approached and walked past the table. The twins were two little girls, skipping and laughing, atop their heads straw hats and red wigs in imitation of the character Anne of Green Gables. He has a ticket for tomorrow's performance of the musical, wishes he were safely in a theatre now.

"We're lucky Mengele didn't live to see this," Julian says, and Hitler shakes his head contemptuously, and the other actor cringes at the tasteless remark.

After some nervous sketching in imitation of Bosch's style, attempting to capture Hitler, unable to do even an outline of the other actor, Julian bursts forth, "No one's told me yet what they'd take on the imaginary train journey."

"We do not need to play parlour games," Hitler says.

"European train journey," Julian adds, droplets of saliva jumping through the heat and striking Hitler's uniform. Julian spits intentionally several times, but Hitler acts as if it is a brief and unannoying summer drizzle.

"I would not require anything on my journey," God says. "I would only desire to watch the beauty of the world through the train's windows."

"I want to discuss Hell and Heaven as depicted in the Bible and the paintings of Hieronymus Bosch," Julian says, a

238 – J. J. Steinfeld

teacher demanding class participation, but neither of the other two respond to his taunting invitation.

"What in the world do you two want?" Julian asks, shouting out his question.

"I am here and not here," God says.

"I have made myself by my actions," Hitler says.

Julian looks at them, the actors with their demanding roles. He whisks his hand across the air in front of their faces. Neither one of them flinches. As if they knew what he was about to do. He hits the table, flagellates the air, spills his drink, its purpleness staining Hitler's uniform, a suppressed rage, no hands reaching for him, to slap or choke. A well-behaved afternoon monstrosity. Julian thinks that God blinks in approval, but his mind is playing a trick, yet another trick.

Who's going to believe him? Maybe if he describes a play or a movie? Calls it surreal or absurd or dark comedy or whatever little phrase he can think of to describe the extraordinariness of the hot afternoon. He'll write a script, then show it to people in Toronto. My soul-soothing, sanity-caressing PEI vacation. The title flashes on the screen. *My Historical, Biblical, Baffling Summer Vacation.* Big cast, small budget. The opening credits roll. Julian laughs out loud, but does not explain his amusement to the other two.

He senses that if he photographs the interlopers, takes the evidence to experts of science and theology, then his sleep would not be as disturbed. Julian pounds at his left forearm, sees himself as a little boy kissing his mother's bruised forearm, begging her not to scream.

Julian asks a nearby tourist to borrow her camera, offers to pay for the film and bring her back two rolls of the best quality film, the woman acquiescing as if trying to placate an agitated intruder. But I've already taken a few photos, she explains, and Julian tells her he will get them developed for her along with his own. When will the police arrive? Can he get expelled from an outdoor café on a hot summer's afternoon in the midst of tourist season? Always the questions. A lifetime of questions. He takes pictures, clicking frenetically away with the unfamiliar camera, an urgency to his photographing as if this tableau will dissolve if he hesitates. With the twenty-fourth and last photograph, Julian turns from the table and runs as fast as he can to a photo shop down the street, thinking that he's going to collapse of heat stroke and then who needs photographic proof? He takes the one-hour service, but offers to pay twice as much for ten-minute service, bemoaning all the waiting people have to do in life, especially when on vacation.

He paces in the photo shop, is told to come back in an hour, you can't believe how busy we are, but Julian insists he will wait. Waiting, he tells a clerk, is always the worst, for answers, for rescue, for the captivity to begin, for the captivity to end, and she says that she has been waiting for two days for a repair person to fix her broken refrigerator, most of her food has spoiled.

Julian returns to the café, again running at full speed, not that full speed is very fast anymore. He had been a distance runner as a young man, and well into his thirties, but those days of strenuous physical activity seemed left in the Stone Age. He places the camera on the woman's table, along with the two new rolls of film and the half-dozen photographs of Province House she had taken earlier, and thanks this tourist profusely.

"These photos I took suck big-time," Julian announces, as he spreads them on the table like a card dealer fearing his cards are about to transform into something hideous and destructive. Bland shots of the tables and other tourists and locals. How could he miss the other two at his table?

"You do not look well," Hitler says.

"I was running fast," Julian explains, and takes several deep recuperative breaths.

"I've written a multitude of poems a second since the beginning of time," God says.

"I almost conquered everyone and everything. I almost undid your multitude of poems and made a mockery of your Creation," Hitler says.

This is small talk? Julian thinks. Where is the guy he met in the pub last night? Talk of Creation was right up his alley.

"How do you say 'eternal verities' in German?" Julian asks. His idea of levity, relief from the heat and assault of his senses.

"History can betray a person, even when you know your destiny," Hitler says.

"We are not embracing the splendour of history," God says.

Julian fights against what he sees, and starts an oration: "The irrational is quicksand. What do we have here, rationally speaking? An actor who is a fully rehearsed, fully costumed Hitler; an actor improvising, I'm sure, God the eternal poet; and me, I just want to know who's going to pay the bill, who's going to clean up all the terrible errors?"

Julian gets up from the table again, this time for good, determined to take a long walk until his thoughts clear, the other two staying there among the tourists and locals and heat, arguing like there's no tomorrow.

Historical Perspective

*H*eadphones securely on, trying to block out the world, creating his own world of movement and music – Glenn Gould's fingers dancing through the *Goldberg Variations* – Louis was taking his morning run along the Victoria Park boardwalk, trying to beat his best time for the run from his house, down to the boardwalk, then along the waterfront, past the other walkers and joggers and strolling dog owners, back again, and home, just about ten kilometres. He'd been disappointed with his last few times, not that they were that much worse than in the previous few months, but he'd recently had his fifty-sixth birthday. He was putting on an extra push, perhaps imagining he was closer to fifty than sixty, and felt this was going to be his best time this summer. Except about halfway through, as Gould's passion hit a crescendo, Louis tripped trying to avoid a yapping little dog attempting to exert its boardwalk dominance.

Louis, in pain and rolling over to his side, shut off Gould's concert, as if sparing the great pianist from the discordance of his fall and injury. The dog's owner, an elderly woman holding a clear little plastic bag with the dog's previous biological imperative, apologized so dramatically and tearfully for her unapologetic, still yapping pet that Louis begged her to get on with her morning walk, no blame, no guilt, merely his knees now painted red.

A tourist couple, much less effusive than the walker or her dog, stopped to ask if the fallen runner was all right. Louis was by then sitting on the boardwalk, looking out to the water, hoping that in a few minutes he would be able to jump up and resume his run. He knew they were tourists. First of all, it was in the middle of tourist season, and he had been running through a touristy area of the waterfront. And the woman and the man both had that where-am-I look. And thick German accents. They were in their forties, Louis estimated, so he didn't have to invoke the memory of his parents, to ask for their advice or forgiveness. But the accents of the tourists scraped his thoughts as much as the wooden boardwalk had his knees. And what about their parents – what wartime memories had they passed on to their world-travelling children? How good sense and the judicious go out the window when you're sitting on your ass on a warm summer's morning with two bloody knees, he thought.

"*Ob nach Auschwitz sich noch leben lasse,*" Louis said, the little German he could still speak. "Barbaric to write poetry after Auschwitz," Louis explained in English, to the puzzled look of the tourists. They must have understood his words, both in German and in English, Louis thought, but not what Adorno meant or what he was trying to say by quoting him. "The philosopher Theodor Adorno wrote that in the same language that Kafka used," he added, trying to flex his legs. Thirty-six years ago, when Louis was a university student, he caused quite a stir over that Adorno statement. It wasn't even a history or a philosophy class, not even a German class, all of which he was taking that semester. Third-year Twentieth-Century Poetry class, and they were discussing poets who had committed suicide. The grey-haired, stoop-shouldered professor seemed to have an affinity for versifiers who had taken the dark door out. That was the expression the professor had used, and a feeble smile that couldn't embrace or even approximate irony: "The dark door out, class ... what incalculable sadness ... the cutting short of one's life and poetic talent." In a German accent. Louis was barely twenty years old then – an idealistic, exuberant, restless twenty – and was not the most comfortable with the German language. That was why he was also taking German that semester. To overcome his problem with the German language. He also wanted to read Kafka in the original. In those days Kafka was his favourite author.

"Where were you during the war?" Louis asked in the middle of a class, near the end of the semester, as the professor was discussing Hart Crane's brilliant poetry and incalculably sad suicide. It was a loud, almost theatrical, questioning. Louis had thought about asking that question all semester, had even written it in his poetry-class notebook dozens of times, phrased in various manners, like a sharpshooter eyeing his target from every angle, but somehow had restrained himself, not pulled the trigger. "What does Hart Crane have to do with the Second World War? He jumped off a ship in 1932. The SS *Orizaba,*" the professor said defensively, as if Louis had asked him for his identity papers at a roadblock. "*Schutzstaffeln,*" Louis said, drawing out the already long word. "SS is for steamship ... steamship," the professor repeated, his back turned to Louis and the rest of the class, his eyes on the blackboard and the words and years, "Born in 1899 ... died in 1932 ... *White Buildings* – published 1926 ... *The Bridge* – published 1930 ... *SS Orizaba* ...," what he had written earlier about Hart Crane.

Louis persisted, even after the professor said Switzerland, he had been in Switzerland, studying literature, and the idealistic, exuberant, restless student stood up, uttering, "*Ob nach Auschwitz sich noch leben lasse*," which he had read and committed to memory the day before. Maybe it was those words, thinking about them, trying to reconcile what he considered his comfortable, protected, middle-class life with the knowledge that his father had spent the war hiding in a forest from the Nazis and his mother had been in Auschwitz that broke down his restraint, made him ask the question instead of continuing to write it in his notebook. The professor asked Louis to leave the class, to return when he had more historical perspective. Hearing the words *historical perspective* in the professor's German accent was like a jab to every part of his memory. His parents were still alive then, with their Yiddish accents and old-world weariness, but both would be dead in another three years. As he was leaving Louis quoted Adorno once more: "*Ob nach Auschwitz sich noch leben lasse*." The student returned a week later, spoke little in class the remainder of the semester, and wound up getting an A in the course, instead of the B or even C that he had expected. Strange form of reparations, he wrote in his notebook.

Years later, a few lifetimes away from that twenty-year-old, Louis can still say that Auschwitz created him, makes him write word after word in protest to the wordlessness of death; makes him sit quietly in a room in a tranquil, tree-filled part of the city writing a poem about his parents' wartime experiences, longing to undo Auschwitz, transform the gas chambers and crematoriums into swaying trees and colourful clouds of God's breath. Can he get away with saying that in a poem, he wonders, this nervous rearranging of words and death numbers and artifacts of destruction just because his mother was in Auschwitz? He has written poems about the hell of Auschwitz he imagined his mother went through. But those poems did not make a great deal of sense to him, no matter how long he worked on them.

During one of his Grade 12 English classes, as the students were struggling with contemporary poetry, Louis said that a poem can be like a comedy routine even if it's a poignant and serious poem, not side-splitting or rollicking off-colour humour; not doing surreal wheelies in clown costume; nothing like that, but comedy all the same – the searching for sense tickles the funny bone in a painful way, call it absurdity, call it civilization, call it a higher or lower calling, an obscene phone call from a poet who makes the obscenities sound like a love sonnet. Now he thinks of that high-school class and his less than successful writing career. A handful of published poems. He is a decent enough teacher, he consoles himself, but he doesn't seem to believe himself sufficiently, as if giving himself an on-the-spot lie-detector test. Over thirty years of teaching high-school English and he has maybe five poems a year to show for it, a fifth of them published in small literary magazines – that is his sudden measurement, his harsh assessment of his life's worth and work.

He doesn't look forward to returning to teach in the fall. He would simply like to spend his time running and writing poetry, writing poetry and running. Running to and running from lands of madness and lands of sensefulness. He feels he is watching himself from a safer vantage point, and shakes his head at the metaphors that are mocking him. He told his wife once that running was poetic, and writing poetry was like running. Then he told her he had his dream again – running around the perimeter of Auschwitz, yelling out his malformed poetry, none of the guards or prisoners paying attention to his speed or words. She had already begun to talk of divorce before then.

Louis thinks more and more about poetry, and his interrupted run. He begins reflecting on his discomfort and the world around him: I jump into the quicksand of poetry, looking up at the historical heavens, starting to wonder what poetry will be like in the twenty-second century how many blunders and horrors and sadnesses will need to be described in horizontal lines. What does this disgruntledness mean, this peculiar looking forward? My God, this century is chugging along, it's a warm, pleasant day, not the imminent end of the world, the world nonetheless damaged, terribly damaged – another insubstantial, inadequate metaphor – but it's baseball season, he reminded himself, the statistics as comforting as ecclesiastical prayers.

There was so much bafflement last century, he had told his students on the last day of class. They already had their twenty-first century war, but he wanted to discuss another century's horrors, using as a pedagogical connection Santayana's observation about being doomed to repeat the past if one doesn't learn from history. "I mean," he had said to the class, "if you take the number of all who died in armed conflicts and from diseases and famines and the barbarity of human misdeeds and divide by the number of days in the twentieth century, 36,525, you get a poisonously high number. Still I need to go food shopping, organic products preferable, and an evening run past the memory gas chambers and crematoriums and later find out the latest baseball scores on the internet, see who's leading in homers, runs batted in, and earned run average, not the number of innocents put on transports and taken into the darkness of history – no *Arbeit Macht Frei* on the gate to any major-league stadium. Centuries belong to historians and filmmakers – couldn't we just discuss kind little hours, or maybe a good hour, not a rushed hour, I don't ask for much."

What started him thinking this convoluted way, in front of his class and now as he sat on the boardwalk? Louis berated himself. Auschwitz, of course, always Auschwitz. Here's the thought process, the journey his sense-thirsty brain went on: In university he received an A for bringing up Auschwitz; but not in high school. In Grade 11, his hormones filling the known universe, he wrote a book report on William L. Shirer's *The Rise and Fall of the Third Reich*. Nothing more profound than the book's title and its more than 1,200 pages were what attracted him. The assignment was to write a book report on any non-fiction book that dealt with a significant event in human history. Louis received a C minus, not the coveted A. He had written that God observed World War Two like a fan in the stands at a baseball game, but not even booing when things went wrong on the field, an error or a wild pitch, not knowing which team to root for. *Preposterous imagery*, his Grade 11 teacher wrote in red pencil, underlined, and then went on: *You used the words "concentration camps" over a hundred times, wrote them every time in upper-case letters, and did not capitalize God's name, not once.* A little judicious editing and a few capital G's, Louis believed, and he would have received a better grade.

In the first week of the twenty-first century, he rented a film video of *Sophie's Choice*. While he was watching the film Louis realized that his Grade 11 teacher had looked like Meryl Streep playing Sophie Zawistowska, Polish Catholic, survivor of Auschwitz. Meryl Streep, acting up a storm, made you feel she was in Auschwitz, Louis had thought during the film, but his Polish Jewish mother was there, not Meryl Streep (and Meryl Streep acted with Liam Neeson in *Before and After* and Liam Neeson played Oskar Schindler but Louis's mother was not on Schindler's list). Louis had to build a bridge of many years between a book report on *The Rise and Fall of the Third Reich* and film video of *Sophie's Choice*, but build he did, like a slap-happy construction worker drunk on his project. How many book reports and films does a person remember in a lifetime? How many teacher's comments and screen portrayals? He turned on the radio, the pre-game show, sat down to write another poem, but he was thinking of visiting his mother in Auschwitz and wait with her to be liberated. Small preposterous world, wouldn't you say?

One of the tourists offered him his hand. Louis felt like he had disappeared into years of thoughts, twenty and fifty-six not all that distant from each other. How much time had passed? He looked at his watch. How long had the tourists stood near him, he wondered, waiting to see if he could stand or would stay unmoving, a newly produced tourist attraction? He had to ask what their parents did during the war. Just as he had to ask his university professor. I should spend more time writing poetry, Louis thinks. And running. He takes the hand of the male tourist and pulls himself up, his legs in great pain. "Tell your parents that you have shown me a kindness," Louis said, and the man responded that his parents had passed away several years ago. "Peacefully?" Louis asked, and turned the *Goldberg Variations* back on, louder than before. "They were old, very old," the tourist told Louis, and he resumed his run along the boardwalk, with as much speed as he could summon. Louis prayed for speed, for swiftness, as he ran to a destination that was farther than the end of the earth.

Paintings

*I*t's my nineteenth birthday tomorrow, forecast is for the most beautiful fall day of 1989 so far, and all I can think about is my older brother, Sean, who died yesterday, a heartbreaking twenty-seven. There was no way I could convince people that Sean didn't want a funeral. He just wanted to be cremated and remembered nicely, and nothing more. But no, people had to give him a big funeral. My relatives were the worst: "A beautiful funeral for dear Sean ..." "How can someone die and not have a funeral? ..." "Only the best for Sean, a funeral no one will forget ..."

People kept telling me to be sensible, that my brother had to have a funeral. Even Mom was stubborn about having a proper funeral and she truly loved Sean. But she never understood Sean or why he had to be an artist. That's a terrible misfortune when you love someone but don't know anything really important about the person. That's the way it was with Mom and Sean. There was so much to Sean; so much love and mystery and sadness. He was eight years older than me, but I was closer to him than anyone else yet there was a ton of things I didn't know. Even when he was surrounded by people he had that lonely look on his face. It was the kind of look that made people come up to him and ask what was wrong or why he was so sad. It hurt him to keep things inside but every time he poured out to someone he was misunderstood or hurt, most times both, so Sean kept most things inside. Except in his paintings. In Sean's painting he wasn't afraid to show his deepest feelings.

I could have shown everybody Sean's goodbye letter but they wouldn't have understood. It said right in the first paragraph about having his body cremated and not wanting a funeral, about just being left alone when he was finally alone. Sean wanted his ashes spread in the sea, not his body buried in the city. No, Sean really hated the idea of a funeral and being buried. But I would have had to show people the whole letter, all six pages, and they would have called it a suicide letter. No one in the family would ever accept it only as Sean's way of saying goodbye. He was weary and felt it was time to leave. In Sean's case you just couldn't use the word *suicide*. It was his way of leaving gracefully. He titled a painting *A Graceful Departure* he did years ago, and if you look closely at it you can see all about his feelings concerning departing from life. He even explained to me once, while we were bicycling together in Victoria Park, that one of the meanings of *departure*, in olden times, was death. I can't have people saying he killed himself. That is what he wanted to do. They all think it was an accident and I won't tell them otherwise. Maybe some people would say he was crazy. Some fools even thought he was crazy while he was alive. A lot those thick-headed fools knew. They were too busy with all kinds of stupid things to know what incredible thoughts were going on in Sean's head.

We were awfully close, Sean and me. More than just

loving brothers, real close friends too. The closest and best of friends. But still there was so much I didn't know about him. We talked a lot and confided in each other but there simply was too much to Sean for anybody to begin to understand. Heaven knows he wanted people to understand him, but I suppose it wasn't possible. This was one of the things that made him weary.

Sean could joke a lot and make people laugh but he never really stopped crying inside. I often told him to try to be happier but he said that's the way he was, sad, and that there were plenty of moments of happiness and joy that made things worthwhile. He appreciated those precious moments. Sean liked to take long walks alone or bicycle around the Island or be with a person he really liked. And let me tell you, he had a lot of women friends. But he was afraid to get too close to any of them after things fell apart between him and Caitlin. It was amazing how many people Sean knew. And he always said how each one was different, important in their own way. Even the drunks. Sean had this thing about painting street people, who I thought were nothing but losers. When I told him to stay away from them he got angry. He told me they weren't bad people deep down inside. It really upset him when I said they were scum or nothings. So I stopped telling Sean not to be friends with the drunks who hung around parts of downtown Charlottetown. Anyhow, he knew so many other people too. All kinds.

Sean said how he lost the two people he loved the most. Dad died and he drove Caitlin away. He didn't mean to drive her away but that's the way they were to each other. They hurt each other a lot but they loved each other more than I can describe. Caitlin is incredibly beautiful. She had magical qualities, Sean liked to say. He painted some great pictures of her, even though he wasn't satisfied with them. Sean was a wonderful artist. His life was completely wrapped up in painting and maybe that was part of the reason for his weariness. He tried to drink his weariness away, but that just seemed to make things worse.

Sean was off the Island when Dad died. He was out west working in some big oil field, making money and getting real-life experience. That's the way he described it, at least. Before Sean finished his first year at art college in Nova Scotia, he quit, and started travelling around the country and working at jobs that had nothing to do with the art things he had studied. First job he got after quitting art college was at a used-furniture store in Halifax; then he headed for Newfoundland and had two or three more jobs there. He even spent some time working on a farm in Ontario. But he'd always come back to the Island, to refresh his spirit he'd say, and he would paint with more energy than you could believe, and spend some time with Mom and Dad and me. Sooner or later he'd get restless and go away for a few months. When people told him to settle down, that he should get some sort of steady work, he told them that if he stayed at a job too long it did strange things to his brain, made it even harder for him to paint.

Going back a bit, it was a damn stupid July morning when Sean left for the oil field job. He had to be at the airport by seven in the morning. He told us he wanted to go to the airport by himself and we would be better off to say our goodbyes that evening. He said goodbye to all of us, Caitlin was over and so were a few friends, and then he went into the backyard with Dad and they talked. Sean was sketching Dad all the time they were discussing things. I was watching through a kitchen window and saw Sean sitting at the foot of Dad's lounge chair. Dad was lying down because he was awfully tired and not feeling the best. Then all of a sudden Sean threw down his sketchbook and pencils. After a minute or two, he helped Dad up and hugged him. I never saw them hug each other for such a long time before. When they came back into the house both of them had really red eyes. Nobody knew what they had talked about. Maybe they knew they would never see each other again. After all, Dad was kind of sick. But the doctor seemed to have everything under control. Yet Dad, even though he quit school in Grade 8, and Sean, who was nearly a straight A student until he quit, were both pretty smart. Maybe they knew.

My room was next to Sean's and I could tell he never went to sleep that night. He stayed up sketching and listening to his favourite music. I sat up in bed thinking about Sean and trying to figure out what he was thinking about. At three o'clock Sean came out of his room dressed and carrying his painting supplies and a little overnight bag. I heard him leave his room so I came out of mine and asked what he was doing so early. He had a smile on his face and commented on my ugly old pyjamas. They had this gigantic hole and I must have looked damn silly with my private parts hanging out at three in the morning. We both laughed, but we were anything but happy.

Sean told me he wanted to walk to the airport, even if it was miles away. "I also have to stop and say farewell to the crows and gulls before I leave," he said. Those were the birds in Victoria Park, not all that far from our house. Sean loved it in Victoria Park, sketching there whenever he could, taking great pleasure in looking out at the water.

He was wearing one of Dad's rings when he left. Dad had arthritis real bad in his hands and couldn't wear rings because his fingers were so swollen. When Sean was much younger Dad gave him two gold rings, one being his wedding ring and the other this fantastic gold ring with Dad's initials on it. The rings were too big for Sean when Dad gave them to him but Sean grew into them. He loved those rings even though he only wore them now and then. That morning Sean was wearing the ring with the initials. He must have had the wedding ring in his pocket or overnight bag.

I stood on the front porch watching as Sean walked away from our house. I didn't see him again for five months, when he came home for Dad's funeral. His face was all bruised and he looked terrible, but Sean wouldn't tell anybody what had happened. He said he would do a painting about it one day and that would explain everything. You didn't have to be a genius to see he'd been drinking.

Sean's second solo art show is ready to open next month. Posthumously, I guess, is what they call it. I wish he could be around to see it. One of his friends got the paintings together and convinced some people at the Confederation Centre Art Gallery after Sean died to look at them, and boy, were they impressed. It took a long time before Sean got his first solo show and it was at a small gallery in an old building downtown, not far from where some of the drunks like to hang out. Only two of the twenty oil paintings sold in the month the show was up, but Sean didn't care all that much about selling his work. What he did care about was the pretty harsh reaction he got to the show, especially when people said nasty things about his subject matter.

All twenty of the oil paintings were of local street drunks, the men either at bootleggers or in their bleak rooms or puking up outside. People misunderstood what Sean was painting. Funny how blind some people are. Now they love Sean. He's really going to be famous. But God, why couldn't it have been when he was around? He would still have been weary, but at least some things might have been different or better. Caitlin never thought Sean would make it as an artist and that tore him apart. She wanted him to go into a secure profession and not into art. He told her he hated security. When he turned down a big scholarship to the University of Prince Edward Island and went to art college instead, she didn't talk to him for weeks, and then he quit art college right in the middle of his first year. Caitlin was scared Sean would never make it. I guess he showed her. He showed everybody. But Sean wasn't out to prove anything. He just wanted to paint and have people look at his work, be moved by it. He loved to talk to people about art and painting, even to the drunks downtown. They were his best, most loyal models, he claimed. I'll never understand why, but Sean liked to drink at the bootleggers with those lost souls.

Too many people asked him why he didn't paint anything happy or cheerful. He sure didn't paint your ordinary peaceful Island scenes, not Sean. But in Sean's paintings there was hope and happiness. Sometimes he painted the drunks as he imagined they were as kids, or painted them living in posh hotels in Europe, and argued that those were his happy paintings. One painting, huge as could be, was of nearly all the downtown Charlottetown street drunks sitting around a fancy table in Heaven, puffy white clouds everywhere, with the biggest bottle of booze on the table. You want happy, a little unadorned ecstasy, look at that painting, he told people who complained that his work was too depressing. Those people who wouldn't or couldn't look beneath the surface of Sean's work thought happiness was a painting that pretended there was no pain in the world. Some people even thought happiness was always telling people you were happy. Sean knew better. Sure Sean painted about sad and dark things, so what, but he never forgot the good things. Sean painted about life.

In any case, one day Sean will be considered a very important painter. I already feel he's terrific, but I'm his brother and no art critic. In just twenty-seven years Sean did over a hundred oil paintings, had enough sketchbooks filled to make you think five hard-working artists had done them, and just about made sense out of life. When he was drunk Sean used to joke that he only wanted to live as many years as Van Gogh had, that would be long enough for him. I hated this morbid drinking talk, and told him he'd live longer than Picasso had. Sean joked back that if I was wishing him artistic longevity, I should use Grandma Moses as the desired goal. If my brother wouldn't have got so weary I wonder how much he would have accomplished, how many paintings he could have completed in a long life. He was improving all the time. There was no stopping Sean except that he was getting so horribly weary.

There are some scary paintings and gloomy sketches Sean gave me that nobody ever saw. It won't be the right time to let people see them for a long while. It's a lot of stuff about Sean's weariness. I cry when I look at those paintings and sketches that he couldn't keep himself from doing. One of these days I'll show this real dark stuff to people. I wonder if they'll cry too. Sean didn't want people to cry unless there was someone near to comfort them. Sean always said tears should be wiped away with love.

I bet this show that's coming up at the Confederation

Centre Art Gallery next month will be a sensational success. When people see such a large display of great paintings in one big room, they'll realize for themselves how good Sean was.

I've been writing down these things about Sean for the last few days. I'm not sure why I'm doing it, only that it hurts a lot more not to write about my brother. I try to express my feelings with paint on canvas too, but I always seem to mess everything up and get myself so damn frustrated. I'm not going to try art college like Sean did, but he got me interested in being artistic. Sean knew a lot about art and helped me with it. I've been working on my own but it sure isn't easy. Maybe if I work hard enough, eventually I'll be able to paint like Sean. But I'm not talented and my brother was as talented as you can get. If it wasn't for Sean I'd be nowhere now, maybe even locked away in some sort of mental hospital. I wish Sean was still around to help me, but I guess he had to leave. Like I keep saying, he was just too weary.

Since I've been in such a writing mood lately, I decided I might as well write out my will. I don't have many possessions so it didn't take me very long. I'm going to stop by a lawyer's office later today and make sure what I wrote is all official and legal. Sean drew up a will about two weeks after Dad died. He told Mom and me that it was just a precaution, but he must have known then that he would be saying goodbye before too long. After Dad's funeral Sean hung around Charlottetown and worked at a bunch of jobs. He wasn't picky, just so long as he had time to paint. It was less than a year after Dad died that Sean made his departure. He left his paintings to me and to some of the people he cared about. My brother knew which ones I would like. He had all the titles of his paintings and their dimensions and dates of completion listed in his will, and the people they should go to. The money Sean had saved over the years he left mostly to Mom. He left something in his will to each of the street drunks he knew. I counted eleven of the drunks at Sean's funeral. I couldn't help but think of that huge painting of them sitting around a table and drinking in Heaven. At the funeral more than one drunk shed a few tears.

Yesterday I went down to Victoria Park, to the place Sean liked so much. It's almost a spiritual place, with trees and flowers and the water that inspired Sean. The crows and gulls were there, even a few blue herons. I'm sure they were some of the same birds my brother used to sketch.

I wish I could paint things like Sean could because Victoria Park and the water are something else. I can't do them justice at all. Sean would walk around by the water or sketch, all year around, it didn't matter to him what the weather was. I bet part of him is still there. Sean never really leaves any place he's been at. If you just met him once there's no way you can ever forget him. He was never the same twice. That's the way Sean was, floating and surging and wandering through life. Anything Sean was at any particular time, sometimes silly, other times serious as could be, a lot of times indescribable, was real. It was Sean at that time. Some people called that immature or unstable. God, were they dumb and scared. Some people were actually scared of the way Sean lived and thought. I'm positive Sean would be angry at me for using the word *dumb* to describe people. *Dumb* was one of those words Sean called coarse. Words that really didn't describe anything too well.

While I was at Victoria Park I bumped into Caitlin and her fiancé. He was a colossal creep. But like she used to tell me and Sean, if she didn't marry Sean, she'd marry for money. That was a lousy thing for a woman Sean loved to say, but Caitlin was that way sometimes. Sean loved her no matter what she said or did. It hurt him a lot when he was mean to her. It was almost that way for Caitlin toward Sean. Almost, but not really. She couldn't let Sean be Sean. Hardly anyone could let Sean be Sean.

Let me tell you, this creep Caitlin was with reeked of money and acted like he owned all of Charlottetown. Now you can have tons of dough and be a great human being, but this guy reeked. He asked Caitlin who I was and she said, *A friend of an acquaintance.* I couldn't understand why she said something so horrible and cruel. I bet she never told this fiancé of hers about Sean, probably afraid that my brother's wild reputation might scare Mr. Moneybags away.

So we talked for about ten minutes, the crows cawing like an excited choir around us, and Caitlin wished me luck. The idiot she was with gave me a fake smile and a weak, insincere handshake. When Sean shook your hand it was warm and genuine. I think Caitlin was beginning to cry as she walked away. Maybe in her heart she was still loving Sean and didn't mean anything bad with what she said. Their love just couldn't have ended when Sean said goodbye. I could hear the jackass she was with ask her why she bothered to talk to a drunk. Hell, I'd hardly had anything to drink that morning.

I tried to get my emotions under control by walking around Victoria Park. I stopped a couple of times to ask the crows if they remembered Sean, and those birds got real enthusiastic. They said Sean occasionally comes back to talk with them. He can be anything he wants to be, Sean's free as the wind now, the crows told me. I smiled because I knew my brother could always be whatever he desired. Sean's mind knew no boundaries. But even with a mind like his, Sean got weary.

I'm sure Sean came down to Victoria Park that day he made his graceful departure. The spot where he actually said goodbye was a fair distance from Victoria Park, way out in the country, but I know he must have stopped by the place he liked so much first.

Sean never rode his bicycle recklessly, even though he loved going fast. He had a beautiful racing bike but he was always careful on it. That's the way he decided to make his graceful departure. Police divers found him and his bike in the water. People thought it was an accident, that Sean lost control of his bike and crashed into the water. But my brother was too good of a rider. And in his goodbye letter he wrote about how soothing the water was and where he wanted to rest his weariness. I guess it's better that people think it was an accident. I already said how they'd get everything wrong if they saw Sean's goodbye letter. You should have seen my brother getting up speed on his bike, his strong legs pumping away. It was a wonderful sight to behold.

Things are sort of getting to me now. I can't seem to paint, or do anything lately that makes sense. Maybe I've been thinking too much about my brother, but I just have to remember all the wonderful things I learned from my brother and his struggles, and not let his sadness or my sadness bring me down. I know I'll find strength by going down to Victoria Park and spending a bit of time there, and then I'm going to start a new painting, one of my brother, full of life, on his beautiful racing bike.

I'm Waiting for You, My Dear Old Friend

Something about breaking in a new pair of running shoes,
even at my advanced age, reminds me of my youth. Not
that I was much of a runner when I was young. To tell the
truth, I was slow and clumsy. But every spring, as if it were
part of the changing of the seasons, I would get my parents to
buy me a beautiful pair of running shoes – or whatever they
were called in the old days – until I was old enough to save
the money myself, and then I would purchase the shoes all on
my own. That, as I look back, was part of my emergence into
manhood: the careful selection and purchasing of my own
running shoes, with my own money. And I would run, not part
of any competition, not against anyone or any clock, merely
run. I did build up a certain stamina and endurance, but not
any speed to speak of.

As I got older, when a friend or someone would ask why
I ran so much, I used to joke that I was running with God, pace
for pace, and time melts away when you're in the proximity of
the Supreme Being. Not that I have many friends anymore, or
talk much to people, but the running is a constant in my life,
from as long as I can remember. Sometimes I think I've run

over the entire Island, traversed every bit of land, and whether you can see them or not, my footprints, like embedded memories, are everywhere. When I was younger, growing up in the country, I ran only in rural areas. Now, retired in the city, a widower – my precious lovely wife, gone a year, was never keen on my endless running, and my two sons and their grown children also never encouraged my running – I run through Victoria Park, along the waterfront boardwalk, back and forth, as though there were no more sanctified terrain for running in this world, the ubiquitous crows, sentinels of the glorious park, often cawing their approval at my exertion.

My most recent pair of running shoes had the smell of my youth, even if they cost many times what running shoes cost when I was a boy. I run regardless of the weather, and a harsh wind can come off the water in winter. The worse the weather, the more of a challenge, and the more satisfaction I would take. But my running has changed. Not because of anything physical – I'll concede eight decades of earthly doings have taken a toll on my body and spirit – but because of an old man on a park bench, looking much older even than I am. I first saw this old man, his eyes as dark as a crow's and a scraggly white beard that he was forever fiddling with, two months ago, the first day of spring. Day after day he would be there. "Nice day," I would say, or "Not so nice day," or some foolish comment about the weather or the less profound aspects of life. Regardless of the weather, didn't matter if the wind was slapping furiously at your face or caressing your weary bones, he would be sitting there on the same park bench when I approached and ran past. At my apartment, I would enter the run in my log, and make a notation about the dark-eyed, scraggly-bearded man.

As much as I like to keep up my steady running pace, one day I slowed down, ran in place, made small talk with the man on the park bench. I started to vary the times I ran, early in the morning, before or after lunch, in the evening – he was always there. Even, on a few occasions, in the middle of the night. "What are you doing?" I asked every time. "I'm waiting for you, my dear old friend," he said without variation. The first time he told me that, I politely said that we had never met, might not yet qualify as dear old friends. Once, during a mild Island night, I asked, "Why do you keep saying you're waiting for me?" but he did not answer, just looked skyward and pulled on his scraggly white beard as if contemplating the number of stars above us.

I changed the times I ran, pushed myself to run several times during a day, and yet he was always sitting there, waiting. I did start addressing him as my dear old friend, and I guess a friendship of sorts came to exist – an odd friendship where we did not even know each other's names or anything of our personal lives. I, to him, was simply a strange old runner and he, to me, the bearded old man on a park bench. I considered him tranquil, serene, if not a most peculiar presence in the midst of Victoria Park.

Then on one of the windiest days I could ever remember, I was startled: *he wasn't there on his park bench.* In the confusion of my thoughts about him and journeying back to my youth, my memory shimmering with all the pairs of running shoes I have run in over the Island, I found myself on the same park bench. I couldn't move, able only to raise my voice in desperation. Words turned to screams, screams to words, but none of my utterances received the slightest acknowledgement, except the occasional crow swooping down a little lower than usual before me, conveying a silent, bewildering message. I ceased my screaming, my calls for help. I looked around me, embraced the magnificence of the natural world, and I sensed, in a most difficult to explain manner, that all my life I had been running to this park bench. In my silence I could hear voices, as if the wind and crows and water and sky could make wordful sounds, and the voices were speaking softly into my aged being – *you have your place, you have your purpose, you are all of your memories* – and when certain walkers or runners pass me or stop, I say, "I'm waiting for you, my dear old friend ..."

Acknowledgements

*T*he author acknowledges with gratitude that many of the stories, sometimes in earlier versions, in *Acting on the Island* previously appeared in the following publications: *The Antigonish Review* (Canada), *Blank Spaces* (Canada), *Bread 'n Molasses Magazine* (Canada), The *Danforth Review* (online) (Canada), *Etchings* (Australia), *Golden Times Magazine* (Canada), *The Fiddlehead* (Canada), *Grey Borders* (Canada), *IslandSide Magazine* (Canada), *Jewish Dialog* (Canada), *Kaleidoscope* (online) (US), *mgversion2>datura* (France), *New Zenith Magazine* (digital) (US), *Passionflower* (Canada), *Pottersfield Portfolio* (Canada), *RED: The Island Storybook* (Canada), *Zygote* (Canada); in the anthologies *The Communication Bridge: An Anthology of Prince Edward Island Writing* (Edited by Dorothy Griffin-Farish, Malpak Arts Council/Crescent Isle Publishers, PEI, 1997), *Gratitude with Attitude* (Bookcraft in Montclair, US, 2006), *Letting Go: An Anthology of Loss and Survival* (Edited by Hugh MacDonald, Black Moss Press, Canada, 2005), *Nelson Literature & Media 11* (Authors/Edited by Neil Andersen and James Barry, Nelson Thomson Learning, Canada, 2002), *Quickfic Anthology 1:*

Shorter-Short Speculative Fiction (Digital Fiction Publishing, Canada. 2016), *Snow Softly Falling* (Edited by Richard Lemm, Acorn Press, Charlottetown, PEI, 2015); and in earlier books by J. J. Steinfeld: *The Apostate's Tattoo* (Ragweed Press, Charlottetown, PEI, 1983), *Dancing at the Club Holocaust* (Ragweed Press, Charlottetown, PEI, 1993), *Disturbing Identities* (Ekstasis Editions, Victoria, BC, 1997), *Forms of Captivity and Escape* (Thistledown Press, Saskatoon, SK, 1988), *A Glass Shard and Memory* (Recliner Books, Calgary, AB, 2010), *Gregor Samsa Was Never in The Beatles* (Ekstasis Editions, Victoria, BC, 2019), *Madhouses in Heaven, Castles in Hell* (Ekstasis Editions, Victoria, BC, 2015), *Our Hero in the Cradle of Confederation* (Pottersfield Press, Porters Lake, NS, 1987), *Should the Word Hell Be Capitalized?* (Gaspereau Press, Wolfville, NS, 1999), *An Unauthorized Biography of Being* (Ekstasis Editions, Victoria, BC, 2016), *Unmapped Dreams* (Crossed Keys Publishing, Montague, PEI, 1989), and *Would You Hide Me?* (Gaspereau Press, Kentville, NS, 2003).

The author wishes to thank all the publishers and editors involved with these publications.

Author's Notes

An earlier version of "The World of Our Hero in the Cradle of Confederation" is based on Chapter One, "Our Hero's World," of the author's novel *Our Hero in the Cradle of Confederation.*

An earlier version of "Paintings" was first published with the title "A Graceful Departure" in *IslandSide Magazine.*

A one-act play by the author, *Godot's Leafless Tree*, based on his short story "Godot's Leafless Tree," was first produced at the Arts Guild (Charlottetown, PEI) by Left Hand Theatre, June 27, 2001, August 7 and 21, 2001; and later produced at the Murray Harbour Community Centre (Murray Harbour, PEI) by Hubris Productions as part of the 2004 PEI Theatre Festival, March 25, 2004.

A two-act play by the author, *A Television-Watching Artist*, based on his short story "A Television-Watching Artist," was first produced by Cape Breton Stage Company at Finishing Touch (Sydney, NS), June 2-4, 2011.

A one-act play by the author, *Flowers for the Vases*, based on his short story "Flowers for the Vases," was first produced at the Arts Guild (Charlottetown, PEI) by Left Hand Theatre, August 14, 2001.

A one-act play by the author, *The Heirloom: An Evidence Play*, based on his short story "The Heart," was first produced at the MacKenzie Theatre (Charlottetown, PEI) by Island Community Theatre, October 28 to November 1, 1986. *The Heirloom: An Evidence Play* was the author's first produced play.

References to the work of other authors are made in the following stories:

In "The World of Our Hero in the Cradle of Confederation," "One feast, one house, one mutual happiness" is from *The Two Gentlemen of Verona* (Act V, Scene iv), by William Shakespeare (1564-1616).

In "Flowers for the Vases," a line from *No Exit* (*Huis Clos*), by Jean-Paul Sartre (1905-1980): "GARCIN: Hell is – other people."

In "Historical Perspective," the quotation "*Ob nach Auschwitz sich noch leben lasse,*" from Theodor W. Adorno (1903-1969), translated as "Barbaric to write poetry after Auschwitz."

About the Author

*F*iction writer, poet, and playwright J. J. Steinfeld was born in a Displaced Persons Camp in Germany, of Polish Jewish Holocaust survivor parents. After receiving his master's degree in history from Trent University and spending two years in a PhD program at the University of Ottawa, he abandoned that program and moved in 1980 to Prince Edward Island to write full-time. Steinfeld lives in Charlottetown, where he is patiently waiting for Godot's arrival and a phone call from Kafka.

While waiting, he has published twenty-three books: two novels, *Our Hero in the Cradle of Confederation* (1987) and *Word Burials* (2009), fourteen short story collections – *The Apostate's Tattoo* (1983), *Forms of Captivity and Escape* (1988), *Unmapped Dreams* (1989), *The Miraculous Hand and Other Stories* (1991), *Dancing at the Club Holocaust* (1993), *Disturbing Identities* (1997), *Should the Word Hell Be Capitalized?* (1999), *Anton Chekhov Was Never in Charlottetown* (2000), *Would You Hide Me?* (2003), *A Glass Shard and Memory* (2010), *Madhouses in Heaven, Castles in Hell* (2015), *An Unauthorized Biography of Being* (2016), *Gregor Samsa Was Never in The Beatles* (2019), *Acting on the Island* (2022) – and seven poetry collections, *An*

Affection for Precipices (2006), *Misshapenness* (2009), *Identity Dreams and Memory Sounds* (2014), *Absurdity, Woe Is Me, Glory Be* (2017), *A Visit to the Kafka Café* (2018), *Morning Bafflement and Timeless Puzzlement* (2020), and *Somewhat Absurd, Somehow Existential* (2021).

From 1981, when Steinfeld published his first short story, to 1986, when his first one-act play was produced, and 2001, when he published his first poem, to the publication of his 2022 Pottersfield Press short story collection, *Acting on the Island*, nearly five hundred of his short stories and more than a thousand poems have appeared in anthologies and periodicals, in Canada and internationally in twenty countries. Over sixty of his one-act plays and a handful of full-length plays have been performed in Canada and the United States, including the full-length plays *The Franz Kafka Therapy Session, The Golden Age of Monsters,* and *A Television-Watching Artist;* the one-act plays *Godot's Leafless Tree, The Waiting Ends, The Entrance-or-Not Barroom, Laugh for Sanity, Back to Back, No End in Sight, Sea Monsters, More Than Money, Imaginative Drinking, A Play of Disbelief, Memory Sounds,* and *In a Washroom of a Prestigious Art Gallery;* and the audio plays *In Becky's Name, A New Map, The Professor's Ashes,* and *Diogenes' Lantern.*

In 2017, Guernica Editions published a book in their Essential Writers Series, *J. J. Steinfeld: Essays on His Works,* compiled and edited by Sandra Singer, which took a critical look at the author's writings of fiction, poetry, and plays. Among Steinfeld's many awards for his writing over the years, four of his works which include stories in *Acting on the Island* have won or been shortlisted for writing awards: Winner of the Great Canadian Novella Competition, 1986 (for *Our Hero in the Cradle of Confederation;* novel version of the manuscript published by Pottersfield Press in 1987); Creative Writing Award from the Toronto Jewish Congress (later The Jewish Federation of Greater Toronto) Book Committee, 1990 (for *Forms of Captivity and Escape*); Finalist for the 2018 PEI Book Award for Fiction (for *An Unauthorized Biography of Being*); and Winner of the 2020 PEI Book Award for Fiction (for *Gregor Samsa Was Never in The Beatles*). Steinfeld was the 2003 recipient of the Award for Distinguished Contribution to the Literary Arts on Prince Edward Island.

Books by J. J. Steinfeld

The Apostate's Tattoo (Stories)
Our Hero in the Cradle of Confederation (Novel)
Forms of Captivity and Escape (Stories)
Unmapped Dreams (Stories)
The Miraculous Hand (Stories)
Dancing at the Club Holocaust (Stories)
Disturbing Identities (Stories)
Should the Word Hell Be Capitalized? (Stories)
Anton Chekhov Was Never in Charlottetown (Stories)
Would You Hide Me? (Stories)
An Affection for Precipices (Poetry)
Word Burials (Novel and Stories)
Misshapenness (Poetry)
A Glass Shard and Memory (Stories)
Identity Dreams and Memory Sounds (Poetry)
Madhouses in Heaven, Castles in Hell (Stories)
An Unauthorized Biography of Being (Stories)
Absurdity, Woe Is Me, Glory Be (Poetry)
A Visit to the Kafka Café (Poetry)
Gregor Samsa Was Never in The Beatles (Stories)
Morning Bafflement and Timeless Puzzlement (Poetry)
Somewhat Absurd, Somehow Existential (Poetry)
Acting on the Island (Stories)